Beagle's Noose

Beagle's Noose

A Novel By
Sam Rogers

Gowen Place Press
Bainbridge Island, Washington

4

Also by Sam Rogers:

The Fulcrum: Selected Poems 2000 - 2010

The Suicide Diversion

Epistle Paternal: A Letter To Our Sons

Cover design by Chris Peters: chrispeters.com

ISBN: 978-0-9847183-5-1
Gowen Place Press
Bainbridge Island, Wa 98110
gowenplacepress@yahoo.com
samrogersbooks.com

Dedicated to those of us whose thoughts distort reality.

I must Create a System, or be enslav'd by another Mans

If the fool would persist in his folly he would become wise

William Blake.

8

Friday, April 28th, 1989

To Governor Paulson D. Renhennie
Governor's Mansion
Olympia, Washington

Dear Governor,

My current life (and death) situation is both
ludicrous and dangerous, like the over-heated dream of
a teenaged writer or a story in one of the horror comic
books from the fifties (found in a cardboard box in the
backyard shed, provenance unknown) that used to scare
the hell out of me when I was a kid. I'm scheduled to be
executed by hanging at twelve midnight, Monday night,
May 1, or Tuesday morning, May 2, depending on how
you want to look at it. The time is now coming up on
twelve midnight, Friday night, April 28, going into
Saturday, April 29, at least in the Pacific time zone.
Probably, knowing how this joint operates, we'll end up
being well into Tuesday before anything actually comes
off (oops, an unfortunate turn of phrase although I am
height/weight proportionate so nowhere near obese
enough for the hangman to pop my head off, I hope).
        Although at that point, what difference would
decapitation make anyway, except to those who have to
observe? Unless, as people speculate, the consciousness
of the severed head lasts long enough for the victim to

watch the world bounce in rhythm with his or her suddenly independent cranium. I wonder if I would actually mind that as it's happening? I can't imagine I'd feel any pain after the severing of my spinal cord so would it be horrible to have my last vision on earth be the equivalent of what a Super Ball would see if it had eyes, a series of swift vertical shifts? A rhetorical question, I assure you, and one I hope not to receive the answer to. Damn, I'm ending a sentence with a preposition but I don't have the time or the literary skill to easily refashion it. Damn, I split an infinitive but isn't that okay to do with an adverb? Concentrate, Isaac!

The imminent prospect of death wakes a man up and, believe me, I needed waking. Here's a quote from my favorite philosopher that applies to this situation. He was a wise old man with spiritual resonance despite his unfortunate years of association with the Nazi party. I have some of his books here but this one I can record straight from the little old memory:

"If I take death into my life, acknowledge it, and face it squarely, I will free myself from the anxiety of death and the pettiness of life - and only then will I be free to become myself."

Martin Heidegger

This is my project, dear Governor, to become myself and you, sir, can be a part if it!

Washington is one of the last states, aside from Delaware, I believe, to allow hanging as an option for the condemned and that's what I chose, not wanting the populace to have the comfort of imagining I will be gently put to sleep like old Duke, the German Shepherd with severe hip dysplasia, for example. Not a dog I'm acquainted with, I hasten to add, but one who popped up in my head, barking enthusiastically, with the broad smile of that breed. Some dogs smile and some don't. Cats hardly ever. A cat laughing is a truly unsettling sight. I won't go into how I know that here. I have to fight against going off on tangents. I have the sense of multitudes milling around me even though I am alone here in my cell. Other realities threaten to break in upon my consciousness yet I press on.

I realize you have very good reasons to be angry with me, and I don't blame you. How could I, given what happened? In the mood I was in up until a few days ago, I didn't care particularly whether I lived or died, but something major has changed. Now I do want to live. I'll outline the reasons for that later but I thought if I put down a bit of my perspective on the death of Dionysius Beagle, you might consider commuting my sentence to life imprisonment. You may not be open to that idea as the crime came quite close to you personally, but you must be fair.

Of all the inmates under sentence of death in the IMU, the Intensive Management Unit at Walla Walla

State prison, I've spent the least amount of time here, yet I will be the first to die. My compatriots (a truly pathetic bunch, by the way, although I must include myself in the pathos), have dragged out their preliminaries for years with the filing of briefs, petitions, and appeals. I seem to be the only one whose case is sliding like an oily key through the rusty mechanism of justice, whose death is being demanded with vehemence by all parties involved, yourself included.

Because I am a guest of the state and have been provided with this domicile free of charge, and you are the Governor of said state, you are therefore, by pure logic, my landlord. Please consider this letter to be an official request that I would like to change living quarters. I want to be transferred out of the IMU, where the condemned prisoners are confined, to a Close Management Unit where inmates with life sentences, but no behavior problems, are housed. I'm not asking for this move because I prefer a better view (no views available in prison), or an enclosure for my toilet (modesty be damned!), or fumigation (cockroaches are the only pets we have). But I have been a good tenant, with no disciplinary actions against me so I'm hoping you will consent to this change in my housing and a minor change in my life status: from doomed to..., well, the opposite, whatever that is.

Obviously, I admit my crime. As Jack Ruby discovered, the presence of television cameras at a homicide significantly reduces the amount of ambiguity defense attorneys can throw around during legal proceedings to befuddle the jurors and win acquittals. The incident took place before the bulging eyes of the wealthiest and most influential citizens of Washington State. They became material witnesses, making my trial as illustrious a social event as the charity ball at which the assassination occurred. Notice that I use the word "assassination." Remember that, because it will give you some insight into my justification for bringing about such a horrendous event.

I did not take a human life without cause and even though I am willing to submit to justice, I think my reasons for transgressing the law might warrant the commutation of my sentence to imprisonment until such time as my life is overtaken by natural events, such as the cardiac illnesses and cancers that do in most people. Here's a thought experiment: knowing what we do now, would you have killed Hitler if you'd had him in your sights in 1930? Now hold on to that thought and, for the sake of my life, don't let it go.

My lawyer, Leonard Main, will be here to visit me at eight in the morning and has promised to drive to Olympia himself tomorrow to present you with this petition (if that's indeed what it is). Leonard is, of course, a court-appointed lawyer with all the limitations you might expect from such a shabby beast. What he lacks in intelligence, as witnessed by the verdict at my trial, is somewhat made up for by his good intentions and his almost pathetic belief in the legal system. Don't be put off by his suit, the only one he owns, bearing the marks of many a spaghetti dinner, or by his stutter that tends to surface during moments of intense emotion (like the summation at my trial, damn it!).

So here I am, staying up all night writing on this legal pad, somewhat ironically named, don't you think, as I'm here under legal orders, and I'm in my pad, that is, my place to live, and I'm using the pads of my fingers to... (oh well, never mind). The other inmates here talk constantly and scream and cry at night but they don't interfere with my nocturnal musings because I block them out by putting in the earphones from my portable radio and listening to the country station, the only one whose signal makes its way through the thick concrete and steel of the walls. George Strait and Rodney Crowell (both boring and dependable in equal measures, in my opinion) are in heavy rotation.

Some of my fellow residents pretend to sympathize with my impending troubles but I know they are to a man eager to be rid of me. They complain that I'm stuck up and aloof but the distance between us is the inevitable result of the fact that I'm a man of intelligence and education whose crime was a humanitarian act rather than one of their sordid, impulsive lunges for sex, power, money, or revenge, usually driven by self-indulgence and substance abuse.

As noted at the trial when Leonard attempted to have me declared insane, I planned my crime, I had my reasons for it, and I carried out the act with a full knowledge of the consequences. Each of the tortured souls in the neighboring cells believes himself to be the victim of uncontrollable forces, if they don't deny any culpability whatsoever. Some of them even go so far as to blame their actions on Satan, so they can distance themselves from their horrible crimes, such as the sadistic rape and murder of a hitchhiker, perpetrated by my neighbor, Tyrone, two doors down, who in the years since has found both an almighty Lord for soothing redemption and a convenient Beelzebub to whom he can shift the responsibility for what happened. To his credit, Tyrone has a lovely baritone voice and sings "Swing Low, Sweet Chariot," every night, in such a sweet tone that his neighbors on the IMU ignore the implications of the lyrics.

I, on the other hand, in comparison with Tyrone's wicked and meaningless act, made a conscious decision to rid myself and the world of an intolerable menace. Pre-meditation? Absolutely. Did I do the deed? You saw me, with your own eyes, as they say (although whose other eyes would one use?), and the news cameras caught me in the act so I would have to be deranged, which I'm not, to dispute the point. My argument for clemency is based on the danger presented by the victim to the world at large. One would imagine I'd be celebrated and not hung by the neck "until dead" (is that really a necessary qualifier? I suppose one can survive a hanging) for ensuring the safety and well-being of my fellow citizens but such is the nature of the political reality we inhabit. I sit on my cot and scribble furiously. I face a wall less than nine feet away but I also have the sense, as if in a concurrent dream, that I'm in another dwelling as well, with long corridors extending to my left and right, a space without cells, filled with others. Is this a vision or a hallucination (and what's the difference, anyway)? You will be the judge of all matters pertaining to my case.

I'm quite aware of the public outcry and caterwauling that went on over the death of Dionysius Beagle. Both Washingtons, the State and D.C., seemed to claim him as a friend, a claim that could only originate from duplicity or ignorance because Beagle was not a friend to a single human soul. In fact, judging from my experience, he was more of a danger to humanity than nuclear waste, the greenhouse effect, or television.

I know the cover story he created for himself: scion of a prominent Seattle family, first in his class at Seattle Prep, crew at Yale, captain of a destroyer in World War 2, editor of the Law Review (doesn't the banality of this list tell you something in itself?), married to one of the great beauties of the Northwest until she died of cancer three years ago. And that makes me wonder: Has anyone investigated the circumstances of her death?

Now might be the time for a good forensics man to exhume her corpse from its palatial vault in Lake View Cemetery on Capitol Hill and see what else she had in her system along with the wildly multiplying cells. I'm not necessarily saying he poisoned her. I'm just pointing out that nothing, absolutely nothing, was beyond the evil machinations of this man, if he was indeed a man.

Beagle created a real estate empire so vast that almost every block in downtown Seattle, Tacoma, and Olympia is connected to his network of holdings in some way, not to mention those vulgar monstrosities, the Beagle Building and Beagle Tower, works of architecture so hideous in shape, color, and texture that I'm surprised airline pilots descending to SeaTac can bring their aircraft safely past these structures without being distracted to calamity.

Of course, one has to mention the story of his son, Bud Beagle, All-American quarterback at the University of Washington, who was driving south for his first pro season with the Tampa Bay Buccaneers when he dove into the wreckage of a burning R.V. on Interstate 5 near Kelso to save a baby. Just as the propane tank blew, Bud threw what the press called his final and most important forward pass, spiraling the screaming infant a good thirty yards, witnesses swear, into the arms of its mother (who should have gone off and negotiated a contract with Tampa Bay herself.) Bud perished in the explosion, floating up to the great training camp in the sky where he is now, no doubt, knocking heads and downing brewskis with the less admirable ghosts of players who died from head traumas, fatty diets, and drug overdoses.

Sorry, I'm going a little off the track here. The point I want to make is this: why did that R.V. catch fire just as Bud was passing (no pun intended but they are always appreciated)? Did Daddy Beagle have any causative relationship with the incident? No? I think he did, although it's undoubtedly too late now to prove it. Maybe Bud discovered the depths of his father's evil and was about to expose him to the world so Beagle arranged the entire "accident," complete with screaming baby, well-calculated to draw forth Bud's sympathetic nature. I don't know where that sympathy came from, maybe his mother's DNA contained the pattern for compassion.

And, you may well be asking, why would Dionysius Beagle plot to end the life of his supposedly only begotten son, Bud? Again, those closest to him were the most likely to discover the depths of his depravity. Is this circumstantial evidence? Not even that, really, but pure speculation on my part although I smell smoke, metaphorically speaking, so have no doubt whatsoever that somewhere Beagle's fire is burning.

Rambling again (multiple apologies) so I'd better move closer to the point. Sitting here in this nine by twelve foot cell (somewhat larger than the cells for the non-moribund in general population, or so I hear) is like my one experience within a flotation tank, in a shabby building up on Aurora Avenue, bobbing on brine as if I were taking a dip in the Dead Sea at night. An article in the Seattle Weekly convinced me to spend some of my meager income for an experience I found anxiety-provoking rather than soothing as I would drift ever so slightly through the salty water until I eventually bumped into one of the side walls of the tank. After that happened once, all I could think of as I lay there was whether I would hit the wall again (not conducive to meditation, I have to say, so, of course, I do say it).

In a similar fashion, I have so little stimulus here that my under-active brain goes off on extended, sometimes overheated journey, bumping into its own walls. Especially with the execution date looming, I feel unusually alive, aware, in touch with all that goes on, in the past, present, and yes, even the future. I feel some spatial dislocation, as if I'm writing both here and in the other space inside my head. Bump.

The imagined collision with my noggin suddenly made me sleepy. The horizontal of my bunk is calling me. I will be sending more later. You can count on that although I'm sure you're not thrilled (as you, no doubt, have many impending issues more important than my continued existence, right?). I'm not nearly done with my argument for life, not by any means.

Sincerely,
Isaac Turbot
Prisoner (not at large)

Saturday, April 29th, 1989

Dear Sandy,

I know you wanted to come out to Walla Walla for what will likely be my last weekend. I refused because I didn't want you to have to endure this sadistic circus. The media death watch is now beginning. I hear that vans with satellite dishes are moving into position out on the highway. I'm sure it will be the Bundy thing all over again: anti-death penalty people with candles and placards, pro-death penalty people with beer, bullhorns, and four wheel drive vehicles. The clamor for death is always louder.

I'm feeling sorry for myself right now, not a pretty picture. When I allow myself to think about what's going to happen, I want to beat the reaper by just dying right now. Big black wadding has fallen around me and crawled into my nose and mouth (metaphorically speaking although, do I really have to add that?). I'd prefer a heart attack that would keep me out of the final scene but no such luck. My chest pains are apparently not due to cardiac issues, the prison doctor assures me, but to anxious depression. Depression is a hungry beast, roaming the earth for its victims, worse than any pissed-off grizzly or mass-murderer. I'm a single digit murderer (and that digit is a one) unlikely, I believe, to be ending the life of anyone else.

I'm now in the process of writing to the Governor and asking for clemency. You kept asking me to speak in my own defense at the trial but I wasn't ready at the time. I'd feel better if the Governor would at least read my letters before deciding to go ahead with the execution. Without some communication, I would die without being heard, not that my broken prose will be changing his mind anyway. I imagined that killing Beagle would suddenly make everything all right, would snap reality back into place with a cartilage-popping click (random chiropractic reference). I didn't think I'd have to fight for my life or, if I did think about it, I didn't care.

I have less than seventy-two hours now. I want to grab each second and hold it to my chest, savor it for a long time but instead the moments keep flowing by, heading to a precipice for the drop foretold in my prison sentence (and in this particular sentence). My heart pumps away, in rhythm with the passage of time, oblivious to the fact that I'm driving ninety miles an hour down a dead end street, as Dylan sings. All my metaphors, cliches no doubt, are mixed together in a big stew in my brain right now. So what? No one is going to grade these final papers. I've been trying to set things straight with a few crucial people. I am determined to explain everything very clearly for the Governor so at least before and then after I die, he'll know what I was about. I'll also try to write to my mother (I told you about her, didn't I?) but I'm afraid I'll only be able to express my extreme anger with her.

You're a different story. I recently read the Kazantzakis novel, <u>The Last Temptation Of Christ</u>, inexplicably lurking on the library cart that comes around to our cells. I thought of you when he wrote about Jesus having a normal life with Mary Magdalene, raising children, working as a carpenter, a vision of what he sacrificed by being crucified. In a similar way (although I'm no Jesus), you were always the greatest danger to my plan because you made me imagine a life without Beagle. In an alternative universe (one of many, I've come to believe), I would live with you, work with you in catering, maybe start our own business. You would give up having other boyfriends although I don't know if you would be willing to do that for me. I remember well your skeptical views on monogamy.

But even if I were to convince you to be mine alone, bitter experience tells me Beagle would find a way to ruin it all. I'm not saying he would corrupt you. I can't believe that, although he's reached almost everyone else I've ever known. Eventually he would find me and nail me, to the floor or to the cross, and I wouldn't want you to be collateral damage. He knew how to predict my every reaction, except for the final murderous one, which he couldn't have known about (or could he?)

Sometimes I wonder whether he let me kill him for some twisted purpose of his own, maybe to force me into this predicament. It was too easy, really. I imagined that killing him would be a battle out of mythology or The Lord Of The Rings (with Beagle as Sauron, The Dark Lord, of course). Instead, ending his life was just another action, like emptying a trash can, or lopping off the heads of dandelions in a lawn. I thought about the deed and carried it through but maybe the utter simplicity of the action explains why I have the feeling he isn't quite done with me. Could he have cloned himself and had a simulacrum accept the piercing I inflicted? But in that case wouldn't I still hear him? I've had only silence from him in the last year but the quality of that lack of verbiage has been ominous.

Sandy, I owe you a great deal because you gave me a vision of the way life could be. I remember the first time we made love, lying in the bed in your Capitol Hill apartment, listening to the drunks yelling in the alley below. I kept slowly running my hands over your body, amazed because every other woman I'd ever been with had been in a hurry to leave, to extract the cash from my wallet and go. You and I were together out of free choice, as equals, friends. I was Elisha Cook, Jr. to your Shelley Duvall, oddballs from movies we liked.

You weren't just a target for my lust. We were constructed differently but fit together perfectly. That's a basic insight but one I'd never had before. Even though men and women are made for each other, we often act as if we're in competition for what we both really want. You and I managed to escape that fate, maybe because we weren't together that long. I'm no expert, but I do know that with you, I finally learned about love. Banal, perhaps, but true.

I don't know what you saw in me. Maybe you projected some kind of image onto the brittle facade I constructed hiding how messed up I was, how deeply I was held in the grasp of Beagle. Part of me was able to enjoy you and our time together but my essential self was intent on death. I'm too tired and sad to think in depth right now. I'm only able to say simple things about how I feel. You're the only human being who ever came close to me. That's why I want you to stay away.

Thanks seem inadequate for what you revealed to me: a world pristine and uncorrupted, where people could live their lives without the vast machineries of deception aimed at me. I wish some miracle had freed me from the web where I lay trapped like that little fly in the movie, with the head of Vincent Price, who was screaming, "Help me!" repeatedly but couldn't be heard. I'm very sorry for exposing you to the jackals of the media who've been hounding you to find out what I was "really like." I only shared the story of my persecution with you indirectly, intimating the difficulties I'd experienced during my life. Selfishly, I didn't want to reveal the depths of my predicament out of fear you would be appalled and want nothing to do with me. That's been the usual reaction from the few people with whom I've shared my story. At least you've been able to tell the police, the prosecutors, and the reporters honestly that you knew nothing about my situation or my plans.

In gratitude, I want to do something for you. I've made a deal with Dr. Fallow, the prison psychiatrist, and I'm enclosing a copy of it. I'm going to be undertaking (the right word in this context) a little writing project he's interested in. I told him to split the profits 50/50 with you. Please find a good lawyer, not Leonard, of course, and put him or her immediately on this because Fallow is not trustworthy. Insist on obtaining copies of every publication contract and make sure your name is included on each document. I don't know how much he will profit from this but it is unique, that I know of, so the profits could be significant. I want you to have enough to start your own business, or at least to provide a cushion for yourself later on. I'm sure Mary has no thoughts of creating pensions for her employees so you need something to put away to retire on. I know you're only thirty-two but you should be thinking about your later years now. I worry about your old age because mine seems to be taken care of.

> All my love,
> Ike

Saturday, April 29, 1989

Dear Governor,

I have returned, if not precisely refreshed, at least alert enough to scribble. I don't sleep for more than a few hours at a time these days, no matter how exhausted I am. I wake up despite the earplugs I use to drown out the snores and screams punctuating the night in the IMU. I'm conscious of wanting to waste as little time as possible in the state of being unconscious. I'm soon to have more than enough time unconscious (although does that word really apply to death? Somehow unconscious implies the possibility of waking up from the situation. As we don't know what happens after death, the prospect seems more like beyond consciousness).

I first encountered Dionysius Beagle at the Seafair parade in July of 1973 when I was thirteen years old. It surprised me when I learned that the whole world didn't celebrate Seafair, that it was, in fact, unique to Seattle. My mother dragged me to the festivities annually from the year of my birth until this particular year, after which I categorically refused to go. I developed a lively hatred for the Seafair pirates, that fun-loving bunch of local yokels who leap from their float, threaten the crowd, and receive vouchers for rum and stuffed monkeys according to how many small children they can make cry. I myself wept copiously under their assaults from the time of my first visit to the Parade at the age of six months until this year that I'm bringing up for a very specific reason (you'll see). I'd never been frightened by the ghosts and goblins of Halloween the way I was by the cursed pirates. Mother, in her typical way, was determined to break me of my fear of them so she would stand us, every year, down at the front of the crowd, after making her way through to the curb with some nasty shovings and scufflings, as we never arrived in time to claim a truly legitimate spot.

I didn't realize at the time just how young my mother was. She delivered me into the world at the age of nineteen, meaning she was only thirty-two at the time of this incident. My last name of Turbot was also her name, given that her involvement with my father was of a highly transient nature. Her first name was Scarlett after the petulant heroine of Gone With The Wind, a movie that impressed her mother, my grandmother, who I called Gouchie, a name I apparently gave her in my toddler years but have no memory of bestowing. After her death, I finally learned that her first name was Agata, the Polish version of Agatha. Through my childhood, we all lived together in a shabby frame house in Ballard, that old Scandinavian neighborhood north of downtown Seattle.

My room was in the uninsulated attic where I would sleep away the winter nights under a mound of old blankets as the wind blew through the gaps between the roof planks under the shingles, freezing my nostril hairs even as the rest of me remained cozily warm (did I really use the phrase "cozily warm" just now? My rampant use of cliched language will show you how distraught I am about my current situation, a predicament only you, Mr. Governor, have the power to resolve).

My mother's last name of Turbot was apparently a mangling of our original Polish family name, something along the lines of Turboski, or Kurboski, altered forever by an official on Ellis Island who was apparently not receptive to complications of nomenclature. Neither my mother nor my grandmother had much interest in life in the old country. My grandfather, Karl, worked for Burlington Northern Railroad in some capacity I never understood and died young of a lung disease connected to the job. Neither Gouchie nor my mother were ever forthcoming with details about the men involved, however briefly, in their lives.

Gouchie survived the Great Depression by working long hours as a maid and cook for a family in Sunset Hills, a wealthy neighborhood close to Ballard but with an expansive view west to Puget Sound (hence the Sunset in the name). No retirement was provided (naturally not) so when arthritis rendered her unfit for service, she was left with Social Security and the support of Scarlett, her daughter, my mother, who returned to the family home after a brief stint in a studio apartment on Capitol Hill, a residence where my conception may have taken place (although she consistently refused to share any details). My mother gave birth to me in that Ballard house.

Because she and Gouchie did not want to incur any hospital expenses, mother was actually delivered of me in the small bedroom where she grew up, surrounded by her dolls and stuffed animals. Gouchie did summon a doctor for a house call, a service that was still obtainable in 1960, but he didn't arrive until I was already out, severed from my mother by Gouchie who to cut the cord used a pair of gardening shears she boiled in a cast-iron pot on the kitchen stove. When I was young and Gouchie was telling this story, I asked why she didn't use the scissors from her sewing basket. She snorted in contempt at the idea of wasting fine scissors on such a messy project.

Am I going a little off-topic? I suppose so but my fervent hope is that by building up for you the details of my less than glorious life, you might feel some regret about taking even my sorry existence off the planet. Gouchie is long gone now but Scarlett lives with her husband, Mitch, in the house attached to his motorcycle shop on acreage down in Enumclaw. Even though we are no longer communicating, I believe (trust? hope?) that my execution would cause my mother at least a pang of regret for the slippery wad of flesh she brought forth in that narrow bed under the signed photo of Frank Sinatra on her bedroom wall (although I've always suspected that some movie studio or record company flack actually signed it rather than Old Blue Eyes). I don't imagine she would have wished for me to end up here, the very last station at the far end of the line.

Mother had a steady job as a waitress at The Kitty Kat, a venerable restaurant on Ballard Avenue, where a motley collection of merchant mariners, local alcoholics, and aging ladies of dubious virtue would gather in the lounge while families with rowdy bands of crying and food-throwing toddlers packed the dining room, famous for large portions of the specialties: Swedish meatballs and chicken cacciatore. On the walls were portraits in oil of ancient Scandinavian noblemen looking dour and disapproving. The kitchen was presided over by a cook named Sven, a man so tall that the pots and pans hanging by hooks over the stoves were constantly swinging from collisions with his cranium. Sven had a handlebar mustache stained dark yellow from the cigarettes he kept hanging from his lips while he was cooking, making ash a seasoning for his specialties, or spe-she-AL-ities, as he liked to call them.

My mother fascinated Sven and he tried many times to win her heart (if not even more of her) but she had no interest in him, despite her usual lack of choosiness in men. She found his smoke-saturated and gloomy demeanor to be depressing and kept a paring knife in the pocket of her apron to ward him off when he made the occasional lunge at her as she inevitably passed by in the course of her duties. Burly mechanics and machinists were more her type because she related to their practical attitudes about life and love-making.

When one such candidate would sit in her section, her usual brisk business-like demeanor would transform as she leaned over to allow him a good view of the deep line dividing her pale breasts. As a young boy of grade school age, sitting in a booth way in the corner trying to do my homework, I would feel such acute embarrassment about her outrageous flirting that I would sink down on the velour bench until my eyes were level with the formica surface of the table, hiding so well that people would sometimes sit in the booth unaware, until the last moment, that I was already there.

Hiding was the theme of my childhood because I was always afraid. I don't know why. Gouchie and mother were brusque in their attentions but kept me fed and clothed and allowed me to entertain myself with television and library books. Maybe the absence of a father or any knowledge of such a person provoked my anxiety. All my mother would say was that he was no good, had used her, and then departed. She wouldn't tell me a name, or give a physical description.

Instead, as her gesticulating hands drew jagged shapes with the red coal of her cigarette in the gloom of our living room, she would allude to my father's charisma and to his insanity in vague terms that left me to fill the void in my mind with anxious imaginings, thinking that at some random moment, in the night as I tried to sleep, or in the morning as I walked to school, he would suddenly be upon me, claiming me for a life I could only find distressing.

I went to the Ballard Theatre on Saturday afternoons to see a double feature of old monster movies, among a raucous crowd of my peers who would send Good & Plenty bullets, propelled by rubber bands, rocketing into the heads of those in front of them, evoking a series of yelps to punctuate the sound track. I would project my fears about whoever my father was onto The Creature From The Black Lagoon, that froggy humanoid with a powerful swimming stroke, or onto The Blob, an oozing jelly pressing itself through the square openings of the projection booth in the movie house to descend upon the audience and remove the flesh of those too slow to escape.

After I saw The House On Haunted Hill, I was afraid to open the drawers of my dresser for fear I'd find my father's severed head staring up at me although how I would know it was his head and not the head of some random murder victim, I'm sure I don't know. Maybe if mother had told me a little bit more about him, my imagination would not have been consumed with such macabre fantasies about who he was and what he wanted. She wouldn't even tell me if he knew of my existence.

I am getting to the point, Governor, don't worry about that. I'm writing to reel out a line of words, like a rope thrown to a drowning man, to save my life. You wouldn't think that with less than three days left (unless you intervene, hint, hint), I would become sleepy but here I am, Morpheus Ascending, in what is likely broad daylight outside the walls of this somber institution. The body is a constant betrayer of the mind. Maybe I'll make some coffee, using water from the sink, instant coffee from the jar, heating it with a plug-in coil from under my mattress that I'll dip into a plastic cup, dabbing a little Cremora (trademark?) on top, creating a congealed mess that only prison life could force upon me.

The heating coil is not strictly kosher around here but the day officer, Bobby Dahlman, known as B-Day, is a good guy and knows I won't try to attack him by shoving the red-hot element down his throat. He's so good I don't even worry (often, anyway) about the potentially ominous association of the "B" in his name with the omnipresent Beagle. Any glance at the record will show me to be a model prisoner, without discipline reports of any kind. I would think you'd take that into account. If the state were to keep me alive for the rest of my natural days, I wouldn't cause you the least bit of extra trouble. You'd never have to break out the riot guns or hose me down in my cell. I'd just sit here quietly writing and explaining myself to all mankind, and womankind, too. Childkind? I don't think so. My story would be too discouraging for the young ones starting out into the world.

The Unit is settling into its afternoon routine, the murmur of televisions tuned to soap operas and talk shows lulling my brethren into forgetting, even for a brief period, the reality of their situations. The lights in the cells never go off so I can always keep on writing. But now fatigue has narrowed my attention down to this tiny circle on the page where the words I've written seem to fade away as I write them. This process keeps me present-centered, dealing with the Now as it emerges in time. You know, I suppose, from the report of the homicide detectives, that I was a philosophy major at the University of Washington, or the U. Dub as it's so fondly called, although I'm probably not an alumnus they brag about.

My senior thesis was going to be on Martin Heidegger, the German philosopher previously mentioned but I never had the rigorously logical mind necessary for writing anything original in the field (although, is logic what's really required or more an ability to endure the almost poetic obscurity of the subject? Anyway...). Since my almost-graduation, I've read more in Eastern philosophy than Western but neither school of thought can fully explain what happens to the Now after death. I'm talking about this moment, in which I'm writing and you're reading, this presence that holds my Dasein, my being in the world. What happens to it? Does it just dissolve, fade back into the blankness from which I seemed to emerge at birth? I don't see any alternative. This is all there is. I haven't encountered any worlds outside the jumbled closet we call reality.

Seafair, 1973 (back on track again, sorry for the digressions), a decade after the World's Fair. Seattle has put itself on the map of the world for the first time, finally rising up from the provincial lumber and mercantile transactions previously justifying its existhence, feeling proud of itself for being able to bring about this massive project. The Space Needle, shiny and relatively new, gleams above us on a Friday night and a particular kind of Northwest magic floats in the air as the beer fumes mingle with smoke from the firecrackers the bored crowd is setting off to while away the time.

My mother is wearing a low-cut red dress that draws distracted stares from the policemen on horseback trotting by. Several of the people she shoved aside for a better view are making comments about her rudeness but she holds her head up with complete disdain for the opinions of others. I clutch her hand shamelessly for I know the torture I am about to endure from the cursed pirates. She allows me to squeeze her hand but when I look up at her (for I was a little guy back then) the lines of her nose and cheek indicate that she is imperiously ignoring me as her eyes slash through the crowd seeking the drug to which she is addicted: the male gaze. From down the block come the howls and screeches of high school bands. The waiting crowds, who've been frisking maliciously in the street, now pull back to make room for the marchers.

I don't remember the exact order of the procession because all the Seafair parades I've witnessed in my life now blend together. I know there were drill teams in their sequined uniforms, floats loaded with persons of dubious celebrity, horsemen doing rope tricks while their mounts left equine souvenirs for the following bands to step in. You know the scene, Governor. On television, I've seen you on top of a float yourself, waving and smiling, making a damn good target if I may be so bold (but I'm not making a threat, no sir, just pointing out a possible security risk).

I first saw Dionysius Beagle on one such vehicle. A gap in the parade gave us time to savor the forward movement of his float. The display consisted of scale models of the buildings he'd constructed. Cutouts in the sides of the building held buxom girls in bikinis. Their legs were tightly crossed as if they'd had a bit too much champagne and were painfully pinching off their bladders until the end of the parade. In the midst of the tallest buildings on the float, a throne had been constructed and on this throne sat Beagle, representing himself as the ermine-collared emperor of Seattle real estate.

At first glance, he was unprepossessing, even to my young eyes. His clothes had been tailored to flatter him but couldn't hide his essential chubbiness. He was constantly trying to smooth down his thinning shit-brown hair that fluttered in the evening breeze. His smile seemed to crinkle from the pressure of having to hold it much longer than he was used to. His eyes skittered nervously across the sea of faces, his agitation standing out in contrast with the sedated demeanor of the girls whose steady gaping grins, bright eyes, and rotating hand waves seemed to be generated by some internal dopey ideal, no doubt derived from the Miss America pageant.

The crowd roared with approval as he passed because, as minor (and to him, irrelevant) by-products of his greed, Beagle had done much to create jobs, modernize the city, and develop the World's Fair. He was on the boards of almost every charity and hospital and was sought after for advice by the top executives of Boeing itself, the one institution which has been and may always be the true soul of Seattle. Beagle seemed taken aback by the enthusiasm of the watchers, who showed themselves to be eager in their approval of someone who'd attained what they wanted (but were unlikely ever to achieve). He waved back at them by flapping his fingers as if saying "bye-bye" to a small child. I thought nothing of him at first. I remember wishing that one of the girls would uncross her legs, allowing me a glimpse of that holiest of temples contained between. I stared at the contents of their tops so hard I was afraid they'd begin to smoke.

As the float came closer to us, I was glancing to the right to see what the next one was (oh, God, the Pirates!) when my mother's hand tightened around mine. I looked up and saw her transfixed. On the float, Beagle returned her gaze with equal intensity. The air between their eyes seemed to shimmer with the energy they generated. The mild, ineffectual mask of Beagle dropped away and in its place was the face of the true man: hard, manipulative, implacable, inscribed with the marks of the many nefarious deeds of his life. My mother's eyes filled with tears, something I'd never seen before.

In that moment of apocalyptic clarity, I knew that Beagle was my father, that he had taken my mother for every pleasure her body and soul could provide and then had thrown her away as casually as he'd toss a gum wrapper to the street (Dentyne, trademark, comes to mind, for no reason whatsoever). I felt no love or filial respect for my newfound father. I felt only hatred for a man who could amass for himself such wealth and power while ignoring the woman who loved him and the son who never knew him. Okay, that's a bit purple but it's the way I felt at the time. I broke from my mother and ran toward the float, brushing past a leather-coated policeman who shouted, "Hey!"

I didn't intend to hurt Beagle. I just wanted to protest, to make a stand, to show him I was human, too. The eyes of the bare and wanton girls widened and their smiles took on funny shapes: oblong, square, parallelogram. A full moon hung quizzically above the parade but was unable to compete with the sadistic street lamps. My corduroy pants made an abrasive sound with every scissoring of my legs. Beagle's eyes dropped from my mother to me. An expression of disgust and horror came across his face as he seemed to realize that I was determined to express my birthright.

He stood up from his throne, hanging on to the radio tower at the top of one of the building models. With his free hand, he pointed down at me. Time slowed and his shout, "Stop him!" seemed to stretch out so every rasp of the bass vibration in his voice was distinct and painful. I reached the float and was clambering up the side, happy to note I'd caused the girls to uncross their legs. I stared eagerly, searching for the recessive mysteries dwelling therein as I sought a handhold in the lobby of one of the model buildings.

Beagle tilted his head back and laughed. I stared up into the tonsures of hair in his nostrils. His jagged incisors looked ready to fall onto my neck and suck out the blood. I swear I heard him snarl, "You're not mine!" just as he was about to drain me of life. Nevertheless, I continued to hoist my hips up onto the float, determined to make a connection even it should prove to be fatal (as it soon may be), when a hot breath of rum enveloped me from behind and made me cough.

"Avast there, matey!" A gravelly voice shouted in my ear. One powerful hand squeezed me by the neck while another grabbed my belt. I was lifted high in the air, up to the eye level of the girls who slapped themselves on their breasts with relief. Beagle turned to fix his laser stare upon me as the float drifted on. I started to spin around as the crowd, in a whirling blur, laughed and pointed at me. I looked down at the bleary pink eye, stubbly cheeks, and red-veined nose of a Seafair pirate, complete with floppy hat and a black eye-patch with a disconcerting smear of crimson upon it, blood perhaps or, more likely, ketchup.

"You're lucky he didn't keelhaul you, squirt," the ruffian shouted. "Beagle doesn't take to punks messing with his women."

Again the crowd guffawed, confirming me in my lifelong hatred of people en masse. I kicked my arms and legs, trying to escape, but he just spun me faster, accelerating until the faces of the crowd blurred together and I was propelled away, twirling like a discus in the air. I landed inside the Pirates' buccaneer ship that rocked merrily on top of its float. The happy drunken fools within were pleased to leave their marks on me with their boots, their fists, and the pommels of their swords. I didn't feel pain, partly because the pirates were too far gone in their collective inebriation to generate much force, but also because I'd retreated far within myself and watched the proceedings as if I were in an impervious bathysphere being attacked by creatures of the deep. They buffeted me but didn't touch my essence.

My field of vision, as limited as the view through a periscope's eyepiece, contained, in turn, a wet handle-bar mustache, a hairy arm with a tattoo of a green dragon, the flash of a sword-blade, a round gut swaying beneath a silk ruffled shirt, the dog shit encrusted heel of a high-top leather boot, a cluster of laughing faces on the street below and, above it all, beyond the glare and the roar, the patient moon looking down at me, with sympathy, I thought, with understanding.

I'm now at mid-day Saturday back at good old Walla Walla. I've used up a large chunk of my remaining time and lots of paper but I'm not sure I've yet successfully pleaded my case. You can't understand another human being in the short paragraphs the newspapers use to crucify their victims, much less in the haiku-like phrases of television "journalism." I'm having some fig newtons now (a trademark, I suppose, although I hope their litigators just relax as I'm merely describing here), a little extra gift from the prison kitchen. An odd phenomenon is that a prisoner with an impending execution date becomes the pet of the cooks who strive to tempt his palate with goodies far superior to the usual slop they pour out from forty gallon drums. I suppose they enjoy a certain aestheticism involved in feeding a man who's not going to live long and therefore does not need to eat to live. The situation must call forth an art for art's sake mood in the kitchen staff.

The unit is relatively quiet. I can hear the intermittent murmurs and shouts along the row, with a deep background bass of whirring machinery. I don't know what the machinery does, probably nothing but prevent us from hearing the purity of absolute silence. I'm sitting up cross-legged on my bed with my yellow pad in my lap and my back against the wall, both literally and metaphorically. I would think the only really effective plea to you would be that I'm alive now, my heart beating, my brain clicking slowly, my lungs collapsing and expanding. I don't want this to end. I've emerged from the Beagle-induced fog and can now enjoy myself with just this: a small space, the always-harsh light, a thread of words I spin out from myself the way a spider extrudes its longing filament (not really a mixed metaphor, or is it?).

My mother's greeting, after the pirates tossed me down, torn and disheveled, and I made my way back to the sardonic audience clustered along the sidewalk, was to crack me across the side of the head, causing groans from those nearby, some approving but others not. The policeman who shouted at me was making his way closer to deliver admonishments and possibly arrest me but nodded his head approvingly at the loud smacking sound her hand made against my skull. He returned to the parade, her blow obviously satisfying his ideal of rough justice.

She accused me of trying to molest one of the girls on the float (of which I was guilty in the Catholic sense, i.e. having lusted in my heart although I was too young to have any idea of how even to begin molesting someone plus I wasn't, never have been, Catholic) but I was convinced of the real reason for her violence. Now she knew that I knew my father, and she couldn't hide her humiliation or her shame. Cursing and snarling, she pushed her way back through the crowd, dragging me by the ear as I tried to ignore the lewd jibes of the inebriated louts around us.

My life began and ended that night. I'd been a normally unhappy boy, yearning for some world, some meaning, beyond the tedium of school in the day and the boredom of my evenings watching TV with Gouchie while my mother served up pints and shots at The Kitty Kat. I did have magic in my childhood but it was all within my head, as I engaged in extended reveries and dialogues with a variety of mythical and fairy book creatures, many of whom more real to me than the people around me. I would talk to Aslan, C.S. Lewis' lion, who I now realize was his obvious stand-in for a redeemer I don't believe in (even though I've always seriously desired redemption). I can't help but recall Nietzsche's statement that "Faith means not wanting to know what is true" but, despite my lifelong skepticism, I found Aslan would answer back in my mind, and maybe in some other dimension I didn't, don't understand, as would the Mad Hatter and Huckleberry Finn and Frodo, the hobbit. Crazy, you might wonder, or not? Just a lonely kid, I think, using my imagination for sustenance.

At my encounter with Beagle, reality thrust itself into my fantasy world and shattered it to pieces. After confronting him, I knew who I was, knew the reason for my pain and isolation, and knew that at some point in my life, I'd have to exact retribution. Let me make it clear, however: I wasn't thinking of murder. That wasn't my intention at all. I merely wanted to let Beagle know, somehow, somewhere, somewhen (I know, but it really should be a word, shouldn't it?) that he had been wrong to let us go, to abandon us to the cruel imperial city of Seattle.

My first impulse was to strive for greater achievement in school, in order to be able someday to buy and sell him. I had fantasies of becoming a wealthy businessman and using dummy corporations to slowly, inexorably, take over his empire until it collapsed, hollowed out from within. I would show up in his office one day, announcing myself to the shocked secretary as his son. I'd intrude into the inner sanctum where I'd explain to him exactly who I was and how I had ruined his fortune. He would stare at the elegantly tailored, handsome young man before him and, at the end of my explanation, stricken by his malicious foolishness in abandoning such a vital young product of his loins, he would clutch at his chest and collapse.

I'd sit in the corner, leaning back in a Barcalounger (trademark again?) with my legs crossed at the ankles, slowly smoking a cigar (Havana, of course), while the Medics occupied themselves by furiously compressing his chest in a futile effort to revive him. (If I survive past this weekend and my letters somehow make their way to the public, I hope the Barcalounger company might send me a free chair in appreciation for this unsolicited endorsement).

After the parade, I couldn't get Beagle out of my mind. I was only thirteen when I met him, albeit a young thirteen, but had been ordinarily happy at my grade school in Ballard where a mixture of kids attended, many of them children of Scandinavians whose parents had signed on for lucrative indentured slavery with Boeings (you could always tell the old-timers because they added the "s" at the end to Boeing, as if it were a mom and pop store. In fact, after the First World War, when the demand for airplanes ebbed, the company actually made furniture, collector's items now).

Also in my classes were the progeny of office workers from downtown, usually workers at a not very high level, given that those making high incomes gravitated to Queen Anne, Madison Park, Montlake, and the waterfront communities in Laurelhurst and Medina.

Ballard remained firmly ensconced in the middle class although back then there were still shacks near the Ballard Locks and run-down houses north of Leary Way. The families of the local poor scraped by on food stamps and government cheese, big blocks of yellow fat that lasted for months and appeared in slices daily, combined with baloney and mayonnaise on Wonder bread, in the sandwiches I assembled for school.

We didn't think of ourselves as poor but mom's waitressing income and Gouchie's Social Security didn't allow for extras. My Christmas presents tended to be clothes I needed and not the plastic toys I wanted when younger, nor the record player I longed for at thirteen. My most precious possession was a transistor radio that pulled in KJR, the Seattle rock station playing the Beatles and the Stones, anthems for the revolution of youth, an illusion I could relate to although I never connected with my peers enough to be caught up in any of their uprisings.

I was undoubtedly odd but was more left alone than picked on. Gouchie always told me I had a scowl on my face that, combined with the bulky build I developed at puberty, may have caused my fellow students to imagine I might somehow be dangerous. However, I was preternaturally timid, not wanting to throw my weight around in any way that might bring me into conflict. In class, I would answer when called upon and my responses were usually correct but I didn't raise my hand the way the intellectually eager would, whispering the teachers' names with great urgency in the hope of being called on. I sat in my classroom at the Leif Erickson grade school, looking out to the adjoining park where the trees were swaying and shedding leaves in the perennial autumn rains of the Northwest. I never was the kind of kid who learned the names of the species of plants and trees, although I have always been someone who wished I knew them. That gives you some idea of how constricted and ineffectual my life has been, at least until this latest chapter.

As I sat there in class, trying to keep from nodding off after staying up reading too late the night before, I'd fall into reveries where I would see Beagle's face forming and dissolving among the remaining leaves. The rustling of branches and slapping of shingles formed a rhythm mimicking the sound of human speech and in this cadence I'd hear Beagle's voice telling me I was never going to be his son so all my claims of paternity would come to nothing in the end. I didn't want to hear his voice. I would much rather have been a normal eighth grade student, wondering if any of the girls in the class liked me, thinking ahead to varsity sports in high school. I probably don't need to tell you that none of the girls passed me notes or plotted to make me their boyfriend. As for sports, I was so inept in physical education that, despite my size, I was quickly benched no matter what game we played.

My fellow students contained a large cohort of future Seafair pirates waiting for their turn in the parade. Like pack animals, they sensed my difference from them and sniffed at me as if I were a sheep in wolf's clothing. When their attentions became a bit too intimate, I'd go down again in the bathysphere, watching with detached interest as they mocked and teased the body they foolishly mistook for me. From inside the deep-sea refuge I created in my mind, I staged entire pageants involving brigades of brave knights using cold steel to dispatch the hordes of barbarians plaguing me at every turn.

At least one of my teachers in Middle School expressed a regard more benevolent than that of my peers. Mr. Grasse, who taught English, was impressed by my compositions but told me I'd eventually outgrow my naive nihilism. That's pretty funny, in light of my present predicament, don't you think? But I don't feel nihilistic now. I take great pleasure in the tiniest details of being alive: the curve in my spine, the meager heft of this pad in my lap, the low buzzing in my head. Everything has been so peaceful since Beagle died. It was only after he was gone that I realized fully how pervasive his manipulations had become, how thoroughly he had permeated my world.

After the calamitous Parade, my mother and I were never close again. The next fall, at an Elks Halloween dance, she met Mitch Prangle who owned, and probably still does own, a motorcycle repair shop in Enumclaw. Mitch is a brooding, taciturn guy who has never said more than three consecutive words to me. My one reason for liking him is that he totally captivated my mother's attention so I didn't have to deal with her intermittent yet intrusive demands upon me. She ended up quitting the Ki Kat and spending most of her time at his house, located on acreage with a massive view of Mt. Rainier. I was left to my own devices, devices I was quite happy to be left with. Gouchie didn't interfere much in my meager activities.

Now I'm able to see the dark hand of Beagle in their meeting. I don't think Beagle actually hired Mitch for the purpose but I do believe he managed to create a situation in which two lost people would inevitably gravitate toward each other. Beagle was a grand exalted something or other in the Elks, and it would be simplicity itself for him to organize a dance and make sure certain people were there. When a man is as powerful as Beagle is, I mean was, he can be subtle. Obviously, his intention was to increase my isolation, making the job easier of cutting me out from the herd and hog-tying me, psychically speaking, of course (not that I ever ran with any herd).

Less than a year after that Seafair parade, my mother was married, pregnant, and living in Enumclaw. I refused Mitch's monosyllabic invitation to join them. Gouchie was willing for me to stay on with her. Her exact words were, "What the hell? Just don't bother me." As usual in this life, at least until recently, I let inertia determine my fate. I moved down from the seasonally sweltering or freezing attic into my mother's old room. I don't remember living there as an experience of what might be called "home." I've always felt estranged from any domicile I've inhabited, including this one (not a plea for pity, just a fact).

I delivered papers before school to contribute toward the household expenses. Gouchie sat and watched TV all day, the fat in her face quivering with either dismay or humor in response to the tragedy and comedy playing out before her. As long as I wasn't noisy, she didn't care what I did. I'm not noisy, never have been. Even less than three days from my possible (probable?) execution, I sit here quietly although no one could blame me or do much of anything if I let out screams of agony. What are they going to do, kill me?

Sometimes, however, I wonder what "they" are up to when I see people who can't possibly be here moving around me, looking down at me as I scribble in my notebook, sometimes commenting on my intensity. They act as if they're real but are mere shadows in my mind. They add a wraith-like dimension to my isolation but are probably just the progeny of my over-active imagination. Don't worry, Governor, I'm not bucking for the insanity plea. I know we're way beyond that now.

Outside my bedroom in Gouchie's house was a cluster of evergreens, inhabited by a host of busy birds, carving sudden vectors in three dimensions. I filled the room with books and kept listening to the top 40 songs of the era through the earphones of my portable radio. I enjoyed the exercise and the isolation of delivering newspapers. I became so adept at the process that I barely slowed my bike at all through the entire route. I'd reach back, grab a paper, and loft it to the steps of a subscriber in one smooth motion, rarely missing, avoiding with my speed and efficiency the problems of human interaction.

Collecting was another story, however. After ringing a door bell, I would stand still, rock-like, on the porch or stoop, confronting the inhabitants through my presence with the fact that they were in debt. I realized then that my self-control had power. People would fumble and falter, sometimes reduced to tears or spurred to verbal abuse by my demanding, silent presence. Needless to say, I was never invited in and only rarely received tips. That was okay with me. I didn't want charity, only my due.

The world around me was in the tumult of the seventies but I was disconnected from its concerns, although I did enjoy the music on KJR with its team of hyper-kinetic announcers. My single, overriding concern was with my father. I read the paper every day, of course, and clipped out any mention of Beagle for my scrapbook.

For example, on November 22nd, 1973, the front page of the Seattle Post-Intelligencer had a photograph of Beagle and wife at a charity auction for some no doubt bogus cause like scholarships for wealthy kids. Exactly ten years earlier, President Kennedy was assassinated in Dallas. A coincidence? I don't think so. Any progressive force was bound to be anathema to his repressive mentality.

Another news photo from 1974 showed Beagle dedicating a new building whose foundations went down into the shifting silt of the industrial area south of downtown, making the structure almost guaranteed to fall at the first minor earthquake. I clipped an article about Beagle meeting with African-American leaders concerning the possibility of construction jobs, no doubt conniving to bring them into the modern form of vassalage guaranteed by the minimum wage. Usually, the camera only captured his fatuous surface, not penetrating to the sinister core. But in one photo that really should have been entered into evidence at my trial, his true self gleams through.

If you are undecided about my fate after reading this, you might want to send a couple of state troopers over to Gouchie's house on NW 60th Street. My mother is still the owner and last I heard she was going to sell it. The police no doubt still have a key. In the closet of my bedroom are a pile of boxes, no doubt covered in spider webs as that house was always the Garden of Eden for arachnids. In one of the boxes is a brown leather scrapbook marked Beagle, Volume 1 (just thought of something. I hope it's been returned by the cops. They may have taken it to document what they termed my obsession with Beagle, completely ignoring his obsession with me. If it hasn't been returned, you'll probably have to look for it in the Seattle Police Department Evidence room).

Anyway (and I realize you are probably not very invested in this project), about halfway through the scrap book is the picture I'm talking about, taken at a panel of city leaders with some silly title like "Whither Seattle?" or "Puget Sound in the Seventies: Boom or Bust?" (We know now which it was, bust, of course, followed by more booms, more busts). All the other fat cats are smiling at the camera but Beagle, standing to the side, has been distracted by something off-camera, something he doesn't like one bit. His mouth is open in a snarl and his eyes are as hooded as the proverbial cobra's. His right hand reaches forward in a claw-like gesture as he looks ready to spit his venom out. He appears much as he did on the fateful night when I approached his float.

Maybe the Indians (Native American) were right and a photograph can capture a man's soul because this shot captures his like no other. If you have any question about why there is crime, sordid violence, poverty, and neglect in this world, you just have to look into the face of Beagle in this picture. I have no doubt this shot alone will convince you I should be reprieved, if not released outright, and I urge you to look for it. If you can't find the damning photo, then I hope you will take my description of it at face value. I'm the man who knows (knew) Beagle better than any other and the fact that someone of my sensitive, poetic, and philosophical nature was driven to kill him should tell you all you need to know about his character. Sorry to brag but no one else is going to do it.

We're sliding toward the end of the day now. I don't have a window in this cell but know from the quality of the sounds around me, from the frequency of the pacings and guttural cries, that the condemned men are waiting for their dinners, one of the few pleasures allowed in the day, no matter that the quality of the food is strictly Walla Walla. A guard who's as bulky as a steer walks slowly by and looks in at me with a flat expression, as if he's glancing into a store window containing items of absolutely no interest to him. They used to yell at me to stop writing, apparently concerned I was composing a denunciation of prison life but I've moved into such exalted status that no one tells me anything anymore. I'm among a group of men condemned to die, guarded by men who will all eventually die (some of them soon given their apparent states of health), yet I'm the only one who knows exactly when it will happen, unless you intervene or unless, of course, the legendary Deity so many in the U.S. claim to admire takes some action.

I hope I'm giving you something here, showing you the roots of Beagle's campaign against me. The point is, he knew I was his son but couldn't admit it, to himself or to me. I began to suspect in high school that he wasn't just ignoring me but was actively campaigning against me (and I soon had absolute proof). I didn't really have any friends back then, aside from a few other victims who felt some collegiality in our estrangement from our peers. I disdained the proms, of course, not knowing any girls well enough to ask and not knowing how I could bear to socialize with my "peers."

My spare time I filled with movies. I couldn't watch many on TV because Gouchie spent most of her waking hours in front of her massive wooden console, even sleeping in her armchair at night to the sounds of talk shows or test patterns. While awake, she would only watch soap operas and comedy shows, the manufactured laughter sounding like the screeching of howler monkeys at the nearby Woodland Park Zoo. I would usually go to 9 PM shows on weeknights where I was often the only customer, enjoying a private screening at the Bay theatre in Ballard, or at the Ridgemont above the zoo, or I'd go to the somewhat more crowded theaters in the University District, the Seven Gables or The Grand Illusion. I couldn't have survived my adolescence without Chinatown, The Godfather I & II, Taxi Driver, Star Wars,

The Conversation, Marathon Man, Annie Hall, and Dog Day Afternoon, most of which provided consolation for an outsider, such as me.

I miss movies here but I refuse to submit myself to the hypnosis of the television that most of the men on the IMU worship throughout the long and boring hours here. (Parenthetically, and you know how I like parentheses, I keep reading in the newspapers arriving on the library cart, weeks late, about new releases I'd like to see, such as Rain Man, Working Girl, The Accidental Tourist, New York Stories, and just last week, Field Of Dreams. The reviews, when positive, make me sad I may never see those films, or any others).

However (back to my youth), even at the movies I found evidence of Beagle's active participation in my life. I'd be sitting with my tub of popcorn, sunk low in the chair, my feet up on the seat in front of me (unless the usher told me to put them down), when I'd suddenly feel I was being watched. I'd look around, half expecting to see one of the trench-coated gropers who even found me, in my pimpled and frowning glory, worthy of attention but no one was there. I'd look around at the other patrons sparsely scattered through the theatre. Someone was watching me, I was sure, but I couldn't tell who. The split-second required to turn my head gave whoever it was more than enough time to pretend interest in the action on the screen. How did I know, you might ask, that it was one of Beagle's emissaries doing surveillance and not someone from the Vice Squad, the Draft Board, or the Publisher's Clearinghouse? The quality of the watching made me certain. The covert surveillance wasn't neutral but oily, insidious, evil in intent. Of the few people I knew in the world, only Beagle had any reason to feel such animosity toward me.

This surveillance continued on my paper route. I'd be biking down a street when I'd feel, more than see, the rustling of curtains as I drove by houses where I didn't deliver. Every neighborhood has its busybodies, old ladies and unemployed men whose only recreation is to watch passing events on the street but this wasn't their doing. The conspiracy was too widespread, involving not just one or a few houses, but a whole series of houses, as if I were tripping invisible wires as I went past, setting off cameras that would give a continuous photographic record of my passage. I could hear mutterings coming from the sky and from inside the trees and houses as I sped down the street. I wasn't able to make out the words but I could hear the intonations involved, suggesting strongly they were talking about me and not in a positive way.

No, Governor, I don't have proof Beagle was involved, or even that anything was happening beyond the idle movements of reality when nothing major is going on, like the ticking of a car after it's been turned off. But I do know in myself that something ominous was in play, something I hadn't asked for, something I didn't want. Reality was a net in which I struggled like the turbot, my namesake (a left-eyed flatfish, in case you didn't know).

Proof finally arrived at the end of my senior year in high school when I attained the second best grade point average in the school and was scheduled to be the salutatorian. The valedictorian was an unbeatable girl, Harmony Dankel, daughter of science professors from the U., who was so machinelike she never received anything but A pluses throughout her entire school career. As isolated as I was, I was happy to be at least a bit more human than she was. Second place was enough, and I'd already prepared my speech, attacking the school, the administration, the community, the country, the human race, and even God himself (in whom I didn't, don't, believe but threw in for the sake of emphasis), indicting them all for their individual and collective blindness and greed, referencing the madness of the Vietnam War, along with a host of other historical inequities, suggesting that all these evils could be traced to one source, a seemingly ordinary business man and real estate developer whose name was..., well, you know what his name was.

I wrote a separate and misleading draft to submit to my English teacher, Mr. Hopewink, a draft encompassing the usual bland platitudes about hope for the future and encouragement for success in college, the military, or whatever vocational courses or jobs the graduates could conjure up. Mr. Hopewink approved this draft but seemed surprised by its tepid affability. I planned to stand up and keep reading my real speech until someone pulled me off the stage. I feared I'd been found out when Mr. Hopewink, with seeming reluctance, asked me to step into the counseling office for a little talk. He said he was extremely embarrassed but had been chosen by the principal to relay his news because he was the only faculty member who had any kind of relationship to me. The message was that a mistake had been made in the grading of a math class. A "B" on Scott Howard's record had been miraculously uplifted to an "A," enabling him to just nudge me out for the honor of addressing the school.

I was furious, immediately knowing this to be the result of the Beagle's conspiracy. Scott Howard was the senior class president, letter man on the basketball team, and the heart throb (not to mention cunt throb) of most of the girls in the school. Without the slight lisp he revealed whenever someone challenged his social status, he would have been totally insufferable. I demanded to know why his grade had been changed and Hopewink could only reply that he was given extra credit by Mr. DiPalmieri, the typically Cro-Magnon gym teacher and math instructor, who no doubt arranged for Scott to solve a set of long division problems that wouldn't tax a moderately intelligent twelve year old while I sweated for my A in pre-calculus.

Why couldn't I work for similar extra credit, I demanded? I'd earned my usual grudging "B" in Phys. Ed. from the same logical half-wit, Dipalmieri. It was too late, Hopewink replied. All grades were now final. I turned without an additional word and left the building even though various "fun" senior activities were scheduled for the day. The rage boiled in my cerebellum and that was the closest I've come to being a true danger to society. Note well, Governor, that I myself am calling this to your attention so you can gauge the difference between what I might have done and what I actually did.

If I'd had access to a rifle or, even better, an automatic weapon that day, I would have climbed to the highest point I could have found and started killing as many of my teachers and fellow students as possible. I would never have surrendered. They would have had to call the SWAT team to take me down and then, as the bumper sticker says, they would have had to pry the weapon from the fingers of my cold dead hand. Maybe not so cold, as they might have had to cut my fingers off to remove them from the barrel where they would have been cooked on by the heat. It says something in favor of the gun control laws you oppose so vehemently that I didn't have access to a weapon or any way of buying one that day.

In a moment of charity, feeling some measure of empathy for those in the school who were as tormented as I was, I resolved to kill myself instead of others. I rode my bike over to the beach in Golden Gardens Park by Puget Sound, stripped down to my shorts, and proceeded to swim out, planning to tire myself to exhaustion and drown. Fortunately (notice I use that word), my plans were disturbed by several factors.

First, it was a lovely mild day, a Friday afternoon in early June and the Sound was full of boats. They kept crossing my path and almost running me over, making me somewhat apprehensive of being struck by their propellers, an encounter that, if it didn't kill me, would send me to the hospital for hundreds of stitches from lacerations caused by multiple blades. I'd imagined my death as lonely and Byronic but they were threatening to turn it into a carnival of horrors almost as ludicrous as Seafair.

Moreover, my bike-riding on the paper route had put me, despite my terrible diet, into pretty good shape. My swimming style was lousy but my wind was fine so it looked like I'd probably be able to swim all the way to Bainbridge Island before I became exhausted enough to die. I would probably end up gasping on the lawn of an expensive waterfront home on Wing Point whose owners would send the butler out to perform artificial respiration. I didn't want to end up at the mercy of one of Beagle's wealthy compatriots.

As I swam, some boaters assumed I was training for a long-distance swim like the English Channel so they swerved close by, offered me sandwiches and beer, and gave me encouragement in typically drunken and hearty fashion, making me think again of the damned Seafair Pirates but without the costumes. Maybe Beagle had hired them to stalk me wherever I went.

I reached what felt like the middle of the Sound, the buildings and vehicles back on shore looking like tiny toys, and treaded water for awhile, my eyes just above the bobbing surface, looking out across the liquidly mobile expanse to Magnolia and downtown Seattle and Mt. Rainier to the south. The setting sun was turning the puffy clouds above to gold while seagulls skimmed low, their heads twisting from side to side in search of food. All of reality seemed to be offering me its wealth, urging me not to die. I relaxed somewhat, realizing my destiny must not be to leave high school in a gurgle of soggy glory. I already knew who had arranged the whole thing, who had the power and the connections to alter a grade long after the grades should have been in, who was so set on keeping me quiet, on destroying me, on stopping me from speaking in public and possibly revealing his darkest secret.

Now you know the answer, too, Governor. A man of your intelligence can make the simple logical connections needed to determine the culprit, the man who was determined to ruin my life. Now you're asking yourself why, oh why, didn't I tell this whole sad story to the police who arrested me, to my lawyer, to the court when I was tried? I stood mute, unwilling to engage with Leonard, my public defender, much less the forensic psychiatrists for hire who were so frustrated when I didn't spill my guts (and insisted on waving around my old hospital records).

Frankly, I was afraid of being misunderstood. Beagle's power would extend, I knew, even from beyond the grave. His final triumph, nullifying my pure stroke of action against him, would be to have a label attached to me so I could be put away in a "mental health" facility. Such places are, I know from bitter experience, actually concentration camps for those who don't conform to society. To be confined there and pumped full of anti-psychotic drugs would be to lose my self, the entity for which I've battled so fiercely over the years. Better to live out my years in prison with my mind intact than to be deprived of my inner awareness years before my bodily death. I'm confident you won't make the mistake of judging me as "mentally ill," Governor. It's really too late now, as I've been convicted of the crime. Moreover, I gather from your public statements that you don't have much sympathy for the insanity defense Leonard tried, so feebly and ineffectually, to use in my case.

Here you and I are in total agreement. If my actions were driven by mental illness then I've unknowingly committed a grave crime, depriving an innocent man of his life. No matter how ill someone is, I believe he or she is responsible for all actions taken. Instead, I hope you will see your Beagle from my entirely rational perspective, see the perfidy the man embodies (embodied, that is, especially as he was cremated and thereby disembodied) and realize he drove me to kill him. Just as a husband can drive a wife to murder by constant beatings, so Beagle, my father, caused me, his son, to kill him but only after I suffered for decades from his psychological, and sometimes physical, abuse. I suppose that resorting to homicide could be considered the result of a mental illness but not when I so clearly thought through the options and only struck when I was sure that the danger to the world, and to me, was so great I had no choice but to act.

Oh, and in case you're wondering, I swam back to shore that June day, napped on the beach for an hour or so to recover from the effort, and then rode my bike home to Ballard. I do have to say that, after coming so close to dying, the beauty of the world jumped out at me from every form. Even the usual aesthetic banality of the cars around me seemed transformed into miracles of engineering allowing humans to wander all over the continent and even down to South America. Someone in a camper van, starting in Seattle, could drive all the way to Tierra Del Fuego to look south toward Antarctica and the end of the world in ice.

Three a.m. now and my bladder and bowels are sending me messages so I'll take a little break with my steel friend against the wall (no toilet seat, just a metal rim, ice cold to the buttocks any season of the year) and you might now want to take some time yourself to think over all I've written. If everything goes as scheduled, you will be perusing this missive well before my scheduled cataclysm. You have plenty of time to send a message of reprieve. You can even send it late if you want to punish me by increasing the suspense, but please send it. I'm beginning to think I might have found a way, through my writing, to help the world and the common citizens I've been dumping on too often in this document. In telling my story, completely and in depth, I might be able to provide solace for other outcasts and misfits, to make them realize they're not the only ones who have suffered, and to guide them in seeking solutions short of violence to their problems. Doesn't that make sense, seem worthwhile, sound okay? You think about it and let me know.

Sincerely,
(at least that,
you'll have to admit,
or will you?)
Isaac Turbot

Saturday, April 29, 1989

Dear Mother,

This may be the last time you hear from me. It's now Saturday afternoon and my so-called necktie party (although who calls it that, I'm sure I don't know?) is scheduled for midnight, Monday night. I've just woken up from a fitful sleep, interrupted at times by guards stopping by to take a gander (but not goosing me) at the man who's about to die. Can't blame them, I guess. Everyone always stops to gape at the scene of an accident. I'm not feeling very well right now, bit of indigestion. Just can't stomach the situation, I guess.

This is the third letter I've written you after Beagle's death and you haven't written back at all. The only communication I've had from you has been indirect, when a Seattle P.I. reporter cornered you at the Safeway in Enumclaw, asking rather crudely what you thought of my conviction. I saw you on the news (back before my sentencing, when I still had access to the dubious pleasures of TV), standing with a pineapple in hand in the produce section, (giving the blonde-helmet head your taking-no-shit stare) asserting finally that you've had no contact with me for years and therefore wanted nothing to do with me or any of my actions. I know you have a new life so I can readily understand why you don't want to be plagued with interviews by the press. I would have thought, however, with me in extremis here, you might give me some acknowledgement of what's happened between us, among us, through us.

You and I never talked about Beagle or his crimes upon you. You were always quick to let me know when you didn't want to talk about something. During our limited and detached time together, we never sat down and discussed anything honestly. We lived by undercurrents and moods, not by the truth. I finally decided that the truth was all I cared for and this decision led me to take the action I did. One thing I hadn't anticipated but now seems to me a possibility given your silence is that you still retain an emotional attachment to Beagle despite all he did to you. In that case, my assassination of him may have seemed like the destruction of your secret love, or some such nonsense.

If that's what you're thinking, all I can say is you would have to approve of my action if you knew all he did to me over the years. The man plagued me in innumerable ways. He was absolutely unable to leave me in peace. Only his death has given me respite from his constant surveillance and harassment. The press tried to portray me as a man obsessed with some imagined slight but they, as usual, had it backwards. Beagle was obsessed with me and I couldn't make him stop.

What's the use? I'm tired of trying to explain myself (even my prose style is breaking down, not that it was very advanced to begin with). I'm writing to the

Governor asking him to let me live but I have little expectation of success. I shouldn't have to beg and wouldn't have to if the Governor hadn't always been a close ally of Beagle. I'm realizing now I may not ever hear from you again. In that case, if that's the way it goes down, and if I were a different kind of person, I might tell you that you were a terrible mother who alternately criticized me "for my own good" (shout out to the brilliant Alice Miller. Look up her work and you might learn something), and then ignored me. I would not have the nerve to say these words except, knowing who you are, I'm sure they won't hurt you. You'll shrug me off and pop open another beer or light another joint and channel surf with Mitch. Not that there's anything wrong with that. Not that you owe me anything. Nothing matters anymore.

I'm sick and depressed. My life has been a farce, pointless and painful. Slugs who get stepped on in mountain trails have more meaning in their existence. I spent almost thirty years trying to avoid looking at this but here it is. The few good things in my life only make the shit smell worse. My bike, the movies, reading, my friend Sandy, plants and trees, what do they add up to? Not much, just momentary escapes from the hell of what's real, the hell you and Beagle (the nightmarish opposites of proud parents) created for me.

Damn, I can't send this. She's an asshole but she's not the cause of my pain. Things as they are, the world as it is, that's the cause. I myself am the cause of my pain. Even Beagle isn't the cause of my pain, unless he's somehow manipulating things from beyond the grave which I doubt because I stuck him pretty good, saw him go down, saw the bubbles of death dribble from his mouth. The truth is that I am very definitely in a bad mood. That's what the jury representing the citizens of the state of Washington wanted when they sentenced me to death. They wanted me to be in a lousy mood as I contemplated the ritual murder they set into motion.

I kept thinking this sinuous line of words would lead me out of all this but now it's just sinking me deeper in the mire. My preoccupation with Beagle used to distract me from the truth but I really have been one unhappy puppy all my life. I should probably stop writing now and do something else, exercise or eat (although, really, in both cases, what's the point?), shoot the shit with B-Day or listen to some music, but I'm afraid to stop the flow of words now for fear I'll never start up again.

If I feel much worse, I'll be calling for the prison chaplain Reverend Tom Acksel who sniffs around here like a dog in heat. He smells a soul going down and wants to talk me into accepting Jesus as my Lord and Savior. I tried once to say, okay, I accept him into my life, now what? It didn't seem to change anything. Acksel's reply was that I had to mean it, which didn't make much sense to me. How can I cross the gap between meaning something and not meaning it? I don't really believe so how can I bridge that gulf to where I do believe? I sense how easy it would be to believe, how reassuring to imagine that as my neck breaks, I won't reach my end but a new beginning. The problem is that I just don't buy it. I don't see the evidence, I don't have the faith, and I don't believe I'm going to be delivered.

Dr. Fallow, the prison psychiatrist, is a much more interesting case. Where the Reverend cares about what I might become if Jesus condescends to whisper in my ear or whatever it is he does, Fallow's only concern is to figure out why I committed the crime. He wants me to admit I was paranoid and delusional when I killed Beagle, as if clearing up that little item will let him rest easy when they execute me. His interest isn't so much personal as it is technical, and professional. He wants to be able to push me, a square peg, into one of his triangular holes of diagnosis, and then publish an article and maybe a book about me. He's a furtive little rat of a man, with his scruffy goatee that must make him think he looks like Freud. To hell with him. I'm not going to finish this letter. Probably best to flush it down the toilet.

Even though I'm not sending this, I may as well finish it by saying goodbye from:

Your son, Ike

Saturday, April 29, 1989

Dear Governor Renhennie,

When I stopped writing early this morning, I was heading for the steel toilet in my cell, and that's where I am again now, with a case of the runs (nerves, do you think?), writing away, always pressing on, like a shark or a politician. I thought for a moment I might be in a grimy men's room in a large facility where people are free to come and go. An odd mental juxtaposition for which I have no explanation. Random neuron firings, probably.

I'm here again, how about you? The guard at the end of the hall is yawning loudly, looking forward, no doubt, to the end of his shift. While I was sitting on the john where, like Martin Luther, I do some of my best thinking, I was trying to imagine what some of your questions might be.

"How?" could possibly be one of them. How, that is, if allowed to live and carry out his mission will Isaac Turbot guide the inexhaustible supply of social misfits of society in solving their problems without violence? One way would be to convince officials such as yourself to take them seriously, to see that problems such as mine need to be addressed. Perhaps I shouldn't bring it up here but I did write you many letters, previous to the fatal event, warning about Beagle and his machinations, messages of vital importance, to which you responded first with a form letter and then only with silence, a silence that turned out to be grave (in at least two meanings of the word).

"What?" might well be another question, that is, what in the world is he talking about? On your part, this question would either be cynical or naive, depending on how much you know. Someone who was an intimate of Beagle would have to be aware of his sorcery-like powers, his control over the basic elements of earth, air, fire, and water, along with electronic transmissions in all their forms. If you did indeed know the secrets of Beagle's powers, then I am doomed, for you are no doubt determined to avenge the death of your diabolical Master. On the other hand, if you were unaware of the depth and depravity of his machinations, then I have the slimmest of chances. I swear by all you believe and all I believe as well (although that doesn't actually amount to much), that I am telling the absolute truth, at least as I see it, and what else do I have to go by?

Following this line of thought, you might well ask, "Who?" That is, who am I that you should believe me? I'm a poor forked thing, as Shakespeare said somewhere, although I'm not sure of the exact wording, or source (King Lear maybe? Sounds like him), a mere mammal walking on his hind legs upon the earth, his consciousness in extremis now, facing the extinction we all have to face, just in a more imminent fashion. Who knows? If allowed to live, I might do something to benefit humanity. I've never been that skilled in math or science so it won't be anything technological, and it certainly won't be cancer research or a cure for heart disease. But maybe in my scribblings somewhere, I will write sentences that will touch someone else, will increase that person's empathy, or give them reasons to go on even when they don't really want to.

As you can no doubt ascertain from this document, I am not a professional writer (although I do come from an academic background, albeit truncated). I won't have time to edit or rewrite. The only story I can tell is the story of myself, a strange tale, I have to admit, but a narrative people may be drawn to by the sheer strangeness of who I am, a strangeness that just might strike a responsive chord in someone equally strange. And aren't we all actually strange in our deepest selves?

We are the final triumph of evolution, with an awareness and capacity for rational thought allowing us to dominate our environment and, in many cases, destroy it. We might be a dead end in the evolutionary process, like the dinosaurs, doomed to become extinct, or maybe this is just the beginning of a larger process where our awarenesses will be able to join together and overcome our essential loneliness. Maybe Beagle with his vast powers was a negative precursor of what will be a liberation for us all, signaling an ability to expand beyond our skulls and the reach of our arms and tools to become one with all of reality but not in a diabolical way, I fervently hope.

And then you will ask "Where?" Where can you find any corroboration for my claims, any evidence sufficient to convince your fellow members of the upper social strata that you would be justified in granting a reprieve to the murderer of one of your own? How can you possibly explain to your own wife, who was deprived of a portion of her anatomy in an unfortunate consequence of my righteous violence that you are allowing me to continue to breathe on this planet? Husbands and wives are naturally bound together by ties of ritual and affection so you are, I'm sure, quite disturbed by the damage I inflicted on your life partner. I can only say that Mrs. Renhennie was not at all my target as I had no reason to harm the spouse of the second most powerful person in the state, next to Beagle, of course.

And then the most basic question of all: "Why?" You may well be asking yourself, why should I spare the life of the man who killed my excellent friend, Beagle, and who maimed my beloved spouse? Why does he deserve mercy when he offered none to two of the people who matter most to me? (I'm assuming they matter to you but no human being can ever gauge the secret movements of another's heart). I have no answer for this final question in the journalistic litany. Either you will find a reason inside yourself to spare me, or you won't.

The choices are life or death, breath or none, health or what's beyond sickness: annihilation. If I were you, I'd probably come down here and kill me myself. And yet maybe you have some inkling in the recesses of your brain, in the innermost chambers of your heart, that Beagle was not who he claimed to be. Maybe you've been feeling the oppression over the years of Beagle's pervasive influence but didn't realize where it originated. Maybe something in what I say strikes a chord on the honky-tonk piano of your thoughts. That's my only possible salvation.

Neither you nor I believe me to be insane. We both know that's not true, as I planned the crime, had reasons for committing it, and carried it out exactly according to my plans, albeit with some collateral damage to your wife. If you don't understand the "Why?" from what I'm writing here about Dionysius Beagle, then I will die late Monday night and no force upon this earth, other than a Presidential pardon, or a meteor strike, I suppose, will save me. Somehow, I don't think President Bush will be any more receptive to my arguments than you are so I won't be sending any missives to the White House by messenger. Either you will save me or I will die (not that I'm especially enamored of states' rights, given how that principle encourages the calcification of local prejudices).

I'm tired now but want to keep writing until Leonard arrives, indeed up until the moment he has to leave to deliver this letter because I want to keep trying for you to understand me, assuming that if you could see this fallen world from my perspective, you wouldn't want my idiosyncratic self to cease. Even if I am going to die, you should at least realize who you are sending to the next world, assuming, which I don't, that there is another world.

I don't want to write my entire autobiography here (sighs of relief in the Governor's mansion) so maybe I should just hit the highlights: chiefly, what led me to plan the crime and what happened, from my perspective, that fateful night (although, realistically, what night isn't fateful, given that every event, no matter how minor, is linked to the entire chain of cause and effect and also to the totality? But this is a discussion we should have in the future, if there is any future for me, but that again is up to you).

Maybe, to relieve the tedium of my repeatedly begging you to let me live, I'll employ an extended metaphor and describe my life in fireworks: a dud for how I finished high school, a rocket through college, bursts of sparklers studying philosophy, becoming lost in the smoke of the mind games there while ignoring the various political movements on campus, a luminescent snake for going to the movies, as I happily drifted back in the years to the classic Hollywood films at revival theaters, an M-80 for falling in love with Garbo, cherry bombs for arguing with my professors, some of whom attempted to move me toward social relevance while others tried to make me lose myself entirely in the world of abstract ideas, leaving me covered by fading showers of sparks.

My high school disaster and abortive suicide attempt made me believe for years I could never overcome Beagle's machinations by direct confrontation. He was too far ahead, too established, had too much control over the system. I needed to be even more subversive than he was, needed to operate under his radar, if resistance was even possible. This was the period that corresponded to sparklers, a hissing glow in the dark. Eventually, I was forced to take direct action, leading to my current predicament. Of course, the night at the Governor's Ball was the grand finale of the entire show, in multiple explosions and fireballs, the sky filling with lingering fizzing strands of brilliant color.

(At the risk of overtaxing the extended metaphor, what's scheduled for Monday midnight will be a hydrogen bomb).

I was always amused to hear campus radicals talk about the evil "system" with no conception of who, individually, controlled it. Of course, you know about this quite well, Governor, as all the press reports said you could have never been elected without Beagle's support. I don't blame you at all if such was the case. Money drives success in this great nation of ours and it would be the rare man who could resist the amount of cash Beagle was undoubtedly offering.

In my search for answers, I studied philosophy hoping to understand the metaphysical context in which such a beast could develop but I never went very far. You might well ask why I didn't undertake my quest in the disciplines of psychology or political science but I wanted to examine the roots of reality itself for the origins of Beagledom. My reading of Marx provided few hints because I didn't think money was Beagle's overriding motivation although he definitely used the mechanics of capitalism to achieve his ends. Of course, he feared the loss of resources and position that acknowledging me seemed, to him, to entail but his persecution had gone far beyond what was necessary to protect himself. He would have thrived in tandem with Stalin, or Mao, or Pol Pot, just as he operated closely with the major corporations that actually run this country.

He even poisoned casual acquaintances against me, ensuring they could never become close friends. As I talked to people in the various places where I found myself, in classes, cafeterias, taverns, bus stops, even in the lines at the bank and the grocery store, I could see the confusion and fear develop in people's eyes as they struggled between liking me (because, despite everything, I'm not completely unlikable) and fearing me because of the evil Beagle's henchmen told them I embodied. Few people were strong enough to withstand this indoctrination in order to become friendly with me, and none were able to bring themselves to admit where their animosity came from, no matter how casually I tried to sound them out about it.

In August of 1980, I was working for the summer in Tony's lawn business where I would eventually be employed full-time up until the year before my current tribulations. I gave up the paper route as soon as I was out of high school, wanting more money and hours of work than slinging the news could provide. Because of my solid A average and my high SAT scores (792 Reading, 650 Math), along with my poverty, my U.W. tuition was absurdly cheap, allowing me to cut back my working hours in the winter time when business was slow anyway, and I needed to study, yet make enough in the other months to get by.

On one particular Wednesday, I was out mowing at the homes of various clients in the North End of Seattle, using the long daylight to work a twelve hour day, as I usually did in the summer months. I returned home to our block in Ballard where the heat lingered into the evening and the neighbors were out on their porches. Kids ran up and down the street, playing tag and hide-and-seek. I could smell the brine from Puget Sound, one of the perks of living in Ballard. The cries of those howler monkeys up at the zoo on Phinney ridge were carried down to us by the still warm air. I waved to my neighbors next door who were sitting on the front steps of their house because they didn't have a porch, only a short flight of stairs leading into the living room. My mother and grandmother didn't believe in being too friendly with neighbors, even though we lived in a dense part of town, so we never did more than exchange short greetings.

I went inside and the air felt close with an odd sweet smell. Gouchie was impervious to heat and often didn't open the windows even in the height of summer so the warmth didn't surprise me but the smell did. The odor was earthy and organic, like the darkest level of loam in a garden. I'd learned about gardening on the job because our yard at home was mostly dandelions that I mowed down every few months. I had already washed my hands at Tony's house where we ended up at the end of every day but I was looking forward to a long shower.

The television was on, playing a re-run of Charlie's Angels, a show Gouchie watched with religious fervor but one I regarded with equal amounts of intellectual disdain and untethered lust. I saw Gouchie's feet up on the foot rest of her leather armchair where she spent most of her hours, so I said, "Hi." She didn't answer and that was strange because she would usually at least grunt at me in response. I turned the corner and looked down. A dried puddle of vomit was in her lap. Her head was back on the chair and her mouth and eyes were open. She had a look of utter surprise, a look I'd never seen on her before as she was usually the most stoic of individuals, greeting all of life's turnings with a grim resignation. Now she looked shocked and amazed by this most radical of changes, her sudden departure from the planet.

I called my mother and she irritably told me to call 911, as if I had somehow violated a required protocol. I asked if she would be driving up and she said she'd already taken a sleeping pill so she and Mitch were in bed. She said she'd come up the next day and told me I could handle it.

So I called 911 and the police and Medics came out, the police to make sure no foul play was involved, the Medics to confirm the obvious. The vomit in her lap worried the Medics so they called the Medical Examiner who came out with his assistant and looked closely at the body before saying that an autopsy would be performed, presumably to make sure I hadn't poisoned her. The police made a report and called my mother themselves, getting an even more irritable response than I had. I could tell by the face of the officer who was on the phone that mom was not giving the kind of sorrowful and cooperative response he expected. But there was no evidence she had been on the scene so she wasn't obliged, as she well know, to be friendly. Her attitude toward the police was soured from years of serving them free meals and receiving minimal tips at the restaurant.

After the Medics and the police and Gouchie were all gone, and the neighbors, who had gathered curiously on the sidewalks outside, retreated to their steps and porches and living rooms, the neighbor to the east of us, whose name was Rose, a plump middle-aged mom, came to the door and asked if I was okay. I thanked her and said I was indeed okay. She invited me over but I told her I just needed to get some rest. She offered to help in any way she could. I thanked her and closed the door.

I sat down in Gouchie's chair, where I almost never sat because she was always there. I arranged myself around the imprint of her body, much smaller than mine, that had been molded into the cushions. I flicked through the channels with the remote control that was connected by a wire to the mammoth console, holding a screen about twenty inches on the diagonal that seemed lost in the expanse of wood veneer. I breathed in both Gouchie's scent of Dial soap (trademark although, seriously, what do I care?) and that of her death, blending the trace of life with corruption.

The Medics had inquired about her age but I had no idea how old she was. They found her Social Security card but didn't show me. I'd have to ask mother but she might not even know as we didn't celebrate their birthdays, and only marked mine until I reached the age of twelve, after which mother told me I was on my own, free to make or buy a cake, to buy a present for myself or not. I suppose it says something about my childhood that this didn't seem odd at all. I didn't have any cousins or friends to compare my life with so I took the bizarre in stride. The Cleavers on <u>Leave It To Beaver</u> were so different from my family that the show might as well have portrayed life on Neptune.

I waited for feelings to arise about Gouchie. She had always been in my life, a stern presence backing up my mother's discipline. She would sometimes show me affection in an offhand manner, throwing packages of cookies at me as if they'd been left over from a more important event. She never said anything that could even remotely be considered as guidance, other than that I should always do as my mother said. On the other hand, she wasn't very critical, in contrast to my mother, who never looked at me without commenting in a negative way about my posture, my hair, my hygiene, my attitude, on and on. As a result, I grew up flinching whenever the maternal gaze turned toward me.

Now I realize she always saw Beagle in my features when she looked at me and felt anew the shame and guilt and embarrassment their relationship evoked, causing her to take action to try to stamp out the Beagle in me. The phlegmatic Gouchie, on the other hand, seemingly impervious to the Beaglian powers, was willing just to let me do whatever I wanted, whether that was watching TV or reading comic books or dozing on the couch as she watched her own shows. For her neutral neglect, I was grateful.

As I sat there that night, watching Johnny Carson on the Tonight show, and the subsequent infomercials, I began to wonder if, in fact, the Medical Examiners would find some evidence of foul play. Gouchie had not seemed sick in the weeks preceding although, I had to admit, she never seemed particularly healthy. Her diet consisted mostly of ordinary foods fried in butter or oil, along with a large bowl of ice cream every night. It was possible that this anti-health regimen had finally caught up with her but I wondered if my nemesis may have had something to do with it. The Medical Examiner might easily find nothing amiss in Gouchie's stomach because Beagle had the resources and the will to research and develop an untraceable poison to administer to her. Given the hours she spent in her chair with the TV sound turned up loud to compensate for her faulty hearing, an agent could easily have broken into the house and poisoned the food.

I hadn't eaten since coming home because of all the commotion but now I was hungry. Usually, I made myself a bowl of pasta or a baked potato, a piece of chicken or fish, maybe a salad after working all day but the kitchen seemed like a mine field to me now. I didn't know what Gouchie had eaten, as I had not yet looked very closely at the sink or the garbage can, but anything and everything could have been tainted.

I sat in the armchair, trying to fit my body into Gouchie's mold, watching an old movie on TV: In A Lonely Place with Humphrey Bogart and Gloria Graham, about a screenwriter with rage issues whose girlfriend begins to suspect him of murder. I thought about riding my bike up to Dick's on Holman Road for a late night meal that didn't involve the food in Gouchie's larder. Tomorrow, I'd have to throw it all out and buy new groceries but realized they could be tainted as well because Beagle likely had connections within the grocery corporations. Nowhere was safe. I decided in the end not to eat. I just sat, watched the television as if I were Gouchie, and listened to my stomach growl.

My mother inherited Gouchie's house. She and Mitch decided to keep it as an investment (hope it's going to pay off for them, or do I?) and let me stay in exchange for keeping it up and paying the taxes. We never did have any funeral service for Gouchie. Mother had her cremated and I placed the ceramic urn containing her ashes on the mantel of the fireplace where they may still be, unless the house has been sold. No one tells me anything. The coroner's report said she died of natural causes but did she? Did she, Governor?

Now I feel like I have to sleep for awhile. My sleep schedule is completely fragmented, no more than three or four hours at a time. Besides, with so little time left, I begrudge any time I have to spend unconscious when I'm about to encounter The Big Coma. More later (I know you can't wait).

Sincerely,
Isaac Turbot

Sunday, May 30th, 1989

To Alan Dershowitz
Harvard University School of Law
Cambridge, Mass. (Sorry, don't know the zip code)

Dear Professor Dershowitz,

By the time you receive this, I may well be deceased, hung by the neck until dead (because you know they won't stop if I'm merely maimed), in which case this letter will not have much relevance to your practice although you may find my situation to be interesting, if not compelling or heart-rending. I'm not really resigned to this fate but I have some sense of what the reality is around me, even as competing claims rise up within my mind, ideas of being elsewhere, in some other situation. I will attribute these ideas to the pressure of impending obliteration, the stress of having to think about the unthinkable.

I know from the media that you're willing to take on hopeless cases, Claus Von Bulow being your client who stands out, of course. Reasonable doubt is a powerful weapon in the arsenal of litigation and you wielded that weighty battle axe with surgical precision. I hope my situation might interest you as an even greater challenge. My case is as hopeless a one as you are ever going to see because I definitely committed the crime of which I am accused. What I would like you to argue on my behalf, if you should accept the job and if I should, by some miracle, be alive to participate in your no doubt spirited defense, is that what I did was justifiable homicide, or maybe self-defense in the largest definition of the term. If someone is about to kill you, standing directly in front of you with a weapon, then almost every legal system in the world allows for the use of deadly force to defend oneself. What if the danger is just as real but is psychological and conspiratorial in nature, danger difficult to explicate to a jury of my peers but just as deadly as the threat presented by the imagined villain with either blunt or sharp instrument?

I would be honored if you would assemble a team of your brightest students who would, no doubt, include future Supreme Court justices, captains of industry, even embryonic Presidents, and put their young energies, physical, intellectual, and moral, to the task of doing something, anything, about my plight. In descending order of urgency, you might work on saving me from execution, on reducing my sentence, on having my conviction overthrown, on having me declared innocent, and on acquiring compensation for me, from either the government or from Beagle Industries, or both. Of course, in return for your efforts (that I have no doubt will prove to be Herculean), you will receive half of any dollar amount I am rewarded and the amount is likely to be substantial given the abysmal depths of Beagle's coffers (abysmal in the sense of abyss deep, not in the sense of disastrous but you're sure to have caught that subtlety so I'll shut up even though it's too late to avoid insulting you so forgive me).

One obstacle might be that I'm almost three thousand miles away, in a state not always impressed by East Coast credentials (although the local aristocracy strive to send their progeny to Harvard or Yale) but I hope that both the imminence and the unfairness of my case will move you to participate, no, more than participate, I want you to be the General Eisenhower for my D-Day (death day, of course), or (in a slightly inequivalent simile) like the Romans sacking Jerusalem, taking no prisoners, showing no mercy. Sorry for the clumsiness of imagery but I hope you see my point.

Rather than argue my case separately in correspondence, I will have my current attorney, such as he is, (Leonard Main in all his lack of glory or skill or imagination but a pleasant individual for all that), forward you copies of the letters I am sending to the Governor in which I am pleading (abjectly, I admit it), for my life.

I would like you to research the background of the afore-mentioned Beagle because I am as certain as I am that my heart is beating (right now, anyway) that he was at the heart of many other conspiracies. Great wealth allows individuals of monumental evil to do damage to the inhabitants of this planet, human and otherwise, either through the massive and comprehensive efforts of corporations, or by having the means and the will to hire beings of low morality to plague the innocent. You, as an attorney, must be familiar with this obvious principle, that the citizens with the greatest wealth and power have the most means to be corrupt. I am poor, always have been, so money played no part in motivating my actions.

The truth, revealed only in the last few days (because of a reticence I will explain to you later) is that I am the offspring of Mr. Beagle, his flesh and blood, as it were, from a brief and tawdry liaison with my mother. I was never recognized by him (of course not), and his name did not appear on my birth certificate (I checked) so anything you can do to make that connection clear would help my case. I know he despised me because I represented his weakness so his aim was not to eliminate me swiftly (because bumping me off would have been the simplest of orders for him), but he wanted to destroy me, morally, intellectually, physically, and I have to say he has more than achieved his goal.

I put on a good face for my fellow inmates and the guards but I am quaking to my marrow at the thought of my impending obliteration, at least if I have any direct access to the nerve endings in my marrow which in this imagery may have turned to marshmarrow. (Puns are a nervous tic with me and, as you can see, I'm not going back to do any editing. I'm like a shark that must move forward or die, except I'm apparently going to move forward <u>and</u> die). I do not want to be dead. I want to live and, if my earthly beingness continues on Tuesday morning, I want you to spring into action to ensure that my Being goes on because Beagle has no doubt left henchmen, sleeper moles, in fact, waiting to act against me if I somehow escape the fate assigned to me by blind justice.

I know this is a long-shot and you undoubtedly have many better things to do than travel out to a profoundly uncivilized state of the Union and give aid and comfort to someone who is best forgotten in the annals of history. That's me I'm talking about because I haven't done much with my life, just tended a few plants, loved one woman, mostly cowered under unrelenting oppression until one day, the day of my arrest (and Beagle's cardiac arrest), I took action to relieve my self and the world of a human pestilence, a man we're all better off without. So what, you might ask? What difference does it make if I die on Monday or not? All I know is that the punishment in this case is greater than the crime because of all the relief I've given the world. It could be that untold environmental and social disasters would have occurred under Beagle's domination of this great land of ours if I hadn't taken action.

Did you ever see the movie, <u>Man Hunt</u>, directed by Fritz Lang, the German director who in escaping from Nazi Germany became an artist of depicting oppression? In that story, the main character is a hunter, played by

Walter Pidgeon, who actually has Hitler in his sights from a position overlooking the Berchtesgaden but is stopped and arrested by the Gestapo. He tells them that he wasn't actually going to shoot the Fuhrer but was merely doing it for the sport, to see if he could get close enough to take the shot (what an alibi!).

Now, imagine me as Walter Pidgeon with the major difference that I actually pulled the trigger (okay, thrust with the knife, big difference) and I was ready to accept the consequences, even if it meant execution in this bloodthirsty commonwealth where I was born (however, only four states are officially designated "commonwealths," and I know Massachusetts and Pennsylvania are two of them. Maybe you could find out the other two and let me know if/when you come out here, although I'm not sure why that matters, sorry, having some trouble keeping the trolley on the tracks).

To sum up, I don't know what I'm doing and maybe you know what I should do. I was born in shit, lived in shit, and maybe I'm going to die in shit, especially if any of the accounts of the aftermath of being hanged are accurate. In some parts of the world, human excrement is used as fertilizer and maybe that's my goal in writing to you, hoping the current state of pervasive fragrant waste matter I'm experiencing might be used to grow something good. That's why I'm reaching out.

You have the intelligence, the training, the resources, and the will to expose the empire of Beagle that I have no doubt extends in every direction, even into space, infecting the solar system and maybe our galaxy (let's just call it the whole universe and be done). I would bet (if I had anything to bet with) that he prepared for his death by setting into motion various plans that will activate over time from unexpected directions and wreak unimaginable havoc upon reality (although I'm trying to imagine it right now and I'm reminded of another movie, The Manchurian Candidate with its sleeper assassins, prisoners of war programmed by the Soviets to lie dormant in American society until set in motion by their evil controllers). The world will, no doubt, experience all sorts of natural disasters, not to mention mass murder by chemical, biological, and nuclear weapons, designed to look like the predictable outcome of cause and effect but actually representing the utter evil that is Beagle, acting even from beyond the grave.

I know what you're thinking (or I imagine I know), that I am obsessed with Beagle, that I have Beagle on the brain, Beagle down to my very bunions, that no man could possibly be so wicked. I would think the same thing if someone else outlined what I've just written to you. All I can do is invite you to test me out. Everyone assumed Von Bulow was guilty and would die in prison but you saw something else. I'm proposing an alternate explanation for my committing homicide that will end up revealing a vast conspiracy underlying the current state of human affairs.

I hope to meet you, if I am still alive past Monday night.

Sincerely,
Isaac Turbot,
the accused,
the perpetrator,
the victim.

Sunday, May 30th, 1989

Dear Governor,

Leonard has arrived and is waiting somewhere in this vast edifice for me to finish my pleas (please!). When I'm done, I will tell the guards and they will pass my stack of letters on to him. For some reason, they don't want me to see him until tomorrow night when I'm about to be hanged (or is it hung? I wish I had my beloved Oxford English Dictionary here, two-volume edition, complete with magnifying glass, a book club deal). But I have a few more things to tell you about my relationship with Beagle and I want to give you my account of the fateful night that had such an effect on your life and mine. But I also feel compelled to set the stage (of my personal drama that became national theatre) by going back to my U.W. days:

I almost always rode my bicycle to campus from Ballard along the Burke Gilman trail that was usually quite crowded with pedestrians and other cyclists. The trail crossed busy streets and even though bicycles had the right of way, at least in theory, cars were invariably not paying attention to anything other than what their drivers wanted to do. So I had near collisions and angry encounters I did not handle well, often giving the finger to more than one of my fellow beings in the course of just commuting to school.

On a cool but sunny day in early October, I was distracted as I pumped the pedals, thinking about Heidegger and Dasein and trying to apprehend the Being at the basis of all that surrounded me, when Beagles' voice began to scream, a scream that continued for a decade. I was tired and on edge. A long-haired young man in a Volkswagen van came driving right at me while I was in the crosswalk on a street just above Lake Union. I had to accelerate suddenly to avoid being hit because he was preoccupied with something on the dashboard, maybe his cassette player while he flipped over a Grateful Dead tape.

As he passed by, mere inches away, I slammed the side of the van with the flat of my hand, hard enough to cause a dent although I didn't actually stop to look. The driver slammed on the brakes and jumped out the front door, looking ready to fight. I stopped some twenty yards away, far enough that I could easily ride off if I had to. He was over six feet tall and very thin so I couldn't tell if he was wiry or weak. We shouted the usual "Fuck You!" and "Asshole!" at each other but then we both weren't sure if we should carry this further. He yelled, his voice straining, "If you've damaged my van, I'm gonna fucking sue you!" I laughed and said his van wasn't worth five minutes of a lawyer's time.

I took off and left him screaming in my wake: "There's a dent, goddamn it. I'll fucking kill you, asshole." I shot him the finger without looking back but seethed as I rode on, unable to let it go. I wanted to turn around and use my bicycle pump to crack his skull but also didn't want to be injured myself so kept on pedaling. As I rode, my anger caused various perceptual disturbances. The path under my bike twisted like a snake in the talons of an eagle. The trees and houses and cars along the path were strobing even more than usual. A muttering began in the wind, with a threatening tone, following me as I rode faster, not looking to either side when I plunged across the streets, causing even closer calls than the one that put me into this state. And those close calls jacked me up even more until by the time I reached the campus and locked my bike onto the rack outside Suzallo Library, I was soaked with sweat and my heart was clacking like a spoon against my rib cage.

I was supposed to go to my class on Immanuel Kant but was reluctant to stumble into the room in my current state. I sat on the grass outside of Ardmore and tried to breathe deeply but, when I did, I found a hitch in my breathing where it hurt to inhale too far, causing me to breathe even more rapidly and shallowly. My anxiety wasn't going away so I decided to try walking slowly across campus to calm down. The sky filled the spaces between the buildings and above with a vivid blue. The temperature was about sixty degrees with a steady breeze from the west and the slight chill made my sweaty shirt feel clammy. Co-eds wearing mini-skirts had goose-bumps along their thighs as they walked past and my anxiety was so intense that I couldn't even enjoy looking at them. My contemporaries inspired no sense of kinship in me, other than an automatic lust for just about every girl, but even that generalized desire had been overcome by the current turmoil.

My fellow students passing by seemed mostly normal and as happy as anyone in college was going to be, coming from stable families into the protected world of academic life to find ways to express themselves. Part of the fun was to protest war, racism, the system, and oppression in general but also to smoke dope, get laid, and hassle with the cops. These diversions held little interest for me, overshadowed as they were by a deeper oppression, noticed by no one but me, filling me with fascination and dread. The very atoms of reality (not that I could see them but I sensed them) seemed charged with menace.

The mutterings in the air contorted themselves and turned into Beagle's voice, telling me how lame I was, how filthy, how bad. I knew he wasn't telling the truth but the sound of his voice, seeming to emerge from loudspeakers placed in the crooks of branches and in the cornices of buildings, inflamed me with rage. I began to see his moon face peering at me from the windows I passed, not so much from inside the rooms but somehow smeared across the reflections, maybe beamed from U-2 spy-craft flying high above the campus, undetectable by normal radar. A burst of adrenaline surged up in my chest and I began to jog, easily sidestepping the pedestrians, accelerating with a jolt and fleeing the campus to sprint across 15th toward University Ave.

The hitch in my breathing snapped free and I felt loose and strong. I thought I'd escape Beagle by leaving the campus, realizing in a sudden shard of insight (how had I never realized this before?) that he was on the Board Of Regents at the University so had control of everything in and around the school. I hoped his influence would decrease when I left University property but I was wrong. As I ran, dodging the maddeningly slow students sauntering on this relatively nice day along the sidewalk, I saw Beagle actually looking through the eyes of those I passed. They didn't seem to be aware of it but he had somehow managed to place cameras inside their eyeballs so he could keep tabs on me from absolutely anywhere.

In every direction, I could see the piercing, condemning gaze of the Master of Evil peering out from the faces of otherwise innocent pedestrians and drivers. Now I knew what all the mythology about the devil and Satan was pointing to: that at critical moments in history, certain individuals took on all the negative and dire elements in the human race, finding physical expression in the red of rage, the horns of aggression, the forked tail of foulness. I glanced behind as I ran and saw Beagle in diabolic form, a cartoon Mephistopheles, chasing after me and gaining with every step. My awareness came loose from its moorings and panic ricocheted from my chest to my head, and back again.

I reached 45th Street at the corner by the Neptune theatre and knew I only had one choice, to throw myself on the mercy of the reality around me with its attendant beings. I ran out into the street, sprinting between cars in the congested traffic, my hips knocking into side view mirrors and pushing them back, breaking one off its mount entirely so it crashed to the ground behind me. I could hear shouts rising in my wake but didn't know if they came from offended drivers or Beagle's sub-demons, or both.

He was rapidly entering the bodies of those I ran past, preparing them to act with the single-minded ferocity of a mob and rip me into tiny shreds of flesh right there on the street. At the moment, a bloody finale seemed all too likely. Now, years later, I know from lengthy and bitter experience that his domination takes subtler and more tortuous forms than obvious demonstrations of violent power. But at the moment, I felt he was hellbent on my immediate destruction. Adrenaline and fear increased my speed so everything was shaped into a kaleidoscopic tunnel swirling around me.

Ahead was a police car but I felt no relief from the sight. Beagle was obviously entrenched with law enforcement the way he was with the Seafair Pirates because all civic organizations, all branches of the government and the armed services, were entangled with his corporations. Cars waited at the light to cross the freeway, the afternoon traffic building up to rush hour. The policeman must have seen me approaching in the rear view mirror, must have heard the commotion of the horns blaring as I passed. His car door opened and he stepped out into the sunshine, his blonde hair giving off glints of light that were obviously coded messages from Beagle instructing him what to do.

With excruciating slowness, he moved around to the back of the car and stood by his rear bumper, in a place where he was going to intercept my forward plummet. His mouth opened and he shouted, "Stop!," the vowel sound of the "O" echoing up to the sky and back. In his mouth (in an image reminiscent of Beagle on the float at the Seafair Parade), I could see the sharpened incisors of a vampire, ready, no doubt, to plunge into my neck and suck out my life blood so Beagle could have it for whatever dire experimentation he planned for me. The cop's hand was on the grip of his service revolver and, with a practiced gesture, he undid the snap holding it down, putting his fingers around the handle. As his mouth closed, with excruciating slowness, I could see the surge of fear in his face, widening his eyes and compressing his lips into a slit that almost separated his chin from his head.

I knew no good could come of our impending collision so as I reached the back bumper of the only car separating us, I ignited my side-thrusters and made a ninety degree turn that took me across three lanes of traffic. The lane closest to the sidewalk actually had cars that were moving as they made right turns. A red Corvette (hello, Prince!) was going by but I didn't want to wait so vaulted up, my foot landing squarely on the middle of the windshield. The forward movement of the vehicle gave me energy I used to spring into the air, landing with grace on the sidewalk at the corner where I ran north. The police car was boxed in as the light turned green and even though the officer set his siren screaming, the cars were so placed that they froze in response to the sound and he was effectively blocked off from pursuit.

Governor, I can only use words to communicate and these potentially uttered sounds signified by marks on paper have a strictly limited relation to reality so will necessarily be inadequate to describe the exhilaration of that moment. I knew Beagle would catch up with me eventually but to frustrate him even for a short time gave me the greatest delight. I passed by the houses in their next-to-the-freeway shabbiness, gliding under the sky that seemed to be swirling its blue in delight at my escape. Somewhere along the way, I'd lost my backpack with its books and notes and now I was hot from my exertions so I pulled apart the front of my shirt and tore it open, the buttons skipping on the street. I twisted my arms out of the shirt without breaking stride and threw it so it landed on a Schnauzer whose owner was walking it on the sidewalk.

I saw the dog shaking its head to remove the blinding hood and heard the owner shouting, "Hey!" That may have been the twentieth, or more, "Hey!" I'd heard since I began my escape and I used one portion of my churning mind to contemplate what that meant. My fellow citizens seemed to be greeting me and noticing my passage on the planet. Maybe they were alluding to the word "hay," indicating recognition that this was a time of reaping and harvest, that the era of Beagle was coming to completion and the world was waiting for a new age, possibly better, probably worse, to dawn (I don't know. It's a theory, anyway).

I looked over my shoulder and saw no one in pursuit so I throttled back to cruising speed. I reached 50th Street and deftly scooted between the vehicles waiting to turn left. Halfway across the bridge over the freeway, I could see that the southbound cars were only creeping forward in Seattle's almost perpetual traffic jam (can't you use your power and position, Governor, to do something about the problem? I know, irrelevant).

My plan was to jog home and regroup. For some reason, the aura of Beagle's domination remained at the same level of intensity as I moved further away from the University, maybe because he was heavily invested in public utilities, giving him access to the wires over my head and the cables running underground. He was always buying up real estate, meaning that the bitter majority of houses I passed were either rented out or owned by one of his companies. I was sure one of his banks held the mortgages providing the so-called owners with the illusion they held title to a piece of the earth when all the while Beagle maintained true dominion.

In any case, my momentary illusion of relative freedom was destroyed by the sight of a Seattle police car, lights flashing and siren piercing, flying over the crest of the hill ahead of me, looking like a stunt car from that silly action movie, <u>Smokey And The Bandit</u>, obviously bearing down to intercept me. Now sirens erupted from behind as well, just in case I should decide to turn and run back from where I came.

A silver cloud seemed to appear in an arch above the only place left for me to run, the on-ramp to I-5. I slipped easily into turbo mode and found plenty of energy, especially now that I was running downhill in the narrow passage between the cars waiting to merge and the retaining wall. I could sense the snap of heads swiveling to follow the flight of a shirtless man, namely me, moving faster than any vehicle on the ten lane freeway. I wondered, in the calm space floating above my churning body, how many horsepower I had inside me. One? One half? One quarter? (Making me a quarter horse, ha!)

I ran onto the freeway, where cars surged forward in short bursts as they tried to prevent any other cars in the neighboring lanes from cutting in front of them. Despite the congestion of the traffic, the police car behind me was undeterred and plowed its way down the ramp, siren howling, banshee-like, as cars edged over just enough to allow passage. I reached the bridge where the freeway soared over the Montlake cut leading to Lake Union. Now the gradient sloped up and my energy began to flag. I was in pretty fair shape from biking and all that gardening but I wasn't a regular runner and I must have run several miles so far. The mere facts of my youth and my agitation weren't enough to sustain me for long distances.

The afternoon sun gave a diabolically red tinge to the clouds gathering above the city, Lake Union reflecting the crimson, the houses on Capitol Hill capturing fire in their sparkling windows. A sea plane descended to the lake, carefully picking its way through the multiple watercraft out on the slightly choppy surface. The ugly tanks and dark machinery of the old Gas Works on the northern shore were surrounded by tiny dots of color representing my fellow citizens congregating in the park for fresh air and views on this cool fall afternoon. In such a massive traffic jam, I expected to see columns of smoke rising in front of me, thinking that only a mammoth bloody crash could be the cause of such an extensive back-up. However, Interstate 5 was so overcrowded that if a single vehicle stalled out and couldn't move over to the narrow shoulder, all traffic in Seattle came to a halt, blocking direct access between Canada and Mexico.

The roadway's ascent to the distant cluster of Seattle's downtown buildings seemed endless and I eventually found myself fatigued, lungs and legs aching. The cop car was making only slow progress, forcing its way through the congestion, but it was gaining on me. Being captured was now inevitable so the question was how to turn this reality to my advantage. I decided that going gently into Beagle's bad night was not how I wanted the game to end. The cars in the left lane were moving the slowest of all as they waited to turn down to the ramp toward the 520 floating bridge over Lake Washington, gateway to the fabulous eastern suburbs, land of upper level management and assorted professionals (all likely in debt to Beagle). The cars in the right hand lanes were inching along, incrementally faster, and I headed toward them.

I jogged over to the railing, easily making my way through the slow vehicles, generating more shouts of "Hey!" from open windows. Who knew so many farmers lived in Seattle? (Am I running the joke into the ground? Well, isn't that where hay comes from? Sorry). I reached the guard rail where I looked out over the truly spectacular view, usually wasted on passing drivers whose minds were focused on the tedious yet dangerous act of guiding their vehicles.

The view from the railing took in the Montlake cut below, busy with boat traffic on this mild afternoon, the expanse of Lake Union, the hump of Queen Anne, the uneven teeth of the Seattle Skyline, and the southernmost mountains in the Olympic range. Looking back over the eight lanes of traffic behind me, I could see the Cascade Mountains stretched across the horizon, catching the full impact of the descending sun.

I'd done some hiking up in the mountains, both east and west, but was not in any way a dedicated outdoorsman. I usually took a bus to trailheads and set out wearing sneakers and carrying the same book bag on my back that I used for school, containing a metal canteen I'd bought in one of the Army-Navy stores on First Avenue, along with a sandwich, some chips, and oatmeal raisin cookies, my usual lunch in any setting. I knew about hiking clubs like the Mountaineers but never wanted to engage in organized group activities. Isolation, then and now, was my faithful companion.

I could see that the mountains had a mere scattering of snow across their peaks after the unusually warm summer. Soon the rains would start here in the lowlands and deep snow would fall in the high passes and above. I straddled the pipe of the railing and felt the cold metal right through my jeans, soaked with sweat from the run. A steady breeze chilled the skin beneath my chest hair. Beside me, a woman with gray hair leaned over and lowered the window of her car to ask, "What are you doing?"

The answer immediately sprang to my lips, "What the hell do you think I'm doing?" The situation seemed pretty obvious to me but she probably didn't know what to say. She would have to feel a true commitment to ask, "What's wrong?" and thereby open herself up to a lengthy discussion. The traffic would soon be flowing so, in order to talk to me, she would have to stay in place and block the lane. Not many people would be so assertive. She chose to continue on. Only the police would have the nerve to stop and delay the onslaught of vehicles in such a circumstance.

Indeed the cops came, as they do on so many other occasions, as they did that fatal night at the Governor's Ball, Governor. I'm sure you remember how they kicked and punched me repeatedly in the head and back in their zeal to "arrest" me. Back on the freeway, the cop following me was slowly making his way up the lane next to the guardrail. I was tired of the gaping stares of the passing drivers so I swung my leg over the railing and sat with both legs hanging over the edge. This felt somewhat precarious as the round top of the pipe was not easy to sit on but I kept myself from falling over by digging both my heels into the concrete surface below the railing.

I'd never been bothered by acrophobia and now I found myself exhilarated by looking down at the drop. If I jumped, some houseboat owner right below my feet would be extremely unhappy. I wondered how often they had someone come tumbling down upon them. From this height and with my weight I could easily kill somebody, not to mention the mysterious entity I think of, somewhat fondly, as myself. However, despite my precarious position, suicide was not on my mind. I knew Beagle's minions were about to descend and all I wanted was to attract as much attention as I could before they muscled me into whatever dark cellar they had waiting to begin the torture. The cop parked his car behind my position, about twenty five yards away, his red and yellow lights flashing. Over his loudspeaker, he said, "Hey, you, move back from the railing and give yourself up."

I gave him the finger, thinking that politeness was not his strong suit. Is this how he talked to a troubled individual? Why not just shoot me and be done with the problem? Another patrol car parked next to him, effectively blocking off the two western lanes of the bridge, presumably so someone more skillful than the first oaf could try to convince me to engage in the uncertain project of continuing to live.

The traffic boiled behind the police as the cars in the two blocked lanes tried to squeeze around them, merging only with difficulty into the already jammed adjacent lanes. Those who were able to accomplish this difficult maneuver then whipped into the empty lanes behind me so they could make a momentary surge ahead to where the traffic stopped again. Many of these drivers were not happy. "Jump, you fuck," was the gentle admonishment offered to me several times. I was also called an asshole and several offered the opinion that I was a pathetic loser. Oddly, despite all the turmoil I was causing, I felt perfectly at ease but kept an eye out by occasionally looking over my shoulder in case some foolhardy soul decided to try to grab me from behind.

I could feel the psychic pressure from the sheer mass of cars backing up to Everett and could also feel the weight of enmity from drivers crawling by when they deduced, falsely, of course, that it was me who was solely responsible for their long wait. I became the target for all the frustrations they'd been building up over the delay, even though it had been well established before my arrival. A storm of disapproval boiled around me and made me laugh because my mother had been the original source of all the disapproval I ever felt so the disdain from these strangers, even when in combination, had nowhere near the impact she exerted on my psyche. I sat and enjoyed the view with the sun on my face, my arms folded across my bare chest. The cacophony of horns and catcalls, even more of them urging me to jump, made a dissonant music around me.

After what seemed like hours but was probably more like ten minutes, another police car rolled up behind the others and a policeman stepped out and walked toward me. He was an older man with gray hair, solid and fit, it appeared, with a drooping mustache. He walked along the railing until he was about ten yards away.

"Hey, how's it going?" he offered, a bland enough approach.

"How does it look like it's going?"

Did I really need to respond to such obvious questions?

"Not so good, actually. Are you really going to jump?"

"That's not what I'm about."

"Maybe you should come with me. We'll go over to the U.W. Emergency Room and connect you with people who can really talk to you. I'm just an old cop, not a counselor, so I don't know if I'm going to say the wrong thing or not. You should have somebody who knows how to talk to you about depression."

"What makes you think I'm depressed?"

He smiled. "In my experience, very few happy people put their legs over the railing of the I-5 bridge. I may be wrong but most of the people I've encountered who were in your position had something wrong in their lives."

I considered. At least with him talking to me, the catcalls had diminished. I figured I might as well begin by telling him what was really going on.

"You're right about that. Something is wrong with my life and I'm upset about it but I know the source. I just don't know how to fix it."

"Okay, so if you want to, tell me about it."

"Are you familiar with a man by the name of Dionysius Beagle?"

"Well, I do live in Seattle. How could I avoid knowing that name?"

"He's the problem. I can't really tell you more because you'll think I'm crazy, but he's been trying to destroy my life for the past thirteen years."

"Lucky thirteen, huh? I know these rich guys can be a pain and I'm just a working stiff but if anything can be done, the doctors can help you figure it out at the Emergency Room. You're not going to solve the problem by staying up here and continuing to screw up the rush hour, and you won't solve it by jumping and making a mess down below. All I can tell you is that there is help and I'll make sure you get it. That much I can promise."

I shook my head. "You're thinking psychiatrists can fix what bothers me. I don't believe that for a second but I do admit staying up here isn't helping. I'll tell you what. You find a reporter from the Seattle P.I. for me to talk to and I'll come with you."

"The P.I., huh? I could call them but I don't know how soon a reporter could get here. How about this? If you come with me to the Emergency Room, I will personally guarantee that a P.I. reporter will come over and talk to you."

"Yeah, how are you going to make sure of that?"

"I don't know. They're probably all potheads. I'll threaten to bust them if they don't."

At least that made me laugh. "Okay, I don't know why but I do trust you."

While we were talking, an ambulance pulled up behind the police cars. The two other officers were standing behind the one I was talking to.

"You don't have a whole lot of other choices right now. How about carefully swinging your legs back and coming over to the pavement?"

"Okay." I did as he instructed but felt wobbly as I swung my legs over, thinking for a second I might roll over the railing and go down. But the moment passed and I was standing up on the pavement. I walked toward the officer. The two cops behind ran past him and right up to me. They knocked me down, slammed my face on the asphalt, and handcuffed me, all very efficient. The older cop shrugged apologetically and returned to his car. His colleagues lifted me up, roughly. The passing motorists honked their appreciation.

"Damn," I said. "You don't need to be so rough."

"We're just making sure you're safe, asshole."

"That's rich. You think I'm suicidal and you're calling me an asshole."

"Fuck, you're not suicidal. If you'd been suicidal, you would have jumped. You're a pussy, that's what you are."

"That figures as the pussy is right next to the asshole, and you're right next to me."

"To the car, funny guy. That proves my point. Suicidal guys don't crack wise. That's a scientific fact."

I didn't feel like cooperating by walking so they escorted me to one of their cars by dragging me along the pavement, the toes of my sneakers making lines in the grime on the asphalt. I could see this because my head was hanging down, allowing me a view of the world turned upside down and threatening to crush me. They stood me up by the car, patted me down for weapons, and pulled my wallet from my pocket to look at my driver's license. After looking back and forth from my photo to my face and satisfying themselves that I was who I was, they threw me forcefully into the back seat so my head banged on the top of the door's opening. I lay for a minute uncomfortably on top of my handcuffed wrists, then wriggled to a sitting position. Outside, the three cops argued about whether to wait for an ambulance.

"We don't need an ambulance," one of the mean cops said. "He's not injured in any way. Let's just take him down to the ER and make sure they strap him on a gurney. This guy has proved he's a runner."

"Yeah, okay," the older cop said.

"What about the P.I.?" I yelled from the back seat.

He heard me even through the closed window.

"That's right. I'm going to call them now and tell them you want to talk and where you are but I can't promise anything."

"You said you could guarantee it."

"Sorry, buddy. That was then. This is now."

He drove off and one of the other cops drove me through the still congested traffic. I was uncomfortable in the handcuffs but felt some relief that the little drama was over. Now I'd see what Beagle had in store for me. The officer turned on the siren and kept heading south through the turmoil of downtown.

"This isn't the way to the U.W. hospital," I said.

"Nope, too hard to work our way back there. You're going to Harborview instead."

That didn't make much difference to me. Harborview was the main city hospital and had a reputation for being kind of rough. Given Beagle's hold over the University, I hoped someone at a different facility would be open to the reality of the situation. I didn't realize until later that Harborview was also connected to the University so no escape was to be had there.

Back in prison world, dinner has arrived so I'm going to take a break and eat it. Hard to wield a spork and write at the same time (in an odd rhyme, the entree is pork). In some other reality, I'm lined up outside, on a sidewalk, in a park, waiting to eat a pre-packaged meal handed out from a truck. Weird that such fantasies should intrude on me but my situation, as dire as it is, must be provoking my brain into random firings of neurons. Don't worry (as if you would), I'm going to send these letters all together and number them so they don't get out of sequence and confuse you. Leonard, my chosen courier, is still waiting but will have to be patient, his only skill.

Sincerely,
Isaac Turbot

Sunday, April 30, 1989

To Mr. and Mrs. Kim
Owners of Kim's Cleaners
Near the intersection of 65th St. and 15th Ave. N.E.
Seattle, Washington (sorry, don't know the zip)

Dear Mr. and Mrs. Kim,

I'm writing because I dropped off a cable-knit sweater, two pairs of slacks, and a sports coat about 18 months ago. I've never returned to pick them up. It now looks pretty certain I will never have that opportunity, no matter what happens Monday night. I don't know how closely you follow the media, but I may be your most famous, or infamous customer.

I've always admired your industry. You stay open at least twelve hours a day and I know you take pains to give good service. You may not remember, in fact I hope you don't, but I caused a little scene in your shop about two years ago. I'd started working for Mary Meals and, for the first time in my life, had need for a dry cleaner. On that particular day, under pressure from a certain entity exterior to myself, I yelled at Mrs. Kim because of a stain on a shirt I claimed was caused by you. I don't know why I did this because I knew I'd caused the stain myself when I was lurching around drunk while trying to make dinner. My only excuse is that I was in a rather sensitive emotional state at the time.

I must have needed some outlet for my anger but I had no right to take it out on Mrs. Kim. She did something on the day of my scene that has stayed in my mind since. At first, she tried to explain, patiently, that the stain had been there when you received the shirt. After it became clear that I was not going to listen to reason and was intent on raving on, she just stood there and seemed to retreat within herself.

Her eyes filmed over as if all her attention was now directed within, not out to the abusive Caucasian in front of her who might well become violent. I recognized her stance quite well as one I've frequently had good cause to adopt for myself. I thought of it as going down in the bathysphere, retreating into the depths of self where one cannot be touched, no matter what storms rage up on the surface. This recognition stopped me from the continuation of my little scene. I couldn't verbally abuse someone who'd been forced to adopt the same defenses I myself had formed. I apologized in a mumble and left a five dollar tip but I still feel bad when I think about it.

As partial compensation, I'd like to suggest a money-making scheme. I hereby give you complete ownership of the clothes I left with you. You could, I'm sure, sell them for a tidy profit. I haven't completely thought out how you'd do it, but I know the world is full

of ghouls who'd want to own the clothing of a murderer.
Perhaps an ad in True Crime magazine, or just a two-
liner in the Seattle Times: "For Sale: Personal items of
Isaac Turbot. Best offer. Call Mr. Kim at ..."

I believe the press has made me notorious enough
that you will receive some enthusiastic responses. Just be
careful in dealing with them because there are a lot of
nuts out there (disclaimer: but I'm not one of them, no
matter what you've heard). Oh, and I hereby certify with
this letter that the items of clothing in your possession
were actually mine. That should clear up any question of
whether they are the real McTurbot. Probably you should
wait until after Tuesday morning to sell them because
they might then be relics and not just souvenirs. Not that
I'm a saint, mind you, but I do feel I'm being railroaded
to the gallows. A man five cells down from me on the
Unit killed sixteen (SIXTEEN!) women and he's been
idling around here for nine years, with no end in sight. I
kill one problematic character and they're eager to stretch
my neck after less than a year.

Mrs. Kim, and probably Mr. Kim, too, you at least
know that life isn't fair. I don't know what happened to
you, Mrs. Kim, to give you the ability to go down in the
bathysphere but I sympathize. Those whose lives go well
can talk about providence, about the good in this world,
and so on, but we who've suffered know it's all a crap
shoot. Feeling blessed for being lucky is stupid. What's
that line from Job? "Whatever I fear comes true, whatever

I dread befalls me." I wanted to have that sentence carved on my tombstone but was informed I don't have enough money for the state to bury me so I'll be cremated instead. I'd arrange to have it printed on my urn except no one is going to want it anyway.

Yes, I do have a Bible, thanks to the good Reverend Acksel who's probably going to show up here any minute. I don't read it for comfort, but for laughs. What a yarn! God as authoritarian ass-kicker throughout the Old Testament, a little reprieve of love with Jesus, and then back to the ass-kicker in the Apocalypse. Human beings seem to yearn for a master and if they don't have one in society they'll create one in the sky. Freud said that religion is merely the family drama projected large across the cosmos. I don't know whether you two are religious. I assume you're Korean and I know many Koreans are Christian. I do hope you're not Moonies. That cult is the furthest outpost of absurdity, although not worse than a few supposedly respectable sects I can think of in this country (if you are Moonies, I'm sorry, in more ways than one).

Hey, it just occurred to me that you can probably sell this letter, too. I've been refusing to be interviewed (although I may soon change my mind) so any communication with me has become all the more valuable. Insight into the mind of a murderer! Turbot discusses his bizarre religious beliefs! Sure, why not? Go for it.

As immigrants to this land, you may also be aware that we are merely immigrants in this life, passing through the world, longing for a home we don't remember, inevitably dissatisfied with the lots assigned to us. I'm talking about myself in the last part, of course, because you may be more satisfied than I am (in fact, you'd almost have to be). Most religions address our essential homesickness, positing another dimension, a greater meaning, containing our true home. I don't know if that's true, which probably makes me an agnostic. I doubt that's true, which would make me a pessimistic agnostic. But when pressed to the limit, as I am now, I can't say absolutely that no greater meaning exists. I may be finding out for sure not many hours from now.

In closing, I wish you well. Thank you for the good work you've done. I hope your business prospers and you receive everything you ever wanted by coming to this large, even if it isn't great, nation of ours. Maybe the best thing after all would be just to give the clothes to Goodwill and throw this letter away. Better for you not to be associated with me. Do your work and live your lives. Take this dirty land and make it clean.

Sincerely,
Isaac Turbot
Confessed Murderer

Sunday, April 30th

Dear Governor,

Back again, had roast beast (random Dr. Seuss reference) that's sitting heavily in my belly so I don't know how long I can write until I become sleepy. But I will persevere as if my life depended on it (irony here, as depending can mean "hanging down"). (Hold on there, Leonard, I'm writing as fast as I can).

As you may remember, I'd just been plucked off the I-5 bridge after what was most decidedly not a suicide attempt. The police car blasted its way through traffic with siren blaring and veered onto the exit ramp to James Street (why the siren? I have no idea). We climbed the steep hill up to 9th Avenue and pulled into the bay of the Emergency Room where several ambulances were in the process of loading or unloading. The cop stepped out and opened the back door, pulling me up and walking me through the glass doors that opened automatically at our approach. He dragged me to the registration desk and spoke to the triage nurse.

"He was up on the I-5 bridge sitting on the railing and threatening to jump. He's a flight risk so needs to be in restraints."

"Actually, I'm not a flight risk. I think it's more dangerous out there than in here."

The nurse looked at me with practiced skepticism. She was skeletal thin with short blonde hair and had the demeanor of someone who'd been working in the ER long enough to have seen everything. She motioned for an aide to bring a gurney over and had me sit up on the surface. After several aides put my legs into restraints, the officer took the handcuffs off and the aides immediately put my arms into restraints as well. They handled the task deftly and I didn't resist so that made it easier (what a good patient I was! As if that meant anything).

They wheeled me down to the end of a hallway where other patients in restraints were waiting. I didn't talk to the officer anymore. He was writing at the triage desk, presumably working on his police report about my "incident." The other patients didn't make eye contact when I was wheeled in. I noticed that some were only in two point restraints and some of those were using a free hand to smoke. The ceiling was low and conversations echoed from other parts of the ER. A heavy-set man in scrubs walked in and scowled at me.

"Are you the guy who was up on the I-5 bridge?"

"Yeah, I guess so."

"Thanks a lot. You made me forty-five minutes late to work."

"The traffic was backed up before I arrived. You can't blame the whole thing on me. Maybe twenty minutes worth."

"You definitely didn't help any."

"That's always been my lot in life."

He shook his head as if dismayed by the folly of the human race. I felt like suggesting he find work in some profession that didn't require empathy but refrained because I was in a somewhat vulnerable position.

A nurse came and took my vital signs. Not surprisingly, my blood pressure and heart rate were elevated. She asked some basic questions about my health but the answers didn't seem to interest her. The other patients stole sidelong looks at me, except for a man in the corner who was talking to himself. He nodded and stared directly into my face as he kept on talking, not making sense, as far as I could tell.

A young woman wearing a Volunteer badge came through and handed out cigarettes, lighting them for those who wanted to smoke. You had to be in two point restraints to receive smoking privileges so those of us in four points didn't qualify. I didn't smoke anyway but was amused at the idea of psychiatric patients being allowed to have cigarettes in their hands but not matches. I hailed a nurse walking by and asked what was going to happen. She said I'd have an evaluation, either by a psychiatrist or a social worker, and they'd decide what to do with me. I asked if I could be let out of restraints. She said she'd be back in twenty minutes and take a couple off if I behaved.

The emergency room seemed moderately busy but not rushed. Each of the staff had something to do and moved with brisk efficiency. My fellow patients accept the wait with resignation.

The man next to me, cigarette in hand, was in his fifties or sixties but his hair and beard were so long I had difficulty telling. He looked over at me and asked, "So you were up on the big bridge? Threatening to jump?"

I thought about just ignoring him but was bored. I didn't see or hear any sign of Beagle although that didn't mean he wasn't there. Even if this man was an agent of Beagle's, I didn't see how any harm would be done by telling him what they already knew.

"Sort of. I wasn't going to do it but had to get away from some people."

"I was up there myself, back in '71. Great view, isn't it?"

A heavy-set woman across the way, who'd looked like she was dozing, suddenly perked up and said, "I haven't been on I-5 but it's hard to beat the Aurora Bridge for views. You're looking right down on Fremont and the Ship Canal traffic with Queen Anne rising up beside you. Very dramatic. I was up there for nine hours one night until they talked me down."

Soon everyone around me was engaged in a spirited discussion of the heights they'd considered jumping from, and of the various attempts they'd made to eliminate themselves from life on earth. Finally, after listening for awhile, a little man in the corner who looked somewhat like an aging Charlie Chaplin without his mustache, spoke up.

"I am one of a select few in that I leapt from the Aurora Bridge in 1969 and am here to tell you about it."

The heavy-set woman snorted. "I don't think so. No one ever survived that jump."

The little man replied, "Actually, while I was in the hospital and then rehab, I learned that a small group of us, four or five maybe, have made the jump and survived. I ended up talking to two of them during my time in the hospital. Oddly, surviving the jump had a salubrious effect, for them at least, in that they may have been somewhat depressed afterward but never made another attempt since the one. The trick, as you might expect, is to land in the water and not on the ground or on a houseboat. If you don't drown, you stand a good chance of being fished out with multiple fractures, like me."

He obviously trumped the rest of us. He pulled up his pants legs to show us the scars on his knees and rolled up a sleeve to reveal where a pin had been put into his elbow. He spent a week on the ICU, a month on a medical unit, and months in rehab where he heard of others who made the big jump and lived.

Unfortunately, after he was released, he found his way back to the alcohol that put him there in the first place. That was why he was in the ER, because he'd been drinking heavily, at least a fifth of vodka, and had talked about suicide in a bar, leading them to call 911. He must have been convincing, given how many suicidal statements bartenders must hear. He was waiting for his blood alcohol level to come down so he could convince the powers that be to let him go. He was probably going to drink again that day but said he knew one thing for sure: he wasn't going to be up on the Aurora Bridge anymore.

After this discussion, people quieted down for awhile. I closed my eyes and let the noises and smells and currents of air swirl around me. I was tired from my exertions and actually glad of a respite from the tortures of Beagle. Of course, even as I was dozing off, I could hear him in the adjoining room, talking to the doctors, trying to convince them to commit me so Beagle could have unrestrained access to my sorry carcass. I thought, thanks a lot, Beagle! Didn't you have enough of me as it was?

And thanks, Governor, for reading this. You may be thinking that my Harborview experience has little to do with why I'm in the IMU. I'm aware that being victimized in itself provides neither legal nor moral justification for homicide. What I want to convince you of is that you were in as much danger from Beagle as I was and so was your wife and so was everyone else in the State of Washington and in the world, for that matter.

I don't have what you might call "evidence" of this but I know, as much as I know I'm breathing, that my plight is universal.

Beagle is everywhere, presiding at the very root of existence. He's Thanatos, the death principle Freud wrote of, the fly in the ointment, the ointment being this viscous liquid we call life. And Beagle doesn't care, the way you and I do. I've been impressed by your statements about your wife and how much you love her in the wake of her unfortunate maiming by yours truly. You obviously have the capacity for love and almost all of us do, except for those sociopaths who wouldn't blink at committing murder if doing so could gain them even the slightest advantage (plenty of those types in my neighboring cells).

Beagle is beyond such human categories, not even a sociopath but more like the demonic figure he presented to me in my flight across campus, the devil himself, inasmuch as he deliberately stands against the good, trying to pretend the good doesn't even exist. He wants us to commit evil along with him just for the sake of the pain that would be spread further across the globe and indeed across the galaxies. You must be gaining some hint of what I'm talking about, aren't you (I hope, I hope)? Although I take responsibility for my actions, the context, the ground, the substratum, of all that happened was Beagle, always Beagle.

In the ER, the social worker eventually came over and woke me up (although how I managed to sleep in the midst of all the activity is beyond me), saying she wanted to talk to me. She had the police report in her hand and asked me what I was doing up on the bridge. She inquired about my sleep and appetite, what the month and date were, who the President was, what my history was, clearly a group of set questions she'd asked many times before. She didn't seem to care what my answers were. I replied as honestly as I could and thought I sounded pretty sane.

I didn't know if I should launch into my tale of woe about Beagle but she eventually asked me what my reasons were for fleeing the police and I didn't feel like lying to avoid consequences. I told her the entire history, going back to the primal Seafair parade, still glowing incandescently (and evilly) in my memory. She perked up right away, her eyes clearing and her mind returning from whatever inner reverie a social worker entertains while doing the boring parts of her job. I could see she didn't believe a word I was saying but thought she had an interesting case on her hands. I had the impulse to unburden myself to someone, so I went into all the detail I could (big mistake).

"I wasn't suicidal when I was up on the bridge but just wanted to bring attention to my situation. That police officer promised me a contact with the Seattle P.I. so I hope you can look into that."

She seemed taken aback by this request. "Oh, no. I couldn't do that. We don't contact the media for any reason. Confidentiality, you know."

"Okay then. Maybe you could just let me go home. I'm not going to hurt myself, or anyone else."

She shook her head. "The problem is the officer wrote his report in such a way that it's not so easy. You did put yourself in danger up there, and all the drivers, too, even if, as you say, you didn't mean to jump."

"So what's next?"

"I'm going to discuss this with the psychiatrist who will also want to talk to you. But I think we'll probably have someone from the county come in and do an evaluation. They're the ones who decide if people should be on involuntary holds. Unless you want to check yourself in voluntarily?"

"To a looney bin? Do people usually check themselves in because they're being harassed?"

"Well, they do if they're putting themselves in danger because of all the stress."

I laughed in what I hoped was a friendly manner. "You have a very nice way of saying you think I'm crazy. The only cure for my stress is for Beagle to stop."

She stood up and tucked her pen into the spiral binding of the notebook. "So let me be clear: I'm not going to contact any news media on your behalf."

She left and, as predicted, a psychiatrist, a tall man with a wispy beard, soon came over and peppered me with questions that I answered in single syllables before finally telling him to go away because I didn't want to talk anymore.

He said, "That's fine but we'll be calling the County officials to come in and see about involuntary commitment."

I roused myself from my question-induced lethargy, pulling myself into a stance with as much dignity as I could muster, given my restraints, and said, "I'll be happy to talk to whoever you want, especially if they're my way out. I regret you can only see me as a crazy person but I understand where you're coming from and I'd probably feel the same way if someone else told me my story. But a lack of logic doesn't necessarily indicate falsity because this life itself is not logical. My mission is to inform the world about the curse we're under and save others from the tortures I've gone through."

He looked at me with interest and said, "Tell me more about Mr. Beagle and what he's done to you."

I shook my head. "No, no, no, I already told the social worker too much. I can tell by the gleam in your eye that you want to call me paranoid and that's not what this is about. I'll just wait to talk to the next person. Quite the conveyor belt you have here."

He looked disappointed but stood up. "I can't predict how long it will be. The County receives a lot of calls and their response time depends on how backed up they are."

"That's fine but I wonder if I could be let out of some of the restraints."

"I'll check on that for you." He went and talked to a nearby nurse who came over and removed the restraints from my right wrist and left leg after eliciting a promise to behave. I felt like giving her a smart-ass answer that one couldn't help but behave and she really should ask for "good" behavior but I refrained. I settled in for a wait. I drank some water that a tech brought me and ate some butterscotch pudding, not easy in restraints, but I propped the plastic container between my knee and the side rail of the gurney and spooned the pudding out with my free hand.

After I ate, I entertained myself with a movie entitled, Psych Area Of The ER, and with a concerto entitled, Symphony of Sounds in the Emergency Department. Of course, Beagle intruded on these works of art as I found his face in the patterns of cracks on the ceiling and heard his voice in the squeaking from the wheels of the gurneys passing by. The sounds seemed appropriate for the rat he was.

I dozed and dreamed of swimming in a winding river, flowing along with the current so every stroke propelled me faster downstream. The riverbanks were lined with trees and the sun playing between the leaves kept me warm but didn't blind me. Fragments of sparkling light danced across my arms and over the undulating surface of the water. This was life, the way it should be, easy from moment to moment, with none of the stress and agitation marring my existence ever since the fateful day of that Seafair parade.

I always dreamt, as I was dreaming now, that my days could flow like this but I didn't know how to apply the dream state to my real life in a positive way. I was actually pondering this dilemma in my dream when I heard a roar in front of me. Mists rising ahead and a line of white froth could only mean a waterfall. I heard a depth in the multitude of sounds, indicating the drop was considerable. I was thinking Niagara steep, or something comparable. I tried to swim to the bank but the river was too wide and the current too strong to do anything but take an angle on the flow.

I exhausted my arms and legs with paddling, to no avail. I resigned myself to the fall and the stream grew faster as I was propelled to the precipice. At least I'd have a moment of flying as I dropped to the roaring chaos at the bottom. I hoped there wouldn't be rocks or driftwood. I went over the edge and was expelled from the water into the air, my legs kicking as I flew through the emptiness, going further down than seemed possible, surrounded by mists so I couldn't see more than a few feet in any direction. I fell for so long that I lost the feeling of descent and found myself weightless, able to move my limbs and change my position in any way I desired.

So I kept falling and that state became constant, as the earth didn't need to support me once the sky became my home. I don't often remember my dreams so I treasured this one, even as I was having it, and didn't even know for sure if it was a dream but I enjoyed floating in a state of Being so buoyant and happy (like Heidegger on a good acid trip).

Beagle had been a huge side track in my life, not that things were going so well before he came along. My mother didn't suffer fools gladly and because I was a kid, I was therefore a fool and didn't matter much. With her not so benign neglect, a malevolently absent father, and an indifferent grandmother, I didn't learn much about love. I knew love was theoretically possible although I'm not sure how I came to that awareness, maybe from TV and the movies, or maybe from an innate mammalian need to bond with something, even a cloth monkey (wish I'd had one). Although I didn't know much about love, I knew that I wanted some, whether it was from a woman or from the world at large, I didn't care. Somehow I equated escaping Beagle's domination with being free and therefore being able to find love.

The endless fall segued neatly into my lying awkwardly on my side as I slowly woke up and found myself on the gurney, still in restraints, being detained among the psychiatrically impaired even though my problems were quite different. While I was sleeping, Beagle had inundated this area and I could see him in the ceiling above me, in the pattern of acoustic tiles, and in the grime saturating the surfaces. As I returned to awareness, I smelled the cigarettes around me and wondered if I could ask for one just to hang onto something real, even if it was bad for me. I was contemplating the prospect of asking for a smoke but didn't know who held the keys to the kingdom of tobacco. I was about to call out to one of the passing nurses when a man came striding across the emergency room toward me.

He looked to be in his thirties, wearing a black leather jacket and boots and carrying a motorcycle helmet under his arm. His gait suggested an easy confidence as he made his way through the various staff people. His long hair was pulled back in a pony tail and an earring was in his right ear. After inquiring of a nurse where I was, he pulled up a folding chair to sit beside me. I was curious about him but he told me who he was right away.

"You're Isaac, right? Good. Hate when I'm talking to the wrong person. My name is Stretch Kelly and I'm one of the County Mental Health Professionals. I'm here to make a decision about whether you should be placed on a seventy-two hour hold for psychiatric treatment. I haven't decided about that because I want to talk to you first but sometimes I put people in the hospital when they don't want to be there so I have to tell you what your legal rights are."

He gave me the Miranda rights and I sat there and watched him. He didn't look like my idea of a psychologist or therapist or whatever but I realized that the image I had was of a man in a tweed jacket with leather patches at the elbows, smoking a pipe. Must have come from a movie. Hitchcock, maybe? This guy seemed more like an outlaw and a troublemaker and I hoped someone like him might be able to see alternatives to locking me up. I decided to tell the truth so I laid out the entire story and assured him I wasn't crazy.

He listened carefully while I talked, looking me in the eye for the most part, occasionally acknowledging members of the ER staff who were walking by. He sat on a folding chair by my gurney, just far enough away, I noticed, that I couldn't reach out and grab him. That was not my intention although how was he to know? I told my story in the clearest way I could and he nodded his head several times as I talked although I couldn't tell if this was in approval or just to keep me going. When I finished, I looked up at him and said, "Does that make sense?"

He nodded again and said, "I hear you and I know you're telling me the truth as you see it. However, I've been doing this work for more than twenty years now and I've seen people who tell me similar things about themselves. The problem is, I've never once found someone whose conspiracy theories and paranoia seemed real to me. Some paranoia just makes sense. Our government will cut us down if we get in its way. Other people will slit our throats just for cash, or if they can see any possible angle in getting rid of us. But the truth is I'm almost certain Dionysius Beagle has never given a thought to you. You believe he's been constantly after you but no human I know of is able to do the kind of plotting and conniving and surveillance you're talking about. I'm not calling you a liar but I do know our brains are funny organs, subject to all kinds of distortions and aberrations we have no control over. The myth that we're always independent entities, able to easily assert our domination over the world, is exactly that: a myth. We're subject to all the forces in and around us."

"The bad news is: your brain is fooling you. Your synapses are misfiring and the chemistry is messed up. The good news is: there is help. The two things that give relief from what you're talking about are the right medications and counseling. The problem is it's often difficult to find the meds that are going to control someone's symptoms. So the doctors have to make guesses and try the best drugs they can think of. If one doesn't work, they'll try another, or several in combination. The most efficient way to do all that trial and error is on an inpatient unit where they can quickly see the effects and adjust the meds as needed. It's possible to do that on an outpatient basis but it takes longer and, from what I can see, you need help right away. What do you think?"

I shook my head. "Everything you're saying makes sense except it's all based on a false premise, that I'm delusional. I know you won't agree with me but everything I'm telling you is true. I know it the same way I know we're sitting here in the ER."

He shook his head.

"We could argue about epistemology all night long but I don't believe we'd accomplish anything. I'd be happy to let you go live your life pursued by Beagle if you hadn't done something dangerous. The bottom line is I have a police report with the evidence to detain you and nothing you're telling me makes me confident you won't be doing something risky in the near future based on your thoughts, deluded or not, so I am going to put you on a seventy two hour hold so you can get what the law was designed for: evaluation and treatment. I'd advise you to keep an open mind about the treatment because you just might find some help there. I'm going to do some paperwork and will come back and let you know where I'm able to find a bed for you."

"I gather there's no way I can change your mind, is there?"

He stood up. "No, I'm afraid not. I know you don't agree with me but I don't make these decisions lightly."

I thought about this for a moment. Then I realized what was happening.

"How much did he pay you?"

He turned and looked back at me, a sympathetic smile on his face.

"I'm paid by the County and no one looks over my shoulder. I make decisions based on people's safety and I'm just not sure about yours."

"It's okay to admit it. This is exactly what I expect anyway. People from all areas of life have been influenced by Beagle and they usually submit when the power becomes unbearable or the temptation is too great."

"Well, thanks for convincing me I made the right decision. You won't believe me but I've never received any communication from Beagle. The fears you're having are part of your illness, whether you believe it or not."

I shook my head, a dead weight shifting from side to side.

"Either you're a good actor or his intimidation has brought you to this point. Or maybe he's rigged my situation so even an experienced professional, such as yourself, thinks I have to be crazy. In any case, I don't blame you at all. You may feel you have to obey Beagle's higher power and that's what most people in the world believe as well."

"Mr. Turbot, I hope that someday, somehow, you reach the point where you see that what your thoughts are telling you are not true."

"And I hope you can find a way to think past the categories in your mind to see the truth when it's in front of you. Just know that what you're doing is not going to help me, no matter what you think."

"This isn't changing my mind."

"I didn't think so."

"I'll be back with the paperwork."

He picked up his helmet from the chair next to him and walked away. Something about finally being driven to the final indignity relaxed me, caused me to lie back on the gurney in surrender and just float on the sounds and sights around me. This was like going over the falls in my dream except I could smell the feet and armpits and crotches of the beings close by, could see their unshaven faces, the open sores, the makeup smeared in the struggles that landed them here. No parent could have foreseen when these beings were babies that one day they would be strapped down to gurneys in a hospital emergency room, unable to decide their own fates, even as the world continued to spin through the vast emptiness where we're both confined and yet somehow free to act.

Beagle's triumph sang in my head as a hissing symphony, his tunes of glory blaring over me. This was what he always wanted, for me to be declared insane. In his Fortress of Solitude, he would be toasting my defeat with jeroboams of Champagne so dry the liquid would evaporate before he could swallow.

I wondered what my mother would make of this. The woman from the hospital registry asked me for the name of a next of kin but I told her I didn't have anyone. I didn't want mother, irritated at the inconvenience, driving up to the ER from Enumclaw with Mitch in tow. If she became involved, Beagle would use her to take advantage of me, would exact retribution on her as the woman who delivered me into this world.

I hoped Mitch, who seemed to be a stalwart fellow, would be able to protect her even though Beagle knew her location, knew every move she made, even knew what she was thinking, because that's the kind of man he was, sitting in his castle on Lake Washington, watching on multiple TV sets as his cameras captured every detail of the lives of the people who obsessed him. No one would concern him more than the woman who was forced to play Madonna to his evil godhead, the maternal vessel who produced the Unchosen one, his godspring (variant of offspring, get it? Of course you do), the ungrateful spawn of Satan, namely me.

Again, I'm not talking about his son (my half-brother, it suddenly occurs to me) who died in the fiery incident on the freeway (more investigations please, Governor) but little old me, whose living presence was a constant rebuke to the image he wanted to present to the world of himself as the kind, civic-minded, generous patron of society. The brand of Beagle, in his mind anyway, was diminished by every breath I took (call out to The Police).

On the ceiling above me, his face oozed from the holes in the tiles, coalescing into a recognizable caricature looking down on me and laughing. The smoke rising from the cigarettes of my fellow prisoners drifted by, transformed into his sulfurous breath penetrating my lungs. Only a god could have his power and I had no choice in this moment but to submit. What was in store for me in the psychiatric hospital could only hurt, no matter what the MHP said, so I needed to harden myself for the various tortures he was undoubtedly feverishly arranging for me right now (two adverbs in a row? That can't be right).

I lay there for hours, like a dog chained in his kennel, dozing at times, waking thirsty and receiving water from the compassionate hands of someone, I don't know who, some veterinary aide, who came with a flimsy paper cup full of ice water with a straw for my convenience.

Eventually, Stretch Kelly returned and delivered my copies of the commitment papers. I knew they would contain lies so I didn't give them any credence and threw them on the floor.

He shrugged and said, "That's fine. You can do what you want with them. You're going to South Seattle

Psychiatric Hospital, a generic kind of psych hospital but they at least can do an evaluation and start medications. I personally recommend you try them because I believe there has to be relief somewhere from the torture you're going through. The only requirement is for you to be a little bit open-minded about the fact they could help."

I stared up at him and saw Kelly's face swimming in a loose kaleidoscopic pattern. Was I merely dizzy and disoriented or was this Beagle tinkering with my field of vision? I didn't know, of course. I had a sudden panic that his face would transform into Beagle's so I shook my head hard, causing a look of concern on what settled down to be Kelly's face. I swallowed some of the bile ascending to my mouth and spoke.

"So I should be open-minded when you're not?"

"I don't want to argue. I'm just telling you what's going to happen. This is now 9 PM on a Thursday night and your seventy-two hour hold doesn't include the weekend so there could be a hearing on Tuesday to see if you should stay for up to fourteen more days. On Monday afternoon, a public defender will see you and ask if you want to stay. If you somehow find the experience is helping, you can sign an agreed order to stay on a 14 day hold, and there won't have to be a hearing. However, if you don't like it and you want out, tell the attorney and he or she will do everything they can to get you out, no matter whether you need to stay or not."

"Don't worry. I'll be released on Tuesday."

"I'm willing to leave it up to the court to decide. I hope you find your way through this mess you're in."

I looked up at him and his face continued to swirl, revealing fragments of Beagle's face. His voice rasped to reveal the edge of Beagle's voice emerging in his words. I knew what was happening but didn't want to scream, despite my urgent impulse. He turned and walked away, leaving a trail of swirling light particles in his wake.

The dominoes of the day continued to fall. My gurney was up at a 30 degree angle so a single sweep of my visual field encompassed the entire proscenium of the E.R. in front of me, including all the bit players Beagle had assembled for his drama: patients in various degrees of distress, nurses and orderlies who ran the gamut from helpful to not, doctors who carried buckets of knowledge in their heads and tried not to spill them uselessly. Eventually, in the swirl of smoke generated both by cigarettes and by Beagle's sulfurous fumes from hell, two ambulance attendants showed up and transferred me carefully from the hospital's gurney to their gurney, with security officers standing by, as if I were going to fight them or run away when I was already beaten into submission.

Now, back at dear old Walla Walla (local Indian word for "many waters," B-Day tells me, although I haven't sensed much rain), some of the infirmary staff are here to measure and weigh me, presumably to give this information to the hangman. I wonder, how many hangmen (or hangwomen, has feminism progressed so far?) are currently employed in the world? And do they have more than one person in that capacity in Washington State? No one will answer these vital questions for me. Maybe, if you ever reply, you could tell me? I'll finish the story of my one hospitalization in the next letter.

To help me muster up some outside support (that I hope will sway you), a good friend here has agreed to send some telegrams for me, at the risk of his job (no, I am not at all willing to tell you who it is). For now, the execution committee has entered my cell, causing its already small dimensions to shrink drastically and amping up my fear.

Sincerely,
Isaac Turbot

TELEGRAM
MAY 1 COMMA 1989
TO POPE JOHN PAUL II THE VATICAN ROME ITALY
DEAR POPE COLON I AM SCHEDULED TO BE
EXECUTED BY HANGING FOR THE DEATH OF A
MAN WHO WAS A DANGER TO LIFE ON EARTH
STOP HUMANITARIAN AND SPIRITUAL
CONSIDERATIONS DEMAND MY EXECUTION BE
PREVENTED AND MY SENTENCE COMMUTED TO
SOMETHING MORE HUMANE STOP PLEASE SEND A
MESSAGE OF SUPPORT FOR ME TO THE
GOVERNORS OFFICE OLYMPIA WASHINGTON AND
A COPY TO WARDEN POUNDER AT WALLA WALLA
STATE PENITENTIARY IN WALLA WALLA
WASHINGTON STATE USA STOP IVE HAD MY
DISAGREEMENTS WITH THE CATHOLIC CHURCH
IN THE PAST BUT DO BELIEVE THAT IF WE DID NOT
HAVE YOU AROUND WE WOULD HAVE TO INVENT
YOU STOP PERHAPS A MESSAGE TO THE
ARCHBISHOP OF SEATTLE WOULD ALSO BE
HELPFUL STOP HOORAY FOR POLAND STOP OKAY
COMMA I AM NOT A CATHOLIC BUT WHY WOULD
THAT MAKE A DIFFERENCE QUESTION MARK
ISAAC TURBOT
PRISONER 321987
INTENSIVE MANAGEMENT UNIT
WALLA WALLA STATE PENITENTIARY
WALLA WALLA WASHINGTON

Sunday, April 30, 1989

Dear Governor,

More grist for the mill here as I think, hope, and pray that I'm heading to a point, sharpened and graphitic and overwhelmingly convincing to you (but, I trust, not a point of no return).

Leaving the ER, we rolled out through the corridors, fluorescent lights pulsing above in a steady succession of illuminated bars, punctuated by a series of faces, some looking deliberately away, others staring at me with curiosity or pity. I was now sitting up at about a 45 degree angle so couldn't see the attendant pushing the gurney. When I was transferred, he'd been a long-haired, mustachioed young man but Beagle could have morphed him into some other being entirely, maybe a horned and scaly sub-demon. I thought I smelled his sulfuric breath, making me think of a dragon with indigestion. The man walking in front of me and pulling the gurney was white-haired, perhaps prematurely, because the skin of his plump face was smooth (mostly). I didn't know exactly what time it was but the sky was dark as we went through the automatic doors and out to the driveway where a wind rose up and blew a cool consoling pressure onto my face (pathetic fallacy? I'm afraid so).

The ambulance was tall, red, and white while the sky was a deep blue creating a mockery of patriotic hues.

Next to several of its fellows, the ambulance waited ominously, like Charon's kayak, to paddle me across the river Styx to hell. The attendants wheeled me over to the back, opened the doors, and pulled a lever to hoist me higher. The white-haired man held the bottom of the gurney, no small matter because he must have been bearing half the total weight. His lips were pressed tightly together so his mouth was a mere m-dash on the bottom of his face. A large white-topped zit close to the end of his nose begged to be squeezed but my hands were restrained so the momentary urge was easily squelched (besides, that was disgusting, both the sight and the impulse).

They rolled me into the ambulance and suddenly my view was of the white metal ceiling and, when the doors closed, of the double windows at the back of the rig. An insect flew figure-eights around one of the lights in the ceiling of the bay. The attendant inside took my blood pressure, the zit hovering perilously close to my face. His cheeks were red, maybe from the effort, and the zit appeared ready to burst on its own. I averted my face to avoid the impending explosion of pus but the moment passed.

He said, "Okay, should be about thirty minutes this time of night. Best thing about night shift is, no traffic. The rest of the day, the rigs spend half their time stuck somewhere." He pulled a tissue from his pocket and took a swipe at the zit. He turned away to soak up the contents and then turned back with a streak of blood marking the crater site.

After that, he didn't seem interested in conversation and I wasn't either. I also didn't think I'd be interested in eating for another day or two. I felt the jolting of the rig, saw the lights flashing across the double windows. I wondered what new tortures Beagle had devised for me at this hospital. I'd seen <u>One Flew Over The Cuckoo's Nest</u> but didn't know if that was a strictly accurate depiction. I didn't have the same boisterous personality Jack Nicholson's character had so I didn't think I'd be leading any revolts. They wouldn't do electro-shock or lobotomies on the usual gang of misfits who came through their doors, or would they?

Probably Beagle could arrange such things if he so desired. Is that what he wanted for me, to be brain-damaged, my intellect reduced to the animal level? The only problem with that plan might be that the smarter I was, the more gratification he could receive from torturing me. We drove over rough asphalt, accelerated onto the freeway for about ten minutes, back to surface streets again and up a grade where, at the crest, we bumped over railroad tracks. We slowed and turned into a parking lot, then stopped under an overhang.

"This is it," the attendant said cheerfully, jumping back and opening the doors. He and the driver slid me out and wheeled me to a covered foyer, where he announcedus by pressing a round gray button on a black box and talking into a set of four serrated openings in the metal surface. Fear rose up in me and gathered inside my chest and head like a thick black wad of tar. I had no idea what to expect, and very little way to protect myself. All I could do was give myself up to the process and hope I'd have some wiggle room for dignity and, if that wasn't possible, find the means for retaliation and escape.

A man in his sixties, white-haired but sturdy-looking, came to the doors and opened them up for us. He began talking as I was wheeled inside.

"Hi, my name is Bill and I'm the charge nurse here tonight at South Seattle Psychiatric. We're going to go upstairs with you still on the gurney but then I'd like to release you from the restraints and settled into bed, if that's okay with you."

I appreciated his easy-going style, even it masked something else.

"Bill, my name is Isaac and I appreciate your talking to me like I'm a human being despite my currently compromised position. What you've outlined sounds like a good plan. I won't cause any trouble if no one causes any with me."

"Excellent, but if any of the other patients does try to start something, come and talk to one of the staff first so you don't have to deal with it. I'll get your information upstairs."

We all jammed into the elevator, with me still on the gurney, and I could smell the fragrance of human bodies, mine with the sharpest tang as I was no doubt the one who'd run the farthest and had been the most frightened today. I wondered if I could take a shower before going to bed.

They wheeled me in front of a nurses' station and Bill looked me in the eye.

"Now, just to be clear, I'm assuming that you're not going to be violent with us when we take off the restraints. There'd be no point anyway because you wouldn't be able to get out and we'd have to call everybody and take you to the floor and put you back in restraints. Besides, you don't strike me as the violent type. Am I right?"

I agreed to be calm so they released the restraints and I sat up. Bill gave me a pill and a cup of tepid water in a paper cup that collapsed in my trembling fingers. He said it was just a mild sedative and I didn't have the energy to argue. He filled out a form that asked many of the same questions I'd answered in the ER. Didn't that paperwork come with me? When he was done, I followed him to a darkened room where he pointed to my roommate who was asleep on the bed against the wall.

"That's Amos. He has some issues but don't we all? I think you'll get along okay. That's your bed there. Clean sheets. The medication I gave you should help you sleep."

I sat down on the bed and listened as my roommate snored, not too loudly but enough to make me think he would keep me awake. The day I had just gone through seemed to have lasted for months. The crazy bike ride on the trail could have been a year ago. I couldn't remember if I'd locked the bike when I slammed it into the rack back on campus. If not, I could wave it goodbye. Now I hoped I'd be able to rest but didn't know if Beagle would be bothering me in the night. He was suspiciously quiet right now. I wondered if my snoring roommate was one of his agents. Bill told me the restroom was just down the hall. He left and I rolled over and stared at the ceiling. I decided the shower could wait until morning.

This felt like the end of an ordeal, or was it just the beginning of an even worse phase? Beagle had been after me for years and now had won. I was locked up in a psychiatric hospital and everyone I encountered thought I was crazy. That's what he wanted and he must be laughing, wherever he was. Maybe in the morning I'd call my mother and tell her what was going on. I didn't think she would provide me with much support as the news would probably just confirm her worst fears about me. But I wanted someone to know where I was.

I stretched out on the bed and tried to fit myself into the ridges of the mattress. That wasn't a problem for me. My bed at home was the same one I'd had since I'd left the crib and my body had carved sharp edges into the mattress that I sometimes had to flatten out by hitting it with a baseball bat so this was, by comparison, comfortable. Through the door came a buzz from the fluorescent lights and I could hear more snoring from the rooms along the hallway. My roommate wheezed in between the snores and then his breath stopped for what seemed like an unnaturally long time until, with a loud groan, it started up again. The hump beneath the blanket seemed large so I imagined he must be fat, his size bringing associations of farm animals being fattened for the kill.

If he'd been planted here as my roommate by Beagle, what was his plan? Maybe to keep me awake with his noisy sleeping, or maybe to tiptoe over and smother me with his weight while I slept, suffocating me in sweaty rolls of blubber. I didn't know him. He could easily be an assassin, a fat assassin, who skipped practicing the arts of combat to engage with the dessert trays and thereby render himself more lethal. Right now, he was giving an excellent imitation of someone oblivious to all the world around him. This was clearly advanced spycraft.

Silly thoughts, I realized, as I finally closed my eyes and followed the swirling dark colors on the insides of my eyelids. The day had been long and the biking and running and stress of the ER had worn me down. I'd eaten very little all day and was feeling quite the opposite of fat, really, was feeling rail thin and fit. If I rested and had a good meal, I thought I could run all day tomorrow if I had to. I didn't expect there would be much chance to exercise in this dump. Such a place was hardly likely to have a track out back or a weight room. I could do push-ups and sit-ups all day and run in place, if I had to, like I was in prison, which I was, but it probably didn't matter if I took a few days off from exercise, barring the possibility of escape. Why did I need to be in shape, except to escape from Beagle?

He now had me thoroughly trapped. I was right where he wanted me and I could do nothing about it. I remembered reading Victor Frankl's <u>Man's Search For Meaning</u> where he wrote about being in a concentration camp and finding inside the torture machine that all he could control were his own reactions, so he made a deliberate choice to act for life and not against it. I supposed I could act in a similar fashion except I didn't know who to trust in this place, and therefore didn't know who was safe to care about. And why should I act to support a life so burdensome, anyway?

The staff was probably in on it too although Bill seemed like a nice guy and reasonable in how he approached me. But his mask of gentleness and civility could be hiding the raging face of Beagle that would quickly emerge if a confrontation were to occur. I hadn't liked being in restraints and my wrists and ankles still felt sore from the pressure of the leather. Here I'd try to avoid conflicts and see if I could prevent being strapped down again.

Sleep was pulling me into its depths as I listened to the snoring and the jingling keys of the guards who passed by, or did they belong to a nurse? More likely some low-paid aide on the night shift was The Master Of Keys. I wondered if lice or bedbugs were hiding in my mattress but, from the little I'd seen, it looked pretty clean. They'd have to change the sheets between patients, and fumigate every so often, wouldn't they? Right now, vermin didn't seem like the largest issue for me to worry about so I allowed myself to be pulled down further.

I didn't take off any clothes other than my running shoes and I lay on the bed with my head resting on my arms instead of touching the pillow. Having my arms above my head felt good, reminding me of when I was a little kid and would sleep that way, completely flexible and comfortable dozing off in any position. I worried someone would come in and assault me but everything was so quiet that the fear didn't seem too real, more like a speculation. Bad things could happen in the night but yesterday proved the same was true of the day. Going further down by the moment, I found myself following a strand of thought that seemed logical as I was having it but then I couldn't remember anything of what it was about. Something about legal action and going to court but the details escaped me. I didn't think hiring an attorney to stop Beagle would help much, given how little the cops or the social worker or the MHP believed me. I was alone and realized that had been true my entire life.

Now I began to hear Beagle's voice again and, oddly (although wasn't everything about him odd?), he was singing <u>Someone To Watch Over Me</u> in a passable baritone. I didn't think he was doing it for me. Maybe he had another victim confined in the hospital. Strange I hadn't thought of this before but maybe I wasn't the only one. Maybe he was stalking many of us although surely I was his only actual child, or was I? Could I have unacknowledged siblings in the same situation as me? I felt an odd pang of jealousy that someone else might be the object of his massive persecutions. A huge thought tried to break into awareness but I was too tired to follow it up. Beagle's singing was restful, lulling me, and maybe that's exactly what he wanted. I sank deeper into the darkness and the colors dissolved to black until, at some point that passed without my realizing it, I was out.

Morning light filtered into my sleep. In the night, I'd put my arms down and now held the pillow over my head to ward off the glare and the noise although both managed to seep through. I peeked out and saw my roommate, a heavy-set troll of a man with a wild shock of rust red hair, sitting up on his bed with his back against the wall. He winked at me. I pulled the pillow over my eyes and willed it all to go away without noticeable results. Of course not, because Beagle wanted this to continue. I tried to fall back asleep but a buzzing urgency in my brain prevented me from finding refuge in unconsciousness. I sighed and sat up, rubbing my face with my hands. My roommate laughed. I looked over and saw him projecting a big smile, revealing yellow teeth that should have had braces long ago.

"First time, I'm betting?"

"That's right."

"My name's Amos. This will be my thirteenth time. Lucky thirteen, ha!"

I didn't really want to talk but figured I should get a read on him if we were going to room together.

"I'm Isaac. What are you in for?"

"The usual, off my meds. I start thinking the CIA is after me and then I make threats to kill government agents. No one in particular, just whoever shows up to assassinate me. You wouldn't think that would be specific enough to commit me but they always do."

"That's too bad."

"Of course, like the doctors here tell me, I should know better. But who wants to live so carefully that all you do is submit, you know what I mean?"

I resigned myself to this conversation.

"It so happens I know exactly what you mean."

Amos stretched his legs out and kicked them, stirring the dust motes, his feet flapping in lime green sandals that revealed long misshapen toenails. I had to look away from them.

"So let me guess what you're here for. I'm pretty good at this game. You're in college, I'll bet, am I right?"

I nodded my head.

"Girlfriend broke up with you and you overdosed. That's it, isn't it?"

"Not even close."

"Damn! I almost always get it. Okay, let me try again. You became obsessed with a female professor and when she spurned your advances, you sent her a threatening letter."

"Nope."

"Shit!" He stood up and paced back and forth in the space between our beds. An aide looked in the door and asked, in a warning tone: "Amos?"

"I'm fine. No problem. I just have to deal with a mystery here."

I sat back, amused at his dismay about his erroneous discernment skills.

"You must be... No, that's not it. Maybe you're... No, yes, I've got it. You're paranoid like me?"

I shook my head. "That's what they said in the ER but what I'm going through is not because I'm crazy."

Amos looked delighted. "Me, too, exactly! Tell me more." He sat back on his bed, put his knees up and rested his elbows on them so he could hold his head in his hands and fix me with what he seemed to think was a sympathetic gaze. I didn't really want him on my side.

"I don't want to talk about it. Let's just say that someone powerful is against me and was able to run me down and put me here."

Amos' eyes widened. "Are we talking about an agent of the government?"

"No, he's actually more powerful than the anyone in the government."

"More powerful?" Amos looked amazed at this news. "Do you think he could be the one who sends all the agents after me?"

I shook my head again. This was too much. Now Beagle had planted an actor here to try and convince me I was crazy by his example. Best not to open my mouth and reveal myself.

"That's all I'm saying. When do they serve breakfast around here?"

"You can't stop now! We really have to compare notes. I bet we'll find your guy is working against me, too. What's his name?"

"I've said enough. Besides, you know very well who it is."

"I do?" He thought hard about this. "Maybe I do but I'm just not remembering. And you think I know because... I'm in on it?"

"Look. Let's just keep to neutral topics from now on. What about that breakfast?"

Amos stood up, his fists clenched.

"I've been turned! The government has been after me for years and now they've made me one of their agents, well, not a Federal agent but an agent of this mystery man who's after you. It all makes sense now. That's why I know so much about you and your situation."

I didn't bother pointing out that he'd been twice mistaken about why I was there. This was obviously an act, a good one, to try to fool me. I stood up and stretched in order to change the dynamic. I moved to the door and he followed close behind me so I caught his odor, a combination of tobacco and old sweat. I looked out to the hallway where several people wandered around, each in his or her own individual daze. They gave each other furtive glances as if to determine who was dangerous or who was attractive.

The truth was that none of us, especially me, was very attractive that morning. The attire ranged from disheveled and casual to stained and filthy, except for one striking individual in a green cocktail dress and blonde wig, in contrast with his handlebar mustache and an anchor tattoo on his forearm. I turned left, randomly, and walked down the hall. At the nurse's station, the staff sat behind the counter chatting and laughing with each other, avoiding eye contact with the patients milling about nearby. Amos came up beside me.

"If you want, I can tell you who's on edge and who's not, although it's pretty obvious if you pay attention."

"No, thanks, but maybe you can tell me how to get breakfast around here."

"The cart should be coming up soon. The grub's not great but it's filling. Even though I seem to be conspiring against you in the big picture, I'll watch out for you while you're here. You can trust me although I know you can't."

I didn't know how to respond to a statement of such profound internal contradictions. We walked together down the dingy hallway, passing other members of the Outcast Society wandering the corridor.

From the P.A. system came a message: "Isaac Turbot. To the nurses' station."

As I headed back there, the elevator doors opened and an attendant pushed the food cart in, piled with styrofoam containers exuding the aroma of bacon and eggs. The wanderers of the hallway followed it down to the common room as if the Ark of the Covenant had been introduced among the faithful.

I identified myself to a large nurse sitting behind the counter. She peered up at me from under an ill-fitting blonde wig, conveying a profound lack of interest.

"Doctor wants to see you."

She motioned me to an adjacent office door that was ajar. Behind the desk was the psychiatrist, in a tweed jacket and looking like Harpo Marx with shorter hair. A muscle-bound assistant in a white coat sat between the doctor and me, presumably for security, at the side of the desk where one could get around it. The doctor gestured for me to take a seat on the folding chair across from him. He opened a folder and scanned through the pages, talking to himself as he snapped the sheets over.

"I'm Dr. Jacobs and I'm just reviewing your information. Mr. Isaac Turbot, up on the Aurora Bridge... Police hold... Dionysius Beagle plotting against you... Doing constant surveillance... Denies being suicidal... Denies homicide... Thinks Beagle arranged for this commitment..."

He lifted his gaze from the paperwork and peered at me, looking me up and down with a care that belied his casual review of my record.

"Does this sound like an accurate description of what's going on?"

I hesitated a moment, purely for the effect.

"It does. The only thing I want to add is I'm quite aware that you, and this gentleman as well, are employed by Beagle so I know what to expect."

"Mr. Turbot, I have a lot of patients to see this morning so I'm not going to mince words. The impression is that you're paranoid and delusional so I'm going to prescribe an anti-psychotic named Haldol, that should reduce your agitation and put you in touch with reality. How does that sound to you?"

I thought for a moment, knowing my answer but unsure of what the response would be.

"It doesn't sound good. I don't need any medication. I want my day in court."

The doctor closed the file and nodded. "I thought as much although your life isn't going to go well until you give up this delusion. But I realize that's easier said than done. We're not going to force the medication on you unless you become out of control or violent here on the unit. I could prescribe a benzodiazepine, however, a mild sedative, kind of like having a few drinks on board. Many people find this place to be stressful so the medication could help you get through it."

"Are you sure it's just a sedative and not something more?"

"Absolutely. Look, you can try a dose and if you don't like it you don't have to take more. I'm easy."

"Yeah, okay. I'll try it."

He was right: the medication had a gradual effect, making me feel I was floating through the hospital. Everything was easy and amusing, including my fellow patients who exhibited an interesting variety of mental problems, from those who were flat and depressed, to the agitated and hallucinating, to those who just seemed like difficult people, some of them assholes, others needy, some manipulative. I interacted with all of them but didn't feel troubled by the exchanges.

Amos would sit by me and speculate about his role in my conspiracy but the words, instead of irritating me as they did originally, flowed over me like water over a river rock. I sat in the common room watching the black and white television that was always on, the set joining in on the flow by going from game shows and soap operas during the day to news in the evening, followed by Jeopardy and the various network offerings (of stunning banality, for the most part). I stayed on through the late night talk shows until the Star-Spangled Banner played and gave way to a test pattern for a few hours. On the second night, I never did go to my room but dozed on one of the couches that seemed less likely than the others to have vermin infesting it. I woke up occasionally to random bits of dialogue or advertising or news, all mixed together in the Mulligan stew of American television.

Much more interesting were my fellow patients (patience? a topic for another time) who came in, sat, stood, talked to each other and to the television, even when no one was talking back. Some of them even spoke to me and I answered as best I could but mostly just listened. In the morning, I had another pill which mellowed me out even more so I began to feel the hospital was one of the best places I'd ever stayed in, not that I'd ever stayed anywhere very much in my life.

Somehow being this relaxed reduced my awareness of Beagle's incursions, making me think he'd previously tunneled surreptitiously into my nervous system so now this abatement of the tensions therein also reduced his hold on me. He didn't go away entirely, however, as I received hints of his presence from the television, in the way the local news announcer looked at me through the camera, in the leer of the cartoon character who advertised cereal, in the football player who mouthed my name as he caught a pass. However, these indicators alarmed me much less than usual and I began to wonder if I could get this medication prescribed to me.

Amos continued to be amused by the idea that he was part of Beagle's conspiracy and kept saying he now understood everything. I wasn't sure what to make of him. For one thing, I found it highly unlikely that an actual Beagle agent would reveal himself so completely. I suspected the aides and nurses much more because they so patently ignored me, in the same way they ignored all the other patients, and that seemed like a better cover-up. I also didn't think Beagle would employ someone so demonstrative and friendly. Sneakiness and malice seemed more like his style. But what did I know for sure? I was locked up in a mental hospital but so were Beagle's multiple underlings.

The lack of windows disoriented me as I floated on my cloud through the weekend. I slept for hours at odd times in my room and then would go out to the common area for more TV and communion with my fellow prisoners. The sure signs of night were the quiet and the snoring and the long hours between meals, not that I felt very hungry for the dry meat loaf, synthetic eggs, and canned vegetables, mainstays of the hospital cuisine. I did, however, develop a strong attachment to the butterscotch pudding served after both lunch and dinner. I found the chalky texture and robust albeit synthetic flavor to be satisfying on a primal level, maybe because this was one of the few recipes Gouchie ever summoned up the energy to make (my very own madeleine, as it were, in a random Proust reference).

Beagle whispered at the edge of my awareness, just beyond my thoughts, perceptions, and emotions but he didn't intrude. I began to think medications might help me bear the burden of his harassment but as I sat through the night by the light of the test pattern, with several people snoozing on couches nearby, I realized this might be yet another trap. Maybe Beagle wanted me to think his evil had been muffled. Maybe he wanted me to accept medications and counseling and pretend he didn't exist, thereby rendering him better able to manipulate me without my resistance.

I realized I had a choice to make, to live unconsciously and at peace, or to live in excruciating awareness. As tempting as the easy path was, I decided to take the path of rebellion, to soak up the pain in order to live in full awareness of reality. At the next med pass, I refused the pill. The nurse just shrugged and said, "Suit yourself." The hospital slowly descended from the clouds and headed for a rough landing on the planet Earth.

On Monday afternoon, a young woman named Marissa, summoned me to the same office where the doctor saw me. She introduced herself as a Public Defender, appointed to represent my rights (ha!) and asked if I wanted to stay in the hospital on an agreed order for fourteen days. She looked tired and sped through her information as if talking about a traffic ticket. She warned me I'd be giving up my rights to possess a firearm if I agreed to the order. I told her I wasn't interested in buying a gun but I didn't want to stay and never intended suicide despite being up on the Interstate bridge. She sighed and said she would try her best to get me out.

That evening, I sat with my fellow sufferers watching Monday Night Football where, in the fourth quarter, the Oakland Raiders were staging a comeback against the Cleveland Browns, in Cleveland, after being down 20 to 10. I amused myself (barely) by imagining I was a "Raider" upon Beagle's dominion, and Beagle was a "Brown"-shirted Nazi bent, always bent, on my annihilation. Maybe I could make a comeback?

One of the patients, a young man named Lester, whose bad sunburn and blistered feet make him look like he'd spent weeks outside before he was corralled here, sat talking under his breath at the television. A commercial came on, with increased volume, featuring a dancing stick of deodorant, apparently the last straw for Lester's vulnerable state of self-control.

He screamed, "It's the devil!" and charged at the television, beating the screen with his fists. The image jumped a few times but the beleaguered set stubbornly maintained its integrity. He looked wildly around the room for something to use as a weapon. He finally stopped and stared at a middle-aged woman who was sitting and nodding off, despite his uproar, in an armchair with threadbare coverings. He ran up to her and turned the chair over with her in it. She fell to the floor with a solid thump and said, "Oof," as if the word were in a cartoon bubble. He picked up the chair, hoisted it over his head, and ran at the television. I felt riveted by this action, more intense than almost anything I'd ever seen before. I wanted the screen to be smashed although I realized everyone here, including me, would be hard-pressed for entertainment after it broke.

Unfortunately for my vicarious thrills, several of the staff, roused for once from their torpor, ran around the corner and stopped him in mid-swing just before one of the wooden legs was about to penetrate into the electronic mysteries of the set's interior. He let out a bellow of frustration as he was taken to the ground. Several of the larger staff members sat on him while another rushed in with a portable stretcher. He was restrained only with difficulty, talking to himself in gibberish the whole time. We, his fellow patients, watched as if the television programming had jumped from the wall into three dimensions in front of us. He was wheeled off to the isolation room as the staff shook each other's hands and congratulated themselves on the successful containment.

I wondered what they would do if we all went wild? They had nowhere near enough staff to take us all down. I realized that the amount of medications in our collective systems made that unlikely. The lady who'd been ejected so brusquely from her chair stood shifting her weight from foot to foot, rubbing her hands together. No one on staff had witnessed her role in the events. She seemed to be waiting for someone to do something for her but when it became clear nothing was going to be done, she went to the armchair that had landed on its feet close to the television at the end of the scuffle and sat down in it. Tranquility was restored and we stared open-mouthed, with some discreet drooling, at a scene in a police station with arguing detectives, the TV set seeming to sigh with relief at its narrow escape.

That night, as I dozed on the bed in our room, Amos talked on in his obsessive way about the Mystery Man who was after me and how he (that is, Amos) must be working for him because that's the only answer that made sense. His voice finally dropped to a muttering drone before he fell asleep, drifting into snores rising and falling like waves. I lay on the bed, unable to lose consciousness, apparently because my body had come to believe it needed that pill. I thought about what I would do if and when I was released the next day. Having a beer and getting a Dick's cheeseburger and fries were high on my list.

I was supposed to work for Tony over the weekend but I'd called him and told him I had an attack of appendicitis and was in the hospital. When he asked which hospital I was in, I quickly said goodbye and hung up. I didn't think he'd tried to visit me, as he wasn't that kind of boss, but I also didn't want to take the chance he'd be checking on me. Voices floated in from the other rooms (but not Beagle's voice), soft-spoken now but with an occasional muted shriek indicating someone was in momentary distress. At least tonight the cries were not sustained, falling away to the ground tone of city noise, combined from the cars and planes and machinery that were always operating no matter what the hour. As I lay dozing, I wondered idly what would become of me, how I would survive the blasts of Beagle's attention?

The next morning, right after breakfast, eight of us, with staff leading and following us, shuffled into the elevator. Amos waved goodbye to me from a position near the nurses station where he was trying to cajole the charge nurse into giving him an extra sedative for what he termed anxiety but was probably just boredom.

He called out to me: "You should agree to stay so we can work on this conspiracy together." I shook my head. Undaunted, he added, "I know I'll be seeing you again." But he was wrong about that.

Our merry band of the pre-adjudicated shuffled down a corridor on the first floor to a loading dock in the back where a van waited to take us to court. We had a short ride up Interstate 5, the city skyline clear against the morning sky. We climbed the hill to Harborview Hospital that loomed over the city as if warning the citizens against excess in gratification and errors of judgment. We parked behind a monolithic building across the street from the main hospital entrance. Inside, Marissa, the public defender came by and asked if I still wanted to leave. I replied, "Absolutely." She said, "Okay. I'll try to have you out of here as soon as possible."

The evaluator from the psychiatric hospital arrived. She was an iron-haired woman in a dark blue pants suit who had asked me a series of perfunctory questions the day before. The exchange was so brief I barely remembered it. She asked me if I was suicidal. I said, "No." Then the prosecutor, a chubby man with gray hair on the fringe of his bald head, came in and also asked me if I was suicidal. Again, I said, "No."

He said, "Do you want any outpatient treatment after you're released?"

"No."

I sat in the hallway with my fellow inmates and waited, hands folded, feeling suspicious. Beagle couldn't possibly want me to be released so soon, could he? I wasn't sure. The only reason he'd want me out is if he had something even worse planned for me later. What could that possibly be? How could anyone be more alone in the world than I was? He'd alienated me from all my friends and family, not that I had many in either category but he'd actively precluded me from establishing any relationships. I knew he'd manipulated my mother into moving away and killed my grandmother by putting poison in her junk food. I now had only brief exchanges with my classmates and professors at school. My boss Tony and I related okay about gardening but his deafness and lack of curiosity prevented familiarity.

No one really cared about me; I had no one I could depend on (I know, boo hoo, but I'm just stating facts, not fishing for sympathy). Being essentially alone was my fate in life although I wasn't sure that state of isolation would always have to prevail. If Beagle was the principle of evil, shouldn't there be a principle of good? Gouchie told me she believed in God but she never went to church or explained what that word meant to her. The idea was a mystery to me but seemed unavoidable. If evil existed (and I'd experienced it first hand), shouldn't there be some countervailing force to keep the universe from degenerating into the sheer foulness of Beagle? I pondered on this occasionally but couldn't imagine a puppet master outside the system manipulating events the way Beagle manipulated them from the inside.

The public defender came down the hall and smiled at me, saying, "You're free to leave. Do you want to go back to South Seattle Psych to get anything?"

"No, I don't. Do you mean I can leave from here?"

"I'll walk you out."

We stood up and walked down the hallway to where a King County Deputy stood at the door, his girth filling the frame. The public defender showed him a form and then handed it to me. It read: "Voluntary Dismissal." She offered her hand and I shook it.

"Good luck to you."

I thanked her. The deputy stepped aside and I walked out to 9th Avenue where Beagle's powers had been momentarily suspended. Everything was bursting out into vivid colors, even on this dull city street. Harborview hospital was faced in beige stone that glowed in the morning light. Above, the blue sky sagged in sections that almost turned to purple. Down toward James Street, the red of the traffic light was so intense it pierced my retina. I felt a presence to my left and turned to see Mt. Rainier looming over the public housing at the end of the street. The peak radiated its sheer power across the distance, looking as delicious as a white ice cream sundae, vanilla with marshmallow sauce and whipped cream.

I felt dizzy from absolute beauty, a feeling not often allowed me under Beagle's domination. I stood on the sidewalk with hospital employees and patients moving past me, exulting in my freedom. I'd never given much thought to what freedom was, just a word thrown around on the Fourth of July and in American History class. But now I realized the truth of what it meant: to stand under a sky, on a city street, without anyone to tell me where to go or what to do on the surface of this planet. I only had about a thousand dollars in the bank, not much in the scheme of things, but enough to take me across the country and even across an ocean.

Of course, I didn't go anywhere although maybe I should have tested Beagle's ability to summon up resources to hound me in other parts of the planet. Instead I went home, had a long shower, and slept for twelve hours, wondering where I could get more of those pills they gave me in the hospital. My head was curiously empty after the tumult of the last few days. For a change, I didn't hear Beagle anywhere. The neighborhood generated only the usual noises of human-related activity, not the caterwauling he usually created to plague me.

Governor, you may well be asking what the point is of all this? To tell the truth, I became so wrapped up in memories of my one experience with mental health treatment that I lost track of how this might influence you toward letting me live. Maybe I'm hoping that the more you know about me, the more the prospect of expunging me from life would seem to be... what?

Distasteful? Inconceivable? Unkind? In any case, I was compelled to tell you more about who I am. Make of it what you will.

Confidingly,
Your prisoner,
Isaac Turbot

TELEGRAM
APRIL 30 COMMA 1989
WORLD COURT
THE HAGUE
THE NETHERLANDS
DEAR JUDGES COLON I AM WRITING TO YOU
BECAUSE I AM ABOUT TO BE EXECUTED IN A
SERIOUS MISCARRIAGE OF JUSTICE STOP I SUPPOSE
YOU ARE ALL FAMILIAR WITH THE NOVEL QUOTE
MARKS THE TRIAL END QUOTE MARKS BY FRANZ
KAFKA STOP WELL COMMA I AM LIVING OUT
THAT NOVEL OR AT LEAST WHAT I KNOW ABOUT
THE NOVEL AS I WAS SUPPOSED TO READ IT FOR A
WORLD LITERATURE CLASS MY FRESHMAN YEAR
BUT ENDED UP CONCENTRATING ON QUOTE
MARKS THE PORTRAIT OF AN ARTIST AS A YOUNG
MAN END QUOTE MARKS BY JAMES JOYCE
BECAUSE THAT WAS THE BOOK I WANTED TO
WRITE MY PAPER ON ALTHOUGH I DID HEAR AND
ENJOY THE DISCUSSION ABOUT KAFKAS GREAT
WORK SO I FEEL I HAVE SOME FAMILIARITY WITH
IT STOP AT ANY RATE COMMA MY
UNDERSTANDING OF QUOTE MARKS THE TRIAL
END QUOTE MARKS IS THAT THE STORY CENTERS
ON A MAN ACCUSED OF A CRIME HE DOES NOT
KNOW ABOUT WHO IS GOING THROUGH A
JUDICIAL PROCEDURE THAT HE DOES NOT
UNDERSTAND STOP THAT IS MY SITUATION

EXCEPT I DO KNOW WHAT THE CHARGE IS
BECAUSE I DID COMMIT A HOMICIDE AND MY
TRIAL IN AND OF ITSELF WAS FAIRLY
STRAIGHTFORWARD AND UNDERSTANDABLE
BECAUSE I DID NOT PARTICIPATE IN MY DEFENSE
AT ALL STOP THE COMPARISON COMES ABOUT
BECAUSE I AM ABOUT TO DIE BUT FEEL I AM
CAUGHT IN A FICTION WHOSE AUTHOR I DO NOT
KNOW AND WHOSE PLOT IS INEXPLICABLE TO ME
STOP I IMPLORE YOU TO INTERVENE TO SPARE MY
LIFE STOP I DO NOT CLAIM TO BE MENTALLY ILL
AND IN FACT I HEARTILY DENY THAT
ACCUSATION STOP MY PLEA FOR CLEMENCY IS
BASED TOTALLY ON THE EVIL OF MY SUPPOSED
VICTIM STOP I CANNOT HELP BUT POINT OUT
THAT I WAS HIS VICTIM FOR YEARS AND THAT IN
ITSELF SHOULD GIVE GROUNDS FOR LENIENCY IN
MY SITUATION STOP I DO NOT KNOW WHAT
INFLUENCE YOU HAVE ON THE JUDICIAL
DECISIONS OF THE UNITED STATES BUT I BELIEVE
THAT YOUR QUESTIONING MY IMPENDING
EXECUTION IN THE WORLD PRESS COULD HAVE A
POSITIVE EFFECT TOWARD SAVING MY LIFE STOP I
ONLY ACTED TO END THE LIFE OF DIONYSIUS
BEAGLE BECAUSE TO ALLOW HIM TO LIVE WOULD
HAVE PLACED EVERY BEING ON THE PLANET IN
SEVERE JEOPARDY STOP WHAT HE DID TO ME HE
COULD HAVE DONE TO EACH OF YOU OR TO ANY

MEMBERS OF YOUR FAMILIES STOP I SEND YOU
THIS COMMUNICATION OUT OF DESPERATION
AND HOPE YOU WILL RESPOND WITH IMMEDIATE
URGENCY STOP MY BEST WISHES FOR ALL YOUR
ENDEAVORS IN THE FUTURE STOP YOUR FAN
COMMA
ISAAC TURBOT
INMATE NOT AT LARGE
PRISONER NUMBER 321987
INTENSIVE MANAGEMENT UNIT
WALLA WALLA STATE PENITENTIARY
WALLA WALLA WASHINGTON

Sunday, April 30, 1989

Dear Governor,

I'm scribbling furiously with Leonard still waiting
somewhere in the antechambers of this concrete
monstrosity and sending me messages wondering when
I will be done so he can make the drive to Olympia and
deliver my manuscript which is now too long for you to
read comfortably before the moment of my execution.
My only hope now is for you to skim through my words
and perhaps something will catch your eye to make you
realize the humanity residing inside me beyond the
crimes I've committed, including the fateful night when I
took the actions affecting you so severely and leading me
to this charnel house.

Does it make sense to eliminate one life because
another was taken? If the state kills, doesn't that set kind
of a bad example for its citizens? How does revenge
function in any way to bring back the person who was
eliminated and does it matter at all if that person
embodied evil? These are all questions deserving of
profound moral debate at all levels of national discourse
from the backyard fence to the echoing chambers of
justice (echoing because they are so empty of morality, in
my opinion). All I'm asking for is to live and yet I don't
know why I want to live other than the vaguest sense
that some meaning might arise during my continued

existence. I must be feeling some visceral and inextinguishable desire to keep breathing, like a rodent desperately trying to escape the claws of a cat.

Nothing to do but press on, endlessly, endlessly (when will this end, you may be asking yourself and the answer could be Monday at midnight?). I decided to go back to school where I ended up only missing two classes, Philosophy of Logic on Friday, and World Religious Traditions on Monday. I resolved from then on to take the bus from Ballard to school to avoid the rage threatening to explode inside me when I was on my bicycle. I found I had indeed left my bike unlocked but it was still there that afternoon when I retrieved it. This was either proof of a God of miracles or evidence of what a piece of shit my bike was, a primitive three-speed contraption. Taking the bus to school provoked various degrees of irritation in me but the inhibitory presence of so many others in close proximity seemed to keep my anger from boiling over and scalding me, or anyone else.

Classes continued in much the same vein as before with the professors usually acknowledging my intelligence but sometimes acting completely befuddled by the conclusions I drew from our readings on the nature of reality. I felt a kinship when I read Sartre on the nausea of existence, expressed in that famous moment when he looked down at his own hand on the seat of a railway train and became disgusted with the sheer being of it. I often felt that way with myself, but not about

Being, which seemed to me buoyant and rather humorous, but from the bitter realization of how completely Beagle had circumscribed my possibilities while I was trapped in this incarnation. I noticed how his name was a combination of the words Be and gull and wondered if that meant he was gulling us about the nature of Being. Of course, a beagle was a dog and what was a dog but God spelled backward, indicating Beagle was an Anti-God, maybe the Anti-Christ so obsessed about by the Biblical literalists?

Meanwhile, Beagle was undoubtedly sitting in his office on the top floor of the Beagle Building, enjoying (as much as he could enjoy anything) his expansive view of the Seattle waterfront and Puget Sound, receiving minute-by-minute reports of my activities from his army of spies and minions (spinions?), and planning out just how to further limit my life. Why didn't he have me killed if I bothered him so much? Maybe he knew the greater torture was for me to remain struggling to express myself but unable to find support for the truth, unable to realize my talents and dreams. Martin Heidegger's work was my only refuge.

I responded to what Heidegger wrote about Being and Dasein even though I had a hard time (that I was reluctant to admit) understanding the literal meaning in his writing (if there was any, and I say this even though I'm a fan), especially in his major work, <u>Being And Time</u>, wherein he used so many made-up terms that he achieved a kind of mad philosophical language entirely his own, almost impossible to pin down, at least for me.

The inability to comprehend this central text was an obvious obstacle to excellence in my field. I came to believe that what he was saying was actually more poetical than logical and Heidegger himself agreed with me when he wrote: "Making itself intelligible is suicide for philosophy" (although I can't rule out that he might have been kidding). What I did manage to glean from his books was that Being was the central mystery of life, that we all shared in it and were individual extensions of its power.

What worried me was that Beagle seemed to be worming his way into the very roots of Being, tinkering with its mechanics, distorting how I was connected to the One. Individual beings such as myself (and like you and the missus) are the fingers of a trillion-digited glove, the expressions of a unity going far beyond what we could imagine yet Beagle managed to saw away at the joint where my individual Being was connected to Being overall. If he could, he would cut my finger from the glove completely and send me spinning off into the void (giving the Universe the finger?) without a connection to what was most vital to me, the power of Being. His influence went so far that he could negate my most essential self. Annihilation was his ultimate goal and disintegration was his method.

Professor Abrams was (and probably still is) a nervous bald man with a Van Dyke beard he pulled briskly when, as now, he was concerned. He was my designated Philosophy adviser and, during a scheduled appointment during his office hours, I outlined to him my plan for a senior thesis wherein I would compare the role of Adolf Hitler in Heidegger's life with the role of Dionysius Beagle in mine. Heidegger had become the Chancellor of a University during the Nazi era in Germany and felt compelled to become a member of the Nazi party. My plan was to write about the similar pressure I felt to bow to the innumerable attacks upon my weakened psyche by Beagle who to a remarkable degree conformed to the very definition of a modern day fascist.

Abrams actually pulled a few strands of hair from his beard and shook his head.

"Isaac, I believe you should go down to Hall Health and seek some counseling. I wish I'd gone myself at certain crucial points in my life. Many students develop, let us say, alternative ideas, under the stress of academics and all the other social forces at work these days. You are obviously intelligent so I urge you to accept help in order to gain some focus in your life."

He wasn't looking directly at me and had pushed his chair back to the window to keep the maximum amount of space between us. Once again, Beagle had managed to co-opt someone in my life. I didn't feel like sparing Abrams in his cowardice.

"Professor, by resorting to the bogeyman of mental health, do you mean to tell me that you are rejecting my thesis?"

He twisted a paper clip around and around in his hand.

"While I don't deny you have a number of interesting ideas about Heidegger, I can't accept your thesis topic in its present form. In fact, I believe you've totally missed what Heidegger was saying by filtering all of your understanding of him through one entrenched and very peculiar perspective. While Heidegger's association with the Nazi party is certainly a troubling aspect of his biography, your analogy of his experience to yours is outside the field of philosophy. I believe you are venturing into the realm of psychology but in a completely non-academic way."

I decided to try at this point to be gentle with Abrams.

"I can certainly understand your concerns because I've been dealing with them for years. You don't need to be ashamed because Beagle's influence permeates the world around us. However, I do wish you'd talk to me about it so I can understand how Beagle works, how you were approached, what rewards or threats he employed to induce you to reject a thesis that, in my humble opinion, points directly to the problem at the heart of

Dasein, that is, Heidegger's conception of Being, and even more than that, to the actual reality of Being itself, a thesis that is more ground-breaking and important than any other work being done in this department."

I'd hit home, I could see. Abrams grew very quiet, even ceasing to pull on his beard. From outside came a monotone of voices punctuated by an occasional carefree yelp, emanating, no doubt, from my fellow collegians (the carefree ones not being stalked by a madman) who were crossing Red Square, a common area soon (no doubt) to be renamed Beagle Square.

Finally, Professor Abrams said, softly, "Isaac, I urge you to seek out help, and that's all I have to say."

I shook my head gently, realizing the intense pain he was undergoing, and the pressure Beagle must be placing upon him. His wife and children, if he had any, or parents and siblings, might be hostages somewhere right now, maybe in a moss-covered cabin down some potholed dirt road high in the Cascades, tied to chairs, only able to hear the wind rattling the wooden shingles.

Understanding this, I lifted my hand in a peaceful gesture, said, "Father, forgive him because he knows not what he does," and left the campus, never to return. I said that, of course, to mess with his head and not out of any religious fervor. I also left the study of Heidegger on that day although I kept his books on my crude shelves made of planks and cinder blocks. No matter what I've gone through, the concept of Dasein has always lingered on the edges of my thoughts.

So you see, Governor, my crime came about because of more than one incident. I underwent years of being persecuted, stifled, and most outrageously rejected because of BEAGLE'S paranoia, not mine (excuse the caps). I represented no real threat to him despite my fantasies of overcoming and exposing his plots. They remained fantasies for years. If he had left me alone, I would have left him alone, I swear it.

I can hear the shift change down at the end of the hall. The day guard, B-Day, my friend, is coming on duty. The night duty officer is telling him the little of what went on during the shift. Now they're talking about me. I know it because their voices are very low. They must feel quite the responsibility for guarding a man who's due for execution in less than two days. I suppose the worst thing of all for the prison would be if I killed myself before the hangman could get to me. Justice would be left in the embarrassing position of staring into an empty cage, wondering where the doomed bird had flown. However, the whole point of this communication is (once again, into the breach) I don't want to die. During the trial and up until recently I felt I'd fulfilled my purpose in life by killing Beagle and preventing him from doing to others what he'd done to me. Now I'm beginning to see how little of my own life I've been leading during the years I've been alive. Even within the limits of prison, my life is better than it was under Beagle's domination.

After leaving college, I went into hiding for seven years, diving deep into the dismal depths (indulging in alliteration) in my bathysphere, working for Tony, doing gardening mostly on Queen Anne and Magnolia and the North End, cutting lawns, edging sidewalks, trimming branches, etc. Tony treated me okay. Our relationship seemed to thrive on his being very deaf so Beagle's voices were apparently unable to reach him. Moreover, Tony didn't take offense at the things I said although some of the customers could be rather touchy when I shared my subtler philosophic observations.

I managed to sedate myself at night with beer and marijuana, finding the right mixture so I could feel loose without thinking too much of Beagle who seemed content, for the most part, with his accomplishment of ruining my life. When I lay awake at night, waiting for sleep to bubble up inside me, I could hear him murmuring in the traffic noise of the North End, talking to himself, no doubt, about my attempts to avoid him. Tony was unusual in that he didn't expand the business in the summer by hiring kids with whom I would have inevitably fallen into conflict. Instead, we just worked more, from first light to sundown near ten PM. The work sedated me as much as the drugs and alcohol.

I knew Beagle could not have forgotten about me because that would be impossible for his vanity. However, I imagined he had at least placed me on a back burner of his raging furnace. I seldom reached out to make friends because he would have inevitably corrupted them. I kept on clipping out articles about him from the paper, watching from the sidelines, not knowing what I would do with all this information in the end.

Beagle suffered some losses in the seventies during the Boeing bust with its corresponding real estate collapse but he rebounded in the early eighties after the first Reagan recession. The Beagle Building was now dwarfed by other structures so he undertook the construction of Beagle Tower, the second tallest building, next to Chicago's Sears Tower, outside of New York City where the World Trade Center reigns supreme. Here in Seattle, citizens protested, architects moaned, but Beagle forged ahead, creating a tall shit-brown edifice that was even more ugly, if you can believe it (and I suppose you can because you, Governor, were at the dedication ceremony), than the original Beagle Building. The shadow of this abomination is so huge it sweeps the entire region in the course of a day, like the darkness of an infernal sun dial. Large micro-wave transmitters on top sap the energy of Puget Sound's inhabitants and stimulate cancer growth in most organisms.

And yet, with all this going on, Beagle somehow came around to finding time for me. I enjoyed a lot of what I did for work. The physical labor of yard care always sweated out the poisons I'd ingested the night before although Tony made a big point of holding his nose around me on hot days. I liked being outside, interacting with the flora, watching the clouds roll in from off the Sound and the ocean beyond, feeling the almost hourly changes in the weather. I appreciated the plants and grasses we worked with, always regretting our daily labor of reducing nice shaggy yards to the uniform smoothness of a golf green.

Of course, the pleasure was that yards were always changing, never static. In the temperate moist climate of our region, vegetation would thrive in our absence, especially the blackberries, morning glory, scotch broom, and bamboo that pushed their way into life with fierce determination. I admired their vigor and began to talk to all the plants we handled. I considered them much more consistent and definitely friendlier than any human I'd ever known. In the course of a day, in various yards, I'd hold philosophical discourses with the trees and shrubbery who would answer me with various qualities of silence. We communicated so much and so intensely that I came to learn their language, understanding on an intuitive level just what they were trying to say.

B-Day, the guard, has come by my cell to ask how I'm doing by giving me an interrogative thumbs up sign with eyebrows raised. I return him an upright thumb for an answer. B-Day is unusual around here, unusual anywhere, really, because he doesn't judge the people he guards. He has a job to do and he does it but the fact that I'm a "vicious" murderer, that we're all murderers here on this unit, doesn't lead him to look down on me as less than human. Instead, we're equal, both okay, all in the same leaky vessel of being alive and waiting for the day we die. He's so good, I'd almost put him in the same category of friendship as the plants, who never gave me any shit, who delivered direct albeit nonverbal answers, who treated me with respect. Governor, you have an excellent employee here in Walla Walla and you might study his example in order to train guards throughout the system although I suspect B-Days are born, not made.

I'm growing tired and have gone even more off track than usual after all. I'm not pleading for B-Day's life (he has a fine one, he tells me, with a wife and four kids at home. I imagine a ranch house nestled at the foot of a dusty hill with roses intertwined in the branches of an evergreen tree). Of course, as you are no doubt by now aware to the point of disgust, I am arguing for my own life but have no idea what to say, even in this onslaught of words.

The trouble in my gardening world began in 1984 (another meaningful date, at least for George Orwell) when Beagle's whispering started growing louder. My nightly pot and booze were causing me to feel mildly ill all the time so I was cutting back a bit. This action put me in a position of vulnerability that Beagle must have been waiting for in order to pounce.

One morning, when I was working in the yard of a large house on Magnolia bluff, a loud persistent voice began abruptly to resound in the sky, telling me, very simply: "You're no good, you're a shit, you shouldn't be here, you're nothing." I looked in shock at the house but the windows were blank. The owners had gone to Mexico for the winter. I tried to discuss this new event with the trees and plants but they were quiet, afraid, it seemed, of this new voice in our midst.

Tony was working diligently, bent over some weeds at the other side of the yard, oblivious, as usual, to the subtler sounds. Above us, a plane flew in a low approach pattern to Seatac airport. I realized what was going on. Beagle had bought his way into the airlines. He'd rigged transmitting devices to the fuselages of the planes so I'd be forced to hear his message outside. The flora were helpless to defend me against him. This form of propaganda was ingenious for it would undoubtedly have the added effect of turning even more people against me when they heard what the voices said. The air traffic into Seattle was so consistent that the voices were almost continuous. As soon as one plane landed out of range, another came into the pattern and took up the broadcast.

Despite Beagle's successes in the commercial world, what must have truly gnawed at him was my existence as the one worm in his apple, the only boil on his butt. The battle had escalated into a new dimension. Heretofore, he'd been content to stifle all my ambitions, to discourage me from thrusting myself into the front ranks of philosophical discourse, to prevent me from acquiring the scholarships and fellowships that would have allowed me to study at Oxford or Heidelberg. He'd managed to convince the police, the Harborview staff, and the MHPs that I was crazy and now he wanted not just the simulacrum of insanity but actually to drive me insane, to make me believe the terrible things the voices said about me.

I tried the usual methods against them: cotton in my ears, noise suppressors while I ran the loudest weed whacker, headphones connected to a Walkman blasting Beethoven at high volume. The problem was that the voices didn't operate just in sound. They seemed to vibrate right into my skull so I could understand them no matter how loud I made the other noises.

Beagle had obviously moved into the area of high-tech research and had commissioned a device transmitting deep penetrating waves with the power to sink into my neurons and bone marrow and inexorably deliver their message. I never actually believed the voices, so they failed in their attempts to undermine my sanity, but I felt rage rising within me. Beagle had gone too far now. He was not content with controlling the outward circumstances of my life. Now he wanted to invade my interior world and destroy it with his thought pollution.

Governor, I gave him many chances to stop. I simply told myself that I wouldn't listen to the voices and I endured them for months, trying to live my life despite the constant criticism and abuse inside me. I fell asleep to their whispers (if I was lucky and they weren't screaming) and woke to them in the morning. They seemed to follow me down into my dreams and poison any cathartic function dreaming might have provided. I tried increasing my drinking and started smoking hash to kept them at bay, but my health couldn't take it. I found myself feeling sick all the time, missing days of work only to have to suffer the torture of listening to the bullshit of the voices all day at home while I was "resting." Beagle began turning his vast armies in my direction. He placed broadcast devices behind the windows of all my neighbors, up on the telephone poles, and in the wires hanging above the street. I could feel a constant tingling from the sheer electronic burden of all the transmissions.

Another reason for you to spare my life is that the constant bombardment by microwaves has put me at high risk for cancer, if I don't have it already. I might as well be very honest about this even though you might calculate that the State would save money by executing me and thereby avoiding expensive cancer treatments. If you want me to, I'd be willing to save you some money and sign a waiver saying that I will refuse radiation and chemotherapy if and when the time comes that they are indicated. I will just stay in my cell and continue to write as those pesky interior cells (cells within cells) multiply madly until my body can't function anymore. In any case, something had to be done. I decided taking action was preferable to this continued passive suffering.

I hear the early risers among our merry crew performing ablutions or doing exercises on the cold floor. I used to wonder why someone in the IMU would bother to work out. Abdul, two cells down, (who killed a police officer during a botched drug bust) told me he runs for miles in place in his cell (like Nelson Mandela, he says, making an entirely inappropriate comparison) in order to be ready to escape. I wondered what that steady thumping sound was.

Don't worry, Governor, he's not really going anywhere. None of us could find a way out of here, no matter how elaborate the plan. The great minds behind the penal system have seen to that. The security here is as tight as at Fort Knox, tighter maybe, because in Kentucky they don't have to worry about the gold trying to flee. Maybe you should just hang us all, no matter what our crimes, and save the taxpayers some money. As far as this mighty nation of States United is concerned, no one outside really cares what happens in the IMU, do they, Governor? Of course, I'm writing all this in the hope, admittedly slim, of making you care but I feel the goal receding with every word. I'm here solely as a result of my domination by Beagle. Even though he's dead, he manages to control me. If I believed in any kind of deity, I'd assume Beagle has paid off Him, or Her.

I have to hurry now because B-Day tells me that Leonard (my lawyer, remember?) is getting exhausted. I can almost hear him whining to himself in whatever office (no doubt most uncomfortable) they allowed him to wait in. Knowing him, he's probably reading a best seller he found at Costco, Stephen King or Tom Clancy, smearing the pages with Cheetos dust from his fingers (no, I'm not exaggerating. His shirt during my trial had orange stripes like a tiger's. Too bad he didn't have a tiger's temperament). He's just a big kid, really, a big, fat, bald kid. Too bad he's such a shitty attorney.

Sorry, Leonard, if you read this but it's true. He's so worried about me he'd probably even be willing to file an appeal based on his own incompetence. What did he tell me about this letter? He said to write the truth and be conciliatory. How can a man be conciliatory about his own life? If I had the slightest inkling of what you wanted to hear, Governor, I'd say it, but I don't know what's behind your public mask. I figure the truth really is the best defense, so I've been trying to tell it as best I can. Not much time now so I'll try not to pontificate (I know, once again, too late), making me think of the great bureaucrat, Pontius Pilate, asking, "What is truth?" Is the truth slippery? Yes. Subjective? Definitely. Is it finally unknowable? I don't know. All I can do is tell my story.

The plan that led me to this place of confinement and punishment didn't come to me all at once but kept rolling around in my head as the voices yammered at me. Maybe, and this is all from hindsight, Beagle's voices wanted me to commit murder so I'd end up here but I couldn't think of another way to shut them up. Another part of Beagle's plan might have been to put mind-altering substances into my food to reduce my cognitive abilities. I have no doubt the local Safeway and its staff could easily have been compromised.

Having made my decision, I went to the Ballard Library and searched the microfiche of past Seattle Times and Post-Intelligencer articles to create a time line of events that Beagle participated in every year (I can understand using "Post" for the name of a periodical as in The New York Post and The Saturday Evening Post, although on closer examination does that mean the information is posted somewhere, like on a telephone pole or is it posted like a letter? We did have the Saturday Evening Post come to Gouchie's house in the mail. But the word "Intelligencer" is more problematic. Does that mean the publication renders one intelligent or is it a comparative term meaning it's more intelligent than similar rags? Is this worth pondering? Probably not).

In a spiral bound notebook, I listed the various charity functions he attended, and tried to imagine how I would penetrate their security. I also rode my bike out to his house, located on a high ridge on the East Side but, after hours of observation, hiding in the thick brush across the street from the entry gate, I decided it was hopeless. A wall the size of the Berlin Wall (will it ever fall?) surrounded the entire estate. Guard dogs patrolled inside. An elaborate alarm system protected both the walls and the mansion itself. A twenty-four hour security service provided at least one rent-a-cop always on duty. "What's he so afraid of?" I wondered, and then realized it was me he feared. I'd have to do an end run of some kind and strike, to mix metaphors (football vs. zoology?), at his soft underbelly. A social event was the only way.

In my planning, I realized I would not be able to count on an effective escape plan. I'd probably have to act in public and that would limit my options after the deed was done. At this point, however, I didn't care. He was ruining my life and God only knew what he was doing to others. He had to be stopped even at the risk of my own health and freedom. Besides, life was not worth living anymore because of the constant chatter he aimed at me from every direction. I didn't sleep well at night, waking up repeatedly after graphic nightmares of being smothered by Beagle himself or one of his diabolic minions (although aren't minions by their very nature always evil?). I was gripped by fear clogging my chest and forebrain, intensified by the voices shouting at me over and over about my profound lack of worth. Pure rage kept me going as I was stubbornly determined to stop him before he ended me.

I narrowed my options down to several events he always attended and chose the one with which you are quite familiar, the Seattle Governor's Ball of 1987, an annual event hosted by the current governor (namely you, in this instance) in order to cement relationships with Seattle's best and brightest. Beagle didn't attend every society function but would certainly be present at this one because Beagle had poured hundreds of thousands into your campaign fund.

I won't even speculate about the intimate ties between the two of you. I only want you to be open to the possibility that this man was not what he seemed to be. I do hope I'm not writing to someone who's already been corrupted and therefore has no intention of even considering any other option than my death. If that's the case, I am lost and merely entertaining myself with this writing (not a bad thing, given the situation, although I do find myself wondering just how real the situation actually is. Walls, floor, ceiling, fixtures, are they what I think they are? Sometimes I imagine a dirty building in downtown Seattle where I try to sleep every night. And what about this place inside my skull where words arise to be fixed upon the page? This emptiness within makes everything outside me seem empty as well).

The decision to eliminate Beagle didn't arise at any one moment but gradually grew from a thought to a possibility to an option to a plan, in a flow not seeming to require an act of will. I was bent over in a yard, pulling a dandelion up by the roots with a metal device when I chose the Governor's Ball as the event I wanted to infiltrate. Why right then? No idea, but the plan seemed obvious, making me wonder now just how free the choice was.

From that decision point, I had to figure out the details. I read the accounts of the past Balls, looking for ideas, and ended up with the most obvious, the catering. I wouldn't be able to disguise myself as a wealthy patron but a waiter? I just might be able to pull that off. I called the Cascade Hotel where the event was always held and pretended to have attended the previous year's festivities. I said I wanted to hire the same caterer for my boss' retirement party. The assistant to the Banquet Manager told me they'd used the Mary Meals Company five years running and were signed up to do it again. I bought a suit and convinced Tony to write me a glowing recommendation, even though he actually seemed to be upset about possibly losing me. He was the one person in the world who had at least become used to me.

I showed up at the little shop on Capitol Hill serving as the headquarters for Mary Meals. I talked to Mary herself, a squat dynamic woman who was thrilled to talk to the news crews after my "incident" and reinforced the media cliche: "He seemed like such a quiet man." I told her I wanted to transition away from gardening (yes, I can sling bullshit, too) and gain experience in food service. I was willing to work for very low pay in order to build up my résumé. I stressed my philosophy degree as a sign of my intelligence, fudging over the fact it wasn't complete, and fed her a line about how my care of the plants demonstrated how I would care for the food and the customers.

Luckily, ever since I decided to take action, the voices had settled down into a quiet murmur so I could present a fairly presentable facade to the world. She gave me a chance on several catering jobs that were difficult for me because they required a great deal of interaction with people but I managed through sheer determination to do well (I'm trying to summarize here so am skipping over dialogue and detail for the sake of brevity. I know. Too late).

While I worked with Mary Meals, I met Sandy who has suffered through undeserved torture inflicted on her by the media. I want to reiterate to you, as I have to the police and the media, that Sandy herself and Mary Meals in general had nothing to do with the assassination. Sandy was one of the few people in my life

I cared for, and my biggest regret is that I hurt her through my actions. However, if you want to find out more about my character, just to back up what I've stated in this letter, you can give her a call.

Leonard has her phone number and will be happy to give it to you. It's Saturday, of course, so if you call her too late in the day, she'll probably be out on a catering job. The one positive element emerging from all this is that Mary Meals has become a big success. Everyone uses them now, partly because of the publicity, but also for the sheer curiosity value of employing people who've known the notorious me. Glad somebody is gaining out of this debacle.

But (and I digress again, for a specific reason: to show you I do indeed have a human heart, despite the attempts in the press to depict me as a crazed monster), I will tell you a little bit about how my relationship with Sandy grew. I first saw her in the kitchen of the Mary Meals shop. Sandy was chopping cabbage for cole slaw with a focused energy. Her hands and arms were slender but strong with the muscles and tendons standing out. She held the knife with practiced ease and the blade moved so fast it was a silver blur in the pale green leaves. Her long black hair was tied in a pony tail that swayed with the chopping motion so, from behind, it looked like the tail of a trotting horse. As she worked, she sang to herself a Stevie Nicks song, revealing herself to be a true child of the seventies.

Her face was open and friendly at all times. She didn't judge anyone. She held no grudges. She forgave slights even before they occurred. In short, she was, is, one of the most amazing people I've ever met (not that the circle of my acquaintance was ever very wide but I will insist to my dying breath, likely soon, that she is extraordinary). I was absolutely riveted. Her only limitation as a reference is that she likes everyone so her caring for me doesn't indicate anything exceptional about me (I may have undercut myself there but I'm trying to be honest. Can you tell? Does it matter?).

Even though her heart is open, that doesn't mean she lacks intelligence. She was invaluable to Mary in her ability to instantly calculate the amounts in a recipe to adjust for the servings needed. She'd studied herbs on a commune where she once lived and was able to give a distinctive and pleasing flavor to the most ordinary dish by applying her knowledge. The image of her face was the only inhibiting factor that might have prevented my actions although I was too far gone (I admit it) for goodness to make any difference.

Another item in the "I'm not a monster" category is that Sandy would take me home sometimes and we'd make love, sweet love (a song I heard?). She made it clear she wasn't exclusive about who she was with and was so open about it that I actually didn't feel much resentment. Some jealousy was inevitable for me given what you've no doubt gathered so far about my personality. In case this goes public, I won't embarrass her by describing in detail how good it felt to be with her but I can say that nothing in my life compares with the experience.

Unfortunately, even when we were entwined on her futon, spent and dozing, I could sense Beagle's presence, in the eyes looking down on us from her posters, in the incessant whispering the cars sent up from Broadway, in the code being tapped out by the footsteps in the hall. I didn't believe, don't believe, won't let myself believe, that Sandy was one of his agents but I knew he had, most likely, wired her apartment for video and sound so he could laugh at the ungainly spectacle of me making love.

Shit, they're about to serve breakfast but I'm not finished yet. My head is spinning and my stomach is churning. Hope I don't have another bout of diarrhea. Anyway, let's proceed quickly to the event itself, about which I can tell you something that is, no doubt, of close personal interest concerning what happened to your wife. As you well know, the Cascade Hotel in downtown Seattle retains some faded grandeur from Seattle's early days. I was required to wear a tuxedo for the first and most probably the last time in my life. Sandy looked particularly fetching in her own version of a tux, modified by a mini-skirt.

A crimp was thrown in my plans when I learned we all had to pass through metal detectors before we started work. I'd been oiling and sharpening a bowie knife for the past six months until it was so fine I could cut a steak by waving it in the air from across the room (a little exaggeration, entertaining, I hope, although I would understand if you don't have a sense of humor on the subject). Now I'd either have to figure out a way around the detector or find another weapon. I knew I only had this one chance so it wouldn't do to be stopped and questioned before I was even close.

In the morning before the Ball, I walked down to the Army and Navy store on First Avenue. I rooted around in the back bins there until I found a plastic knife perfect for my purpose. It was made of some kind of hard polypropylene but was still razor sharp. For $15.95, I bought myself a murder weapon. I followed the controversy about this knife in the papers with some interest. I have difficulty seeing what real purpose it has for the sports enthusiast other than to pass through metal detectors. Some letter-writers talked about its light weight and portability, as if that made some kind of difference in hunting. Usually hunters carry around an extra 10 to 50 pounds (or more) of ugly fat they'd do much better to lose before they worry about an extra ounce they're toting on their knives. In any case, I found the fateful blade and bought it, not needing a firearm to accomplish my goal.

They're shoving the breakfast tray through, a heaping mound of bacon and eggs for me, the death day boy. The way my stomach feels now it would just make me puke. Best to flush it all down the toilet so the cooks won't feel bad. They really are excited about this upcoming execution but I hope you'll feel free to disappoint them.

Where am I? This doesn't look like a prison. What is it exactly? I can't believe I've been scratching out these words for so long. My fingers are becoming numb but I'm hanging on to this thread of words. Words and memories are all I have to take me out of here. Maybe if I write enough of them, they'll snake themselves out through some tiny crack in the wall, expand there, and create an opening large enough for me to crawl through. I'll be able to slide down with them to the ground and follow them as they frisk merrily off to the horizon. My task will be to figure out how to obtain a normal set of clothes and how to find the Greyhound station in Wenatchee, not to mention how to raise the money to buy a ticket.

This isn't what I want to say. The Ball, yes, I have to tell you about the Ball, but that reminds me of Lucille Ball who I watched relentlessly in reruns when I was little, imagining that she was my mom and I could be little Ricky's brother. Of course, I was fascinated by big Ricky Ricardo, Lucy's husband, the straight man, the stooge, who stood in for the mystery parent whose identity I longed to know, at least before I encountered my real father with his unaccountable loathing for me. But I loved Lucy.

I arrived early in the day with the rest of Mary's crew, along with the temporary help she hired for the occasion. I helped set up, positioned the tables for the maximum access to the food and drink (lots of champagne, as you may remember), arranged the elegant serving dishes. Mary and her team worked well together with little friction, and I have to say I miss the camaraderie and the synchronization, even though my mind was dark with my intention.

I handed out beverages and hors d'oeuvres to the movers and shakers who were as hungry as if they'd just come in from the shelter for the homeless (which reminds me of something...). Their heads floated above their finery like crude clay sculptures on frameworks of fabric. They wolfed the food and swilled the drink (mixing lupine and porcine metaphors, am I?) saving money on their astronomical food bills, I suppose. The Harry James Orchestra, or its present incarnation, was wailing away at the far end of the room while Seattle's elite performed the favorite dances of the early nineteen forties. Why the era of World War II should be the Valhalla of American ballroom dancing is beyond me but I'm not a dancer so what do I know?

I watched you and your wife enter with a team of security people. Can't be too careful nowadays, can you? (In an alternate universe, you might actually want me to be on your security staff, given my skill at scanning the environment for signs of danger). To tell the truth, I didn't take much notice when you entered. I hope you never believed the prosecution's absurd attempts to prove that you and your wife were also my targets. I remember you reminded me somewhat of Robert Bork but without that silly beard.

As for your wife, I remember thinking she looked like she could be a real pistol if she didn't get her way. Lovely, of course, but demanding and high-maintenance, I'm sure. Hope you don't mind. That remark is just between us; please don't relay it to her. I shudder every time I see her name in the paper for fear she's launched into me again. The voices I heard were mild compared to the opprobrium she's heaped on me since that night. Reminds me of dear old mom. Ha, ha. Insert a smiley face here (I have no idea why I wrote that as it's not my usual brand of humor).

Leonard is anxious; Leonard is distressed and wants to go (I just know. Hey, a semicolon, maybe my first?). Must press on, scribble, scribble, making the sound of a rat trying to dig his way through a wall. Okay, so I'm working in the Ballroom, plates of stuffed crabmeat turnovers in my hands, smiling at the movers and shakers, but really keeping a weather eye out for

Beagle's arrival (More mixing of metaphors but, news flash, I don't care). When he entered, the band played "My Way" (the very cliche for a wealthy man) to usher him in, his presence causing a greater commotion than you generated with your entire party. Because of his wealth, his influence, his wife's "tragic" death, his son's "heroic" death, his breeding, his bearing, his everything he had and I had not, Beagle, despite his perfidy, had managed to touch the hearts of the entire crowd, as I was to discover to my pain just a few minutes later.

Sandy nudged me out of my fixed stare and told me to take a plate across to Beagle and the people around him. This was like a message from the fates Federal Expressed (trademark again) directly to me. I nodded and smiled. Sandy smiled back happily. She isn't a beautiful woman by magazine standards but her smile, even through the crooked teeth she can't afford to fix, could power turbines all the way across the country. The fates were telling me to act, although the voices were now urging me to refrain, saying that killing him would be the end of me, and they may, in fact, have been correct. I held back for a moment, knowing my next step would take me irrevocably away from her. A decision point had been reached in my life, one of the few I was allowed to have under the oppression of Beagle. My next thought was to wonder if Sandy was actually a fail-safe device on Beagle's part to keep me from acting against him.

Maybe he reasoned that if love held me back, he would be out of danger. In fact, thoughts of Sandy and the possibility of a different life made me hesitate. The voices told me I was bad, and damned, and too weak to act. All that was left to me after Beagle's domination was the power to choose what to think and how to act in this moment. The damage Beagle had done was irrevocable so I had no way to build a life apart from him. My only recourse (or so I believed at the time) was to separate him from his life (if such a division is metaphysically possible).

I placed my tray on the corner of the banquet table, bent over as if to adjust my sock, and pulled out the plastic knife attached to my leg with duct tape. The pain of the tape tearing away from the hair on my leg woke me up to what I was about to do. I had to be relaxed yet certain, completely clear yet ruthlessly efficient. My entire life had been aimed like an arrow at this point so I couldn't fuck up (or at least I didn't want to). I picked up the tray again and held the knife underneath it.

Beagle stood in a group of people including your wife. I hate to tell tales out of school (or rather, out of jail, hah) but as I approached I had the definite impression of Beagle flirting with her in the manner of a man covering up a deeper attachment by pretending to be harmlessly teasing. I sensed something was going on between the two of them from the brightness of her eyes, the heaving of her ample bosom, the slight sheen forming across her upper lip. Of course, even if she had been flirting, and even if something was going on between them, what happened to her next was certainly not justified but I merely want you to have the entire picture as I see it. I couldn't discern what Beagle was feeling because his walls of deceit were up, as always, enabling him to conform to the social occasion in a way I've never been able to do. Certainly, I could see the malevolence radiating from his every pore.

He looked over at me, distracted from his dalliance by the tray of food coming his way, bearing steak tartare on crackers, an appropriate (and disgusting) dish for the carnivore he was. The flesh of his brow and jowls jiggled eagerly in anticipation of the raw meat he mistakenly believed would soon be ground between his teeth (ground round, of course). The knife rested easily between the bottom of the tray and the palm of my hand in what I hoped was a natural manner.

As I moved closer, I grew afraid that in any instant he would drop his mask, shout "Stop him!" and point at me the way he had twenty four years before. I couldn't have endured the replaying of that scene. I'd have had to cut my own throat right there on the spot. I turned sideways to slip between two of his admirers and murmured the words "Hors d'oeuvres?" I kept my eyes lowered in a simulation of respect and noticed the damp area around his pants zipper, undoubtedly from a hurried trip to the men's room before he entered the Ball.

I've read all the media accounts and heard the conflicting testimony about what happened next. I wonder how judges and juries can stand dealing with such feeble approximations of the truth. I definitely did not shout "Sic semper tyrannis" although it would have been appropriate in its denotation, given Beagle's status as a world-class tyrant. Its connotation would be that the victim was as innocent as Lincoln which in this case is pure bullshit as I hope I've amply documented.

What I did shout as I dropped the plate and grasped the knife was, "Now you'll stop!" I hadn't planned the remark but it did reflect the feelings behind my action. In the heat of the moment, I'm afraid it came out more like "Arrrgh Urr Ragh!" a Rorschach blot of a statement that witnesses felt free to interpret according to their own neuroses, if not psychoses. The nearby judge who swore I yelled, "Marx forever!" must look under his bed for Commies every night before he goes to sleep. Your wife testified that I called her a bitch, an error I'm afraid must be due to a guilty conscience because she was only a shadow on the periphery of my awareness and intent.

As I yelled, an expression of violent recognition came into the face of Beagle. He stretched out his hands to ward me off. In the intensity of the moment, it seemed the Ballroom held only the two of us. In an instant, he knew who I was and why I had come. He began to raise his hand to point and his mouth opened to yell, but before he could utter the same words from so many years before, the energy I'd been building up from millions of instances of unanswered oppression came uncoiled inside me.

Quicker than a cobra, or a bullet, or a light wave, faster than imagination itself, I thrust forward with the knife, slipping it between his ribs with ease. His surprise was complete, his eyes as round as silver dollars. In the past decades, he must have cherished the illusion of invulnerability as he killed off those closest to him and tried to grind me down. Now he looked like an atheist who had just received undeniable proof of the existence of God. Within five minutes he came to know the answer to the question no one on earth knows (no matter how much they insist otherwise): what happens after the breathing stops. In my opinion, the choices are binary, either nothing or everything.

My turn came to be surprised. He looked into my eyes and said, "Isaac, my son." This admission shocked me so much that I whipped the knife out of his chest as violently as I'd pressed it in. My hand flew back behind my shoulder. After a second, as I stared at the dying Beagle crumpling before me, I felt a warm sticky shower hit my neck from behind. Unfortunately, I'd cut off the end of your wife's nose on the recoil and she was now pumping blood all over me.

With my first shout, a KING 5 news cameraman, scrounging nearby for some stray shots for the late broadcast, panned rapidly around and caught me in action. My thrust into Beagle was hidden by the crowd but the decapitation of the nose was perfectly framed (I know decapitation is not the right word but the cutting off of a nose happens so seldom I don't know if a word has been invented for it. De-nasal-ation? That couldn't be right. A dictionary and an Encyclopedia Brittanica are in the prison library but only for reference use and we can't leave the IMU so, well, you get my drift). In a way, it does look as if I was thrusting back at her, but ask yourself this. If she was my intended victim, why am I staring intently in the opposite direction, at Beagle?

I swear on my life, which is all I have right now but may not last for long, that I did not mean to attack her. I felt far worse about her accidental maiming than I did about my intended murder. If the wounding of your dear wife and her subsequent need for plastic surgery (quite successful, I may add, at least from the photos I've seen in the press) play any part in my present precipitate rush to the gallows, I ask you please to reconsider. I again send both you and Mrs. Renhennie my sincere apologies for the injury and for any pain and humiliation I may have caused by bringing about the sudden absence of the fleshy apparatus allowing the free passage of air into her lungs. I won't point out the obvious, that we can easily breathe through our mouths when our noses are stuffed up. We're born with the inherent ability to breathe through two different orifices (three if you count each nostril separately) and no one should be deprived of that basic human right so I again apologize most profusely for my most unfortunate but entirely unintentional backswing.

On a lighter note, that you really should entertain, I did provide your lady with the perfect excuse for plastic surgery. Her former proboscis was somewhat on the large side which may have accounted, at least in part, for its being in the path of my knife. I notice she did not choose to return her nose to its exact former shape but took the opportunity to have it replaced with another in a rather elegant style. The recent news photographs make me wonder whether she might not have also taken the opportunity to have crow's feet removed and some breast and buttock work performed at the same time. At any rate, she looks lovely now and, if you notice any improvement in the scenery, if there's been any recent heightening of intensity in your love life together, you might send a kind thought in my direction as the unwitting instrument of your new happiness.

B-Day tells me Leonard is, in B-Day's words, "having a cow" about being able to drive to Olympia in time (Leonard is a dedicated meat eater so needn't look further than his belly for bovine possession). I have to wrap this up and if you've made it this far, I'm sure you will be relieved. I wonder if they'll ask me if I have any last requests so I could ask to be set free (silly, of course, sort of like my wondering when I was a kid whether one could survive a plummeting elevator by jumping up at the moment before impact so one would only have to fall a foot).

What else can I tell you? You may be thinking that no one else seems to have noticed Beagle's final words. Most of the other witnesses remembered it as a surprised grunting sound except for that senile judge who claimed Beagle called me "Judas" which, if it were true, would at least indicate he knew me. Yet I was the one closest to him and I know what he said. If I can't depend on my own perceptions, what can I depend on?

I'm glad he finally admitted his link to me although I'm grieved it took his murder to force it out of him. I can't help but wish things had turned out differently, that on the long ago night of Seafair, he had scooped me up to ride high with him in splendor on his float beside the cross-legged bikini-clad girls. He could have had two sons then and one son now because I would definitely not have rushed into any burning recreational vehicle, or performed any other selfless yet hazardous act, no matter how urgent the provocation. But recognizing me would have required admitting his link to my mother, thereby bringing us under the umbrella of the Beagle name and family fortune, an eventuality his Satanic pride could not countenance. His twisted thinking led him to attempt to stifle and control me from afar rather than acknowledge the weaknesses against which he constantly struggled.

The voices stopped for me at the instant of the murder. Whatever broadcasting Beagle had arranged must have been designed to end immediately with his death. His minions had no reason to torture me after their boss was gone. As the cameras recorded, your wife's wound was much more visually horrible than Beagle's. He actually bled very little although I sliced right through the center of his heart. Apparently I stopped the muscle so quickly the blood just sat where it was, congealing internally.

Because of the disparity in the visual impact of the wounds, the crowd gave succor to Mrs. Renhennie and pretty much ignored Beagle for some long minutes. Meanwhile, the beefier males entertained themselves by throwing me to the floor and kicking me. The staccato rhythm of the blows reminded me of that long ago night of Seafair when the pirates entertained themselves with me in a similar fashion. In fact, at least some of my attackers at the Ball may have been the same Pirates who stomped me so thoroughly so many years before.

Another faction of the crowd launched a search for your wife's nose which, as you know, disappeared in the furor and indeed never was found. They apparently imagined it could be sewed back on and thus preserved. I suspect someone snatched it up for a souvenir and then didn't have the nerve to admit they had it. I was strip-searched by the police so I obviously never had possession of any part of your wife's body. I will not dignify with a denial the scurrilous rumors printed in the tabloids accusing me of eating the nose as part of a demonic ritual. A supposed psychic came up with the idea. I've asked Leonard whether we might be able to sue those infamous rags but he seemed so overwhelmed by my appeals that I didn't press the issue.

Now I really must be closing. B-Day has come back yet again to see if I'm finished and I can almost hear Leonard grinding his teeth in the room where he's been waiting. I've written this with as much honor and candor as I can muster up right now. I hope you will respond to that. I believe if you know the entire truth, with certain elisions due to the time available and the inevitable limitations of language, you might find it in your heart to let me live. As I mentioned, I participated in my trial in a very limited way because, at the time, my life had little meaning for me.

Now I'm waking up, coming to myself, for the first time in my existence, and I find I don't want to die. You can keep me behind bars until my natural death but please let me live. I realize the harm I've done to you and your family but maiming Mrs. Renhennie was not my intention. Beagle tortured me, abused me, dominated me from that moment of recognition at the Seafair parade of my childhood, a moment that has structured my life in the intervening years until today (and believe me, as I hope I've shown, I was intervened with plenty. Not grammatical, I suspect, but I press on). Please break this cycle and don't allow him to win from beyond the grave. In this matter of imminent mortality, please don't let me lose by a nose (can't help myself).

Yours faithfully,
Isaac Turbot

P.S. I want to add the words of Martin Heiddeger, not as a narcissistic display of empty erudition (although I realize I've displayed plenty of emptiness so far) but in the hope their utter mystery will call forth some form of compassion from your soul:

"Everyone is the other, and no one is himself. The they, which supplies the answer to the who of everyday Dasein, is the nobody to whom every Dasein has always already surrendered itself, in its being-among-one-another.

Monday, May 1, 1989

Dear Sandy,

I'm afraid the news right now is not good. I stayed up all last night finishing my personal appeal to the Governor. Leonard picked it up this morning and drove down to Olympia. Then Leonard called and left a message for me an hour ago. He said the Governor wasn't home. He left suddenly with his wife for a fishing trip in Alaskan waters and isn't expected back until Wednesday. Now Leonard has to turn around, sleep-deprived, and drive back to Walla Walla in order to be with me as I die.

Didn't I see this in an old John Garfield movie? In that plot, the man is on Death Row while the Governor is out fishing. How will he be saved? Well, maybe he won't. Oddly enough, movies in the thirties were willing to have unhappy endings, or at least endings in which the star died, as long as the moral lesson was clear. Now the morals are confused but the star always lives, to conquer, to look good, to appear in the sequel. Unfortunately, I'm no star.

I've paused because something odd seems to be happening as I write. I keep hearing laughter but when I put my head by the bars, it doesn't seem to be coming from anywhere on the Row. What's going on here?

Oh, shit, the voices are back. After being absent for two years, they're here again, laughing and saying "He's won! He beat you!" Beagle's accomplices have somehow managed to start transmitting into the prison. They've probably worked out a deal with the Governor, but why? What good will it do them to torture me now? Too late to go for an insanity defense, not that I ever wanted it anyway. But the irony is the unwillingness of the State to kill anyone who's sick or outright crazy. It's almost as if the accused would have it too easy, would be taken prematurely out of his misery, so they have to wait until the poor slob is sane enough to be scared shitless, healthy enough not to want to die.

Now Beagle's voice is being broadcast throughout the prison. He's saying he's alive, I didn't kill him, I fell into his trap! But he couldn't really be alive. I felt his heart stop at the point of my knife. This must be a recording, a computer-generated voice of some kind. His people are fabulously wealthy. They can do all kinds of tricks, but why? I'm going to die anyway, for God's sake (or, more likely, for no one's). Why do they want to make my last two days miserable?

Now he's saying it wasn't him I killed. I eliminated a double, the clone I was just talking about. That's why it was so easy! He's saying he committed the perfect crime: he wanted me dead, he lured me to murder, and now the state is going to kill me for him.

He'll continue to be alive but he's going to expand beyond the identity of Beagle. He'll be everywhere and able to use his power, his fortune, to float at will and do anything, be anyone he wants. No, it can't be true, it can't! 1 won't let it be true. I'll kill him again. I'll choke the voice in my head. I'll kill you, you bastard!

Well, that was exciting. I really pitched a fit in here. I started by throwing my legal pad to the floor and screaming at the top of my lungs. Then I banged my head on the wall until the blood ran down onto my face and clothes. The guards came running, an activity their collective bulk didn't make easy. All the other death day boys woke up and started yelling. Dr. Fallow came racing up from his Bat Cave, wherever that is. Four guards, suited up in kevlar, carrying plastic shields, burst through the door and restrained me (no big whoop, the record is eight guards). In minutes, I was a bug on my back with my ankles and wrists in plastic ties connected behind me. I managed to destroy most of my meager possessions while throwing my tantrum.

Fortunately, when I calmed down and was released, I found this legal pad bent and oddly folded but not torn. They patched up my head in the infirmary but didn't bother with x-rays. Not even any stitches, despite the severity of the gashes, just dressings on my forehead that feel like the beginnings of a mummification process. What if, after Monday, I wander the prison in mummy's bandages, like Boris Karloff in the old movies? I suppose cremation would put, not a damper but an accelerant on that plan. No head x-ray, of course, because no one, including me, cares if I have a head bleed.

While I was being examined, Fallow took pleasure in telling me what I already knew (having just written it above somewhere. You know I'm not going back to find it) that I have no chance of winning a postponement of execution on the grounds of mental disorder. He said I was experiencing a perfectly natural reluctance to die, demonstrating proof of sanity, not insanity. I told him he was preaching to the choir. He is such a tedious man. Meanwhile, the voice, Beagle's own it sounds like, is chattering away all the time. Plus I have a terrible headache.

This is just perfect, the fitting end to a life of shit. What happened at the Ball? I know I killed someone but maybe it wasn't Beagle. He owns research labs doing cutting-edge work so his scientists could have cloned him. Or he could have found a look-alike and perfected his doppelgänger with plastic surgery into an exact duplicate, fingerprints and dental work included. Or maybe it was even an android, a facsimile of a human being (although I'm sure you know what an android is). That would account for the lack of blood. The aid car attendants and the hospital staff and the medical examiner's office would all have had to be conspirators but that's not impossible. Nothing's impossible if he runs everything and if he can be in my head right now.

I'm tired but I don't want to sleep anymore. I don't have enough time left, although sleeping might stop the voices. It would be better if they dragged me from the cell and strung me up right now. I'm sorry to lay all this on you but I am going to send it off. Someone should know what's happening to me. I'm also going to send that letter I wrote to my mother. Even if she doesn't care, she should know what I think. Even worse than dying would be to die without telling anyone my story.

Sandy, if Beagle has somehow come alive, you're not safe. My advice would be to go far away, don't tell me where, a place where he can't find you, although I don't know exactly where that would be. I don't think you're a threat to him but it's impossible to predict how he'll see it. Live quietly and simply in some backwater village. With your skills, I know you can find work just about anywhere.

I'm sorry for ruining your life but I do have that scheme going here that could make you a chunk of cash. Please take care of yourself. Find someone worthy of your love. Try not to remember me with the knife in my hand and the Governor's wife's blood shed all over me. Instead, remember how I learned awkwardly but earnestly how to be a caterer, carefully following your instructions. Remember me making love for the first time in my life with you. But also remember to call Dr. Fallow, here at the prison, and get every last cent of the money he owes from our little project.

With love,
Your Ike
(You're the only one I know
who would say, "I like Ike.")

Monday, May 1, 1989

To Dionysius Beagle:

High time for the two of us to have a talk. You've been droning on in my head, polluting my final time on earth, so I'm going to try to engage in dialogue with you, tell you what I think, just as you're always telling me what you think. You've invaded me from every direction. I can't escape. Maybe some night while I slept, you took me away to some private dungeon in this vast facility and had little transmitters placed inside my skull so you could talk to me as if you were a voice in my head.

My hatred for you is now the single emotion in my brain. My hate is much more limited than yours because my resources for acting on it are so much less. Your influence is everywhere. You've permeated reality. You seem to be able to manipulate life down past the molecular level to the pure energy field that brings all this madness into being. You impregnated my mother and brought about my birth. You're bringing about my death. You've directed everything that's happened in between.

The only thing you haven't controlled is this tiny shard of self, here inside my skull, holding out against your voices and defending itself against your attacks. You've done everything you could possibly do against me, except for one thing. You haven't won me over. You haven't convinced me to enlist on your side, although you've apparently convinced everyone else to join. Even Sandy I'm not absolutely sure about. She could have been a mere tool you used to draw me unsuspecting (is that an adverb? Unsuspectingly doesn't sound right) into your trap, or she could be more deeply involved. But I'm not going to believe it because I want to keep one thing for myself. I may never know for sure whether or not she did betray me. However, I choose, freely, not to believe it.

How did you acquire so much power, and why do you want it? Wouldn't it be better just to set the world free to do as it wants? Why not let us all be? But you can't because you're determined to be the force of evil in reality. Does your existence imply the existence of good? I have felt the good, out working in the yards, in Sandy's bed, in the movies, but I don't know if good is an actual force or just the absence of you, a mere accident in the chaos. You won't tell me, I'm sure, but I have to ask. Why are you here? I want to know.

"To kill you," is your reply.

It looks like you're going to accomplish that, but why? What good is it going to do you?

"I'll defeat you, just as I defeat everyone."

Still, why should you want that? I'm your son, for God's sake, even if I am illegitimate.

"You're part of me but you think you're separate and you insist on rebelling. That brings on its own punishment."

I know I sound like a five year old asking the same question over and over, but why do you hate me?

"Because you hate me. Your hatred is your destiny. Just accept it."

That's no answer. You could just as easily love me as hate me.

"Who says I don't love you?"

Nothing could be more obvious but... It strikes me that you're thrashing around the planet, ruining people, killing them without much idea of why you're doing it.

"In other words, I'm a lot like you."

No, I knew why I killed you, because you wouldn't leave me alone. You kept persecuting me.

"Are you sure it was me?"

I thought so. Who else could it be?

"Think about it. Who's the most powerful person in the world?"

You were, apparently. Now maybe it's Bill Gates, or President Bush, or one of those Japanese billionaires.

"No, the answer is closer than you can imagine."

Don't play word games with me. Why don't you show your face and we'll see what happens? Give me another chance to kill you.

"Brave talk, but you're the one who will die soon. Or maybe we both will."

That would be fine by me.

"Me, too."

Maybe we should close on that note, a rare moment of accord between us. Nevertheless, my point is: we'll always be enemies. I still have a day left. Maybe I can do something to thwart you.

"Knock yourself out."

I will.

Hatefully,
Isaac Turbot

TELEGRAM
MAY 1 COMMA 1989
TO GOVERNOR PAULSON D PERIOD RENHENNIE
OR HIS STAFF
GOVERNOR'S OFFICES
OLYMPIA WASHINGTON

DEAR GOVERNOR RENHENNIE AND BACKSLASH
OR YOUR STAFF COLON MY EXECUTION MUST BE
POSTPONED STOP I HAVE GOOD REASON TO
BELIEVE DIONYSIUS BEAGLE IS NOT DEAD STOP I
NOW HEAR HIS VOICE AND SEE EVIDENCE OF HIS
PRESENCE STOP I MUST NOT BE HUNG FOR THE
MURDER OF A MAN WHO IS STILL ALIVE STOP
FIND THE GOVERNOR STOP USE SEARCH PLANES
AND HELICOPTERS IF YOU MUST STOP HAVE HIM
SEND NOTICE OF A REPRIEVE IMMEDIATELY TO
WARDEN POUNDER AT WALLA WALLA STATE
PENITENTIARY STOP JUSTICE AND MERCY
DEMAND THAT I LIVE STOP

ISAAC TURBOT
PRISONER 321987
INTENSIVE MANAGEMENT UNIT
WALLA WALLA STATE PENITENTIARY
WALLA WALLA WASHINGTON

(The following is a transcript of a taped interview from May 1, 1989 by Cindy Connors of KOMO-TV Seattle with condemned murderer Isaac Turbot)

CINDY: This is Cindy Connors of KOMO 4 TV Seattle reporting from Walla Walla, Washington at the State Penitentiary. We've been granted a rare pre-execution interview with Isaac Turbot who is set to be executed at midnight tonight for the murder of Dionysius Beagle, Seattle real estate developer and philanthropist. Mr. Turbot, thank you for this opportunity to speak with you.
ISAAC: You're very welcome.
CINDY: We also thank Warden Pounder who allowed this extraordinary interview on the very day of your execution. All through your trial and year of imprisonment you refused to speak to any of the press. Can you tell us why you agreed to an interview at this extremely late hour?
ISAAC: Um, yes, I have several reasons. I agreed to speak with you because I'm about to be executed for the murder of a man who is not, strictly speaking, dead. I have reason to believe Dionysius Beagle is alive and well somewhere.
CINDY: Mr. Turbot, you must understand that people will be very skeptical of this claim, coming so close to your execution. Mr. Beagle's family, the Medical Examiner's office, and the undertaker who buried Mr. Beagle have all issued outraged denials, not to mention

the millions who watched the videotape of his death on their televisions.

ISAAC: I'm not surprised by their skepticism.

CINDY: Do you have any kind of proof to substantiate your claim?

ISAAC: Yes, I can hear Beagle's voice. In fact, I've talked to him.

CINDY: You've spoken with Dionysius Beagle?

ISAAC: Yes.

CINDY: Where did this take place, and when?

ISAAC: Just this morning, right here in my cell.

CINDY: And what did he have to say?

ISAAC: He said bringing about my death would be his final triumph over me.

CINDY: Did this voice continue to speak with you?

ISAAC: I'm hearing it right now.

CINDY: What's he saying?

ISAAC: Um, actually, he's saying some things about you I'd better not repeat on television.

CINDY: About me? Ah, yes, uh, you know, Dr. Fallow, the prison psychiatrist, says that this is just a conscious attempt on your part to postpone your execution.

ISAAC: That's correct.

CINDY: You admit it?

ISAAC: Absolutely. I am conscious and I'm attempting to have the execution postponed if it can't be cancelled altogether.

CINDY: Actually I think he's saying that you're making all this up about the voice.

ISAAC: No, I'm not. The voice is as real as you are, as I am.

CINDY: Are you attempting to be declared insane in order to avoid execution?

ISAAC: No, that's obviously not going to work at this late moment. I'm just saying what's happening. It's not my fault if the truth creates a problem.

CINDY: The other possibility is that the voice is a symptom of mental illness. What do you think?

ISAAC: No, if that were true then everything happening to me would be unreal, delusional. I've maintained for years that I am as sane as anyone, as you are.

CINDY: If Mr. Beagle is alive, what happened on the night of the Governor's Ball?

ISAAC: Several explanations are possible.

CINDY: What are they?

ISAAC: I would have thought it was obvious. Either I killed somebody who looked like Beagle or Beagle's people were able to revive him after they left the hotel.

CINDY: Frankly, I find it very difficult to believe either of those explanations. The murder itself was recorded on videotape and looked very real.

ISAAC: I agree that the viewing audience saw someone who looked like me killing someone, or some thing, that looked like Beagle but he has the power and the authority to create any kind of illusion.

CINDY: If Beagle is alive, how is he able to speak inside your head in a maximum security prison?

ISAAC: Nothing could be simpler for a man like him. Beagle has many resources and access to technology about which the general public knows little.

CINDY: So he uses some kind of device to broadcast inside your head?

ISAAC: That's my speculation, anyway.

CINDY: What's he saying now?

ISAAC: He's saying our talking isn't going to help me one bit.

CINDY: And what do you think about that?

ISAAC: I'm afraid he's right but I do have another reason for giving this interview.

CINDY: Okay, what is that reason?

ISAAC: Dr. Fallow, the prison psychiatrist, and I have arranged for a literary experiment. I'm going to keep a journal up to the moment of my execution. I hope to record my final thoughts in the interest of science, supposedly, and to expose Beagle for the evil he embodies. Dr. Fallow has agreed that my friend, Sandy Harding, will share in any proceeds.

CINDY: I assume you know about all the speculation concerning Sandy's involvement with you.

ISAAC: I'm going to repeat for you what I've been saying all along, that Sandy is a good friend who had nothing whatsoever to do with my crime.

CINDY: Did you know that the Governor's office issued a statement today saying the Governor has no intention of issuing a reprieve, no matter what desperate measures you come up with?

ISAAC: My attorney informed me of that.

CINDY: The execution is scheduled for twelve midnight tonight, a little more than twelve hours away. Are you at all able to put into words for us how you feel?

ISAAC: I've been living in someone else's dream all my life. For some reason, a few days ago, I just woke up. Or maybe I started dreaming my own dream.

CINDY: Do you think the execution will happen as scheduled tonight?

ISAAC: I don't know. Waking up was something of a miracle. I'm open to the idea that another one can happen.

CINDY: Has any religious faith or spiritual belief sustained you during this difficult time?

ISAAC: I don't have any.

CINDY: But you just spoke of miracles.

ISAAC: The way I look at it, if you have any expectations, or what they call faith, an unexpected occurrence isn't really a miracle. It's more like payment due. Even though Beagle is a poison throughout reality, I still hope this world retains the ability to surprise me.

CINDY: What do you mean when you say Beagle is poison?

ISAAC: All I can do is speak from my own experience. He ruined my life, kept me from living for myself, prevented me from developing my potential.

CINDY: What do you think his motivation was?

ISAAC: I really don't know. Maybe your question can't be answered. Maybe it's like asking why there's disease, or why hurricanes kill people. Maybe something happened to make him cruel, but I don't think he'll talk about it. Whatever pain is inside him, he will deny it and try to say it's my fault. He's a man who's been driven out of himself to wage war against the world.

CINDY: Would that be a good description of you as well?

ISAAC: Maybe. The first part applies but by waging war against him, I don't think I'm fighting the world, I'm fighting a devil, taking the last human stand against evil.

CINDY: So you think he goes beyond the human?

ISAAC: Yes, I'd say so. He goes beyond anything a human can do.

CINDY: Well, it has been most interesting to get your perspective on this. I understand you've been doing quite a bit of writing while in prison.

ISAAC: Actually, I've only recently taken it up. Everyone needs an art form in order to bear this life.

CINDY: Does the writing help you through this ordeal?

ISAAC: Not really, it's more like something I have to do, no matter what. But, yeah, I guess it helps.

CINDY: The state was thrown into great controversy by your decision to choose hanging over lethal injection as the method for your execution. I wonder if you have any regrets now about that choice?

ISAAC: No, I'm glad to cause all the discussion. Lethal injection might have been easier on me, but it would cover over the reality of what's really happening here. If I have to die, I don't want it to be easy for anyone. I want people to realize a human being is being put to death and won't depart peacefully via some euphemism, such as "going to sleep" or "passing over to a better place." The sheer gruesomeness of hanging makes it hard to ignore, hard to deny the reality.

CINDY: For my final question, is there anything you can tell us that might help us understand how you ended up in this position? Before he died, just last January, Ted Bundy said pornography was a catalyst for his crimes. Was there anything like that for you?

ISAAC: I'm doing this interview to tell you that Beagle is alive so your question is irrelevant. If I hadn't been sinned against, I wouldn't have sinned and I'm not sure anymore that I did sin, although I did intend to commit murder so it's a crime of thought alone which would make me just as culpable if I were Catholic, which I'm not. Beagle is alive. He's watching you right now and watching everyone who's watching this. What happened to me could easily happen to you if he decided to make you a target. You'd have no way to escape. In fact, I believe Beagle will destroy you and everyone other living being some day. I'm the proverbial canary in the coal mine, tweeting away until my last breaths.

CINDY: The warden is signaling me to end our interview. Any last words for the world?

ISAAC: I haven't shared this before but I don't see any point in hiding the truth at this late moment. Dionysius Beagle was my father and just as Abraham in the Bible had to kill his child, I, who bear the name of Abraham's son, had to kill my sire. My only crime was to do what the universe impelled me to do so why should I die for it?

CINDY: Warden, can I follow up on that. No? But... Okay. Thank you, Isaac Turbot, for a very interesting interview. I am sure your friends and family are praying for you.

ISAAC: No. I don't believe they are. But that's okay.

(end of interview)

Dead Man's Diary
by
Isaac Turbot

Monday, May 1, 1989
6 pm.

    I'm starting now. This document is an experiment I suggested to Dr. Sanford Fallow, Staff Psychiatrist at the Walla Walla State Penitentiary, Walla Walla, Washington. My name is Isaac Turbot, and I am a resident, for the next six hours anyway, at the same institution where Dr. Fallow is employed. The Doctor wants me to write out a record of the final thoughts of a condemned man during the hours leading up to his execution. He thinks he can make some kind of name for himself by publishing this journal with his own commentary. He has agreed to print my writing in its entirety, without editing of any kind, but he reserves the right to say whatever he wants in his afterword. Fair enough. All I can say at this point to my future readers is that it would behoove you to ignore his fucking words. If his writing is anything like his medical abilities, you're better off reading Mickey Spillane or Beetle Bailey for an understanding of my situation.

    Despite my low opinion of Dr. Fallow, I agreed to participate in this project for several reasons. The first is I want people (specifically, you the reader) to know the details of what's happening to me, to realize this is the termination of a human being, not a rabid dog or a horse with a broken leg. Another reason is that I want to use this journal as a way to deal with the sheer terror I feel at the prospect of my own annihilation. We all know in a general way that we're going to die, but I must be one of only a handful of people in the world who know pretty much when it will happen. I don't know what other executions are scheduled for tonight across this great globe of ours, but right now I may well be the only human being who knows the hour of his end, and it scares me. A miracle or a bureaucratic fuck-up of some kind may take place, of course, but I'm not allowing myself to hope. If it happens, fine, but I'm not going to delude myself that it's likely. A third reason is, if by chance this makes any money, I want my friend Sandy Harding to benefit from it. She deserves to have some cushioning in her life which I've already messed up enough. If you want to add some real misery to your days, have your name broadcast in the media in connection with a notorious killer.

The business of my life is coming to an end. I've sent off letters to the important people in my life and I've written to the individuals with the most power over me, Dionysius Beagle and Governor Renhennie. I've said goodbye to the staff and inmates here in the prison this afternoon, telling them I'd like to spend the last hours alone, doing this writing, as preparation. It was hardest to say goodbye to my friend B-Day, the guard, when he went home from the day shift but I'm glad he's not going to be around for the end. His humanity would be too incongruous set against the execution itself.

Members of the kitchen staff came up and wept in the corridor outside my cell. Some of them knelt and prayed. I didn't know any of them as the guards always brought the trays of food but their demonstration was quite touching, although I suspect they were grieving more for the loss of the source of their recent culinary inspirations than for me myself. They left a tray of various treats (although I have little appetite), including a chicken-fried steak, onion rings, a six pack of soda, and several bottles of beer.

The warden stopped by to ask if there was anything "feasible" he could get for me. I responded that the definition of feasible was subjective. For me, avoiding execution was eminently feasible while I'm sure he thought it was necessary. Everyone seems sympathetic and that must be because I'm being rushed to the chopping block much faster than the usual resident around here. I told the Warden that the writing is enough for me. He nodded and told me to carry on. My scribbling feels meditative, ritualistic, sacramental even. I've allowed myself to imagine that this activity will be my way out of here, my path to freedom.

You (whoever you are) may be interested to know how this project is going to be handled. Dr. Fallow has given me a black and white composition book, the kind we used in grade school but smaller, 8 1/2" by 5 1/2", that should be sufficient for everything I have to say. I've also been assigned three excellent ballpoint pens, two of them as back-up systems in case of engine trouble. An administrator (but not the executioner himself; I won't meet him until midnight) came up to tell me the prison has no problem with me having my hands free to write as I walk to the gallows, as long as I don't give them any trouble. I assured him that if I could keep writing, I would have all the trouble I needed and wouldn't have to cause them any more.

One difficulty was about how I was going to write while actually standing on the trapdoor with the noose around my neck. They didn't want me to have my hands free because I might (certainly would, actually) hang on to the rope when the trap opened beneath me. I thought about this problem a bit and then suggested they shackle my upper arms to a chain around my waist but leave my forearms free to continue writing. That way I couldn't reach up far enough to save myself but would be able to keep scribbling away until the final moment.

Apparently this was unprecedented (just like the entire project) but, after several intense phone calls through the levels of hierarchy, to whatever authorities exist in the prison system, they all agreed it was a fine plan and should work perfectly (just giving you the story as told to me by the Warden). Dr. Fallow made a special point of congratulating me for a "most ingenious idea." So here I am, by myself, the clock ticking away, pen in hand, the black ribbon of ink uncoiling across the page. I'm finding the cliches about being close to death to be true: everything does seem extraordinarily vivid and precious. Even this cell, made with the minimum of consideration for comfort and human feeling, would be a paradise were I to be allowed to stay in it forever. I can feel my fear of death, my fear of the unknown, rising up within me in waves.

How can I "be" one moment and not "be" the next? Human life is certainly a strange proposition. Beagle keeps chattering away in my head, but softer now. He's not a problem. In fact, I feel kindly toward him as another sign I'm still alive. So what if he says terrible things about me like an old bag lady who verbally abuses me as I walk by her on the street? If I react with hostility, she's pulled me into her pathetic game. If I react with compassion in whatever way seems appropriate, the encounter has some potential for becoming a healing for both of us.

I miss Sandy intensely. I know it's better she's not here, but I could use someone to hold onto. The good Reverend Acksel threatened to spend the entire evening with me but I voted the idea down vehemently. He will, however, be here to mutter his incantations during my long walk. I don't mind because he needs to play his role and I want to cover all my bets. I would have requested it even if he hadn't offered. Maybe I'll tell him I really have accepted Jesus Christ as my personal savior. That would make him happy and certainly wouldn't do me any harm. I'm not a stickler about accuracy (or ethics) at this point. Whatever gets me through this night is all right.

Despite my fear, I'm intermittently in a mellow mood, although my mind shifts faster than a go-go dancer's hips. If I had my life to live over again (idle but inevitable fantasy at this point), I would not kill whoever it was I killed at the Governor's Ball. I certainly wish I hadn't cut off Mrs. Renhennie's nose, a major tactical error reverberating against me tonight. But regrets are pointless now. I made a decision and I'm following the consequences to the end. Guess that's just the way the cosmos unwinds and how things crumble, cookie-wise (from a favorite movie, The Apartment). I knew about capital punishment before I made my decision to end Beagle's reign of terror so I'm a living demonstration of how much the deterrent theory is worth.

What do I want to say to the world in my final moments? Don't do as I do? Beware the Beagle, his shiny jaws, his piercing teeth? What do I really believe about my old adversary? I don't know. He's been with me for so long he's like my arm (long and hairy? no), very much here, unquestionable in its reality. Or maybe he's more like the plantar's wart on the bottom of my foot. I tried to cut him off but he simply emerged bigger than ever. Maybe I should try addressing him again to provide some analytic fodder for Fallow.

Who are you, Beagle? Why have you done this to me? I'm completely caught by you. I'm wrapped tight in your webbing, watching you come toward me on your eight legs, your red eyes gleaming, your mouth open and slavering to eat. Your victory is complete, except for these words dancing their way across the page. This is mine. Yes, let your voices disparage me, cut me down. I am still here. Even if they take away my pen and paper (over Dr. Fallow's dead body at this point), I could slash my flesh with my fingernails and scrawl words in blood across the walls of the cell. Even if they put me in a straight jacket, I could let my own words, not yours, march across the blank sheet of my mind. You can't beat me at this game and that's what drives you wild, isn't it?

You're the complete control freak but when you strip me down to my essence, I'm uncontrollable. I don't know what I'm going to say next and neither do you. These words are the last act of pure creation in the universe or at least in my universe (and, really, what's the dif?). You've dominated everything in my life except this thread of sentences inching across the page. I've actually won, haven't I? I can go to my death knowing that even though you live, you've been defeated because you never touched ME, the real self inside, what the religious call the soul. An ironic twist: first I kill you and think I've won. Then you resurrect yourself and I think I've lost. Finally, I win by dying. I will leave you empty-handed on the playing field, contemplating your loss.

I am the other you require in your universe. Without me, you're caught in your own trap. You need me but I'm leaving, goodbye, so long, farewell. With my death, you'll be shrinking, screaming, dissolving into a puddle below my swinging feet (joining the urine and shit I will no doubt emit). So chatter on in your tedious voice telling me incessantly that I've lost, you've killed me, I'm completely worthless. The story is not growing more convincing through repetition. Now I know the truth of your irrelevance. On the last day of my life, I make the big discovery, that all of your manipulations were actually demonstrations of your impotence against the real me, the thin shivering spiritual strip within where these words arise.

You haven't destroyed my freedom because freedom is in the reality these words create. So what do I want to make with these words? I don't want you any more so I declare you gone within this world of words. I give myself all of your wealth and power and I use it for good. The noble son of a bad father, I take over and redeem reality. I use my power to support people, to make connections, to infuse beauty into recalcitrant matter. I embrace this planet, this solar system, this universe, this entire reality, each quark and parsec of it.

You've backed me relentlessly into a corner, compressing me into a smaller and smaller space until finally I can be squeezed no more and I've reached a dangerous level of density. I'm exploding and everything has flipped to its negative image, tearing the fabled fabric of reality apart. Do I really have five hours left? I hereby declare this time to be an eternity.

Let's go through it all. I hereby join in on the creation of all the people on this planet and I love them equally and saturate them with my love but I give them the choice of whether to accept my love or not because, if I force it on them, I become like you. I hear you snarling in anguish. You know I've discovered the secret you didn't want me to know.

I have omnipotent power in my hands, in this pen scrawling across these blank pages. I declare this cell to be the container for the universe. Everything is inside here and you can't do anything about it. I understand what my power is now. The meek shall indeed inherit the earth. The oppressed shall become victorious. In dying, I shall live.

These words become a flexible roving eye across the universe like an infinite fiber optics cable with the power to penetrate the most inaccessible recesses. I look at the rings of Neptune, the sty on a child's eye in Delhi, the berry stains on a grizzly's hide up in the Brooks range, the blowhole of a whale off the coast of Antarctica, the sweat in an anchorman's armpit as he delivers the news at the ABC affiliate in Roanoke, Virginia. What a show! You may control it all outside but in here I participate in perfect communion with everything. You are completely irrelevant.

Now what? Having finally been given access to my own power, I can relax a bit. I've been so worried about defending myself that I've been scribbling desperately along. I can slow down, take a breath, stand up, and stretch. I can just imagine good old Fallow yammering away in his commentary: notice how the writer turns to megalomania as a defense against what's going to happen. Well, why not? I feel very good now, as good as I've ever felt in all my days. Life is pouring through me. My skin tingles all over. Energy pours out of my hands, covering these pages in cascades of delight. I use the pen to rewrite my story:

I was born of two loving people on a farm near the Pacific Coast where my dad calmly and skillfully taught me about machinery, construction, animal husbandry (although the old me chimes in wondering who would want to be an animal's husband?), and crops. My mother introduced me to all the domestic skills, including sewing, cooking, and baking. I was a voracious reader who excelled in high school and became the valedictorian. I attended an Ivy League college with brick buildings atop a New England hill bejeweled in autumn colors (all year round, oddly enough). I decided to be a writer so traveled to Europe, working on a freighter to pay for my passage, writing on deck at night while looking out across the luminescent sea (okay, okay, but cliches carry some resonance). My facility with languages helped me find work in all the major capitals. I wrote fine sensitive novels about Americans having the sharp corners knocked off them by coming in contact with other cultures.

Several of my novels were sold to the movies so I soon had plenty of money to follow my inspirations as I explored various disciplines (swordsmanship, falconry, soufflés), made friends with odd people (a Paris waiter, a London cabbie, a Venetian gondolier) and engaged in interesting quests (to climb Mt. Blanc, to go on pilgrimage to Mecca, to explore the source of the Nile). In the middle of my life (at thirty-five years of age or so, after many steamy liaisons), I met a lovely woman who combined elements of Barbara Stanwyck, Claudette Colbert, and Katherine Hepburn. We married and had children, a boy and a girl, Mark and Isabel. We settled by the ocean in Malibu (why not?) where I rose every morning to run on the beach, along the edge where sea, sand, and sky came together.

In the mornings I wrote, looking out on the pulsating surface of the water, following the sun as it climbed high above me. In the afternoons, I puttered around the house, using my hands to make furniture, to repair appliances, to nurse the stuff of life along. In the evenings, in the light of the setting sun, I met my friends (movie people, music people, artists, scientists), laughed and played. My wife and I traveled at least twice a year to foreign lands, not rushing around to see the sights but settling in somewhere, a small village, a quirky city neighborhood, a riverside, to watch the life flow around us.

This is all too perfect, I know, and kind of abstract. I'd have to fill in this outline with lived experience to make it real. But at least I've created a starting point. I hereby construct everything I never had. Towers of imagination rise up in each corner of the cell. The pressure from my fantasies intensifies and begins to crack the walls. Just a little more and I'll be out of this cell, striding to freedom through the rubble of shattered concrete and twisted metal.

The guards walk by and look in (curious to see how I'm doing on the very threshold of annihilation). They offered to let me spend my final hours in a more private box somewhere in the prison but I know this space. I've made it safe with my ragged breathing, my farts, the stench of my armpits. Besides, location is irrelevant now. I feel intoxicated with the power of the writing. Make what you want out of that, Fallow. I've actually defeated Beagle by putting these words down on paper. Impossible, but true. Veritas! Freedom! You may kill me, will kill me, in fact, but the writing will keep going, telling stories to itself, describing faces, recording the rhythms of time and the sinuous meandering paths of personality. I know, I'm not creating a complete fictional world like those of Tolstoy or Tolkien or Nabokov but I'm creating myself here.

I'm going back to the night of the Governor's Ball. I'm leaving the knife at home. I'm dropping the plate of hors d'oeuvres with a startling crash and embracing Beagle. I'm telling him he may deny me to the end of time but he is my father and I love him. He pushes me away initially but breaks down and cries despite all those powerful people around. He hugs me and invites me to go with him back to his mansion, hidden behind the high walls and guard dogs. We talk for days about who we are, what we want to do in the world, how to spend his money for the greatest good. Another life begins:

I walk up to the front porch of a house in Enumclaw. Motorcycle parts are strewn across the front yard. The brooding green mountains hang above the town, humbled before the sheer mass of Rainier, staring down like the eye of God. I knock on the door and my mother answers, wiping her hands on her apron (must be thinking of June Cleaver here because that's so not my mother). I tell her I know she may not want to see me, may want to sever all connections between us but I have to tell her I love her. She slowly pushes open the screen door, grabs my shoulders, and pulls me into a fierce embrace. I give her money so she can do whatever she wants in life. I befriend my step-father, step-brother, and step-sister, helping them decide what to do about their careers, their lives. We all drive to the Presbyterian Church on Sunday to worship together (avoiding, I hope, the most tedious hymns).

Okay, I may have gone a bit far there, but you get the idea. I hold an ink-filled magic wand in my hand and I transform the world. Scribbling is the only power I have right now but it's enough to help me through the next few hours. I'm writing so fast that time is having difficulty keeping up with me. Maybe if I write even faster, time will stop entirely. No, I don't think so. There's some point, like the limit of the speed of light, beyond which time cannot slow down. It never comes entirely to a halt, no matter what you do to expand your experience. I have to cram as much as possible into the last few hours, try to fill them with a lifetime of experience in these words. What I won't be able to capture is the pulsing beat of day and night, day and night, the ordinary life of someone who doesn't worry about death, who feels himself living in an endless piece of music carrying him along. I do have compensations for that loss. Few people without the immediate prospect of death (and I'm not sick, as physically healthy as ever!) could live, think, write, or dream as intensely as I am right now.

Memories explode in my brain. Twenty years have passed since I visited the zoo with Gouchie but now the ripe smell of penguin fills my senses and almost knocks me out (she took me to the zoo? Amazing in itself). I just took a shower so I don't think it's me. I once sailed on an old schooner to Blake Island with my high school class. From that trip, the waters of the Sound and the skyline of Seattle fill my vision as if I'm back on that day with my cratered face, nylon jacket, and unwashed jeans. Separate from my classmates, I went to the bow of the ship, leaned far over the edge, and watched the sharp wedge of prow bite into the water, eating clumps of seaweed, bright clusters of froth, bits of bark and driftwood. If I stretched far enough out, I could pretend that the boat behind me had disappeared and I was flying, fast, just above the water, transformed into a seagull, a bolt of feathered flesh, free from the prison of being Isaac Turbot, the figurehead of a ship destined to sink tonight at midnight.

Even though I was physically free until recently, I've been in prison all my life (cue the violins). The pain of my childhood, the neglect from my mother, the constant fear of Beagle, these all constructed a box of the mind even more confining than the actual box I'm sitting in. I'm trying to speak directly. I won't have time for rewrites so you'll have to excuse any awkwardness or inelegance. I'm not coming this way again. I want to leave something for everyone who lives on after me but I don't know what it could be.

My advice: Don't have an unhappy childhood. Be born of sane and loving parents. Believe in yourself and your power, no matter what kind of abuse you've had to go through. But how do you get there? How do you go from pain to release? Therapy, est, religion, push-ups, politics, swimming? Whatever works. For me, being on the IMU, about to die, and scribbling furiously in a notebook, gathering every element of my life into one living presence, this is working wonders although I don't necessarily recommend it for anyone else.

Birth thrusts us into a vast game where we have to figure out what the rules are or make them up on our own. All manner of obstacles and opposing forces try to stop us from achieving our goal. And the goal, ah yes, what is the goal? The only sure goal is the one I'm going to reach at midnight. Everything else just sort of happens along the way to this certain end. I don't know when you're going to die, or how, but the effect will be the same as my hanging has on me. Whatever you've been hoarding, whatever you've built, whatever you've achieved, you're going to have to let go of it all, the way I'll drop this pad and pen, my final treasures, as my neck breaks. I just hope I don't shit all over these pages. However, that's Fallow's problem. He'll have to clean it up. The thought of him sponging my final excrement from this manuscript makes me laugh.

Grim thoughts but it's that kind of period for me, you know, kind of dark, thoughts of death, stuff like that. Just a mood that will pass. The way I will. What time is it? Eight thirty now. Good thing I can't hear very much from inside. What if I had to listen to the carpenters building the scaffold the way prisoners had to in some of those Westerns? What if I could hear the world outside so I'd be anxiously listening for the sound of sirens coming closer to the prison with news of my pardon? Maybe a miracle would be okay with me. Couldn't hurt to ask:

If anyone is here and listening, if anyone has divine powers, if anyone sees the Big Picture, listen to me, let a miracle happen, let me live after tonight. This is a bit embarrassing after I've denied you for so long but you have to admit the situation fits the definition of an emergency. And you might look in your Book (not the Bible but the cosmic one where everything is recorded) to note I've never asked you for anything before (at least not that I remember and, if I don't remember, how could it count against me?). How do I have the nerve to pray when I don't believe in you? If by chance I was wrong and somehow, although I don't see how, you really are real (I won't say "exist" because your existence seems to me a logical impossibility), let me live. I've certainly put up with enough shit in my life.

If you are indeed omnipotent, I have to conclude you had something to do with my crime, not denying my own complicity, of course. So why not give me a break (not a neck break, mind you), and let me live, especially now that I've found something I want to do? I just want to sit and write. I don't care what I write. I just want to let it flow, burble out from my underground springs. The possibilities are endless. How about a relationship saga like <u>Madame Bovary</u> or <u>Anna Karenina,</u> or a novel of spiritual search like Walker Percy's <u>The Moviegoer,</u> or a playful novel of myth and personality like Robertson Davies writes? Why not go whole hog and cough out another <u>Ulysses</u> or <u>Pale Fire</u>? Poetry, essays, travelogues, screenplays, cookbooks, you name it, I'm ready to start scratching away (but no romance. Did you ever read any Barbara Cartland? Every sentence is a new paragraph. Absurd!).

If I'm spared, I wonder who I could convince to purchase a computer to help me with this writing and how I could talk the warden into letting me have it? Maybe Sandy would buy it for me in the following scenario: I keep scribbling away up until the minute they put the noose around my neck. Just as they're about to drop the trap door, a beefy state patrolman (is there any type other than beefy? Must be, somewhere) comes puffing in with a stay of execution. Perfect! This document would still be valid as the record of a man about to die, except I'd be around to enjoy what comes after.

Oops, maybe in that case, I shouldn't have jinxed it by writing about the possibility of a narrow escape. Oh, well. I haven't been very good at avoiding bad luck. I just want to get through this. I feel strong enough to keep on writing until it happens, whatever it is, although I'm not as ecstatically happy as I was some pages ago. I'm afraid I peaked a little early. Would have been better to wait until the final moment to get so thrilled because such exultation is impossible to sustain for too long. Life has its own rhythms and may not be scheduled around my execution. So where am I?

Oh, yeah, in the cell, sitting on my bed, writing away. How could I forget? It's like the way I've heard meditation described. These words float up in my mind, I write them down, let them go, and move on to the next words. No point now in going back to my previous pages. I'm here to write, not read. Am I paddling down the stream of consciousness, is that what I'm doing? No, not exactly. My consciousness contains a lot of other things aside from words. I'm hearing the noises along the unit, the footsteps of the guards, and the bantering of the prisoners, many of whom seem quite cheerful because they're not the ones who are going to die today. Some of them may be depressed because my upcoming execution reminds them of their own but obviously I don't hear them being depressed unless a certain undertone of sibilant sighing represents their mood. More likely it's the steam pipes. I smell Lysol and shit, the Siamese twins of prison life. I feel the cold concrete against my back, the rough blanket under me on the bed, the scratchiness of my woolen shirt, the tension in my head from staring hard at this notebook for so long. Not to mention the cramp in my right hand.

Typing would be a lot easier than clutching this pen but one must use the means at hand. On the opposite wall in front of me are a series of Chinese landscaped I tacked up in order to derive some relief from their synthesis of art and nature (elements sadly lacking in prison life), along with an interesting pattern of cracks, reminiscent of the scratches on my eyeballs that float in my vision when my eyes go unfocused. To my right is a steel ledge serving (poorly) as a chair while to my left are the toilet and the sink neither of which I've cleaned lately. Maybe I'll leave it for someone else, the next murderer who is assigned to this cell. Better luck to him as he scrubs away at my most intimate grime (him and Fallow both having to sanitize after me. Ha!). In front of me, on the page, is my hand holding the pen, the center of creation right now, the navel of the belly of the universe.

Right now I feel quite different than the mood Sartre described in <u>Nausea</u> (mentioned previously, as if you cared, oops, letting my bad attitude slip out again) when his own hand in its sheer being and essential separateness from himself disgusted him. By contrast, I love this hand in front of me with its chewed-up fingernails, the hair on the knuckles, the dirt-lined cracks from gardening everywhere on its surface (cracks that don't clean out no matter how much soap I use). I love the way it holds the pen, as if about to throw it like a dart. I love the way words flow out from the tip of the pen. I find myself hurtling to an inevitable yet surprising conclusion:

This is it.

This is what I've been searching for all my life: this moment, this feeling, this activity. I don't love what's soon to happen but I love this globe of reality I sense in every direction. I'm reminded of the Zen story of the woman who goes into the butcher shop and asks for a cut of the finest meat. The butcher throws down his cleaver and exclaims, "Madam, this is all fine meat!"

Reality is, in reality, indivisible. All of time and space is one huge mass of bubbling energy (chime in here, Einstein) and all that really changes is how we see it. I've read somewhere that Original Sin resides in the thoughts we employ to make ourselves miserable with judgment and resistance. I don't know if I buy that entirely. If you've had the shit kicked out of you as a kid, you may have difficulty in seeing your pain as part of the fine meat but maybe the point is that the mind can heal those wounds, or maybe the mind isn't the healer but whatever lies beneath it, the space where all things arise.

What did Uncle Martin say? (Heidegger again. You knew I was coming around to him again, didn't you?): "Transcendence constitutes selfhood", one of the most intelligible things he ever wrote and yet fairly mysterious if you stop and ponder what it actually means (don't bother right now, just humor the one who's about to die).

Back to stream of consciousness: words can't keep up with all the mind's activities, with all the happenings of reality. Reality is repetitious so it would be tedious to record over and over again the quality of this light from the recess in the ceiling as it strikes the sheet of paper (beautifully golden, by the way). Words are a separate stream from the flow of life. They're the finger, not the moon (yet, mysteriously, the shapes of the letters and the sounds of the words are composed of moon dust). When someone reads these words, he or she will have to use imagination to construct the experience I'm attempting, feebly perhaps, to write down on paper.

You are that someone. I don't know who you are exactly but I can guess who will read this. You, Sandy, will be sure to read these words so let me say the ultimate banality because it happens to be true: "I love you." The Governor may read these as well so, in case he does, let me tell you, your Eminence, your Highness, that if you don't pardon me, you're a shit (pardon me for being blunt). I hope one of those salmon you're supposedly catching takes a sudden lunge and bites your dick off unless, of course, my reprieve arrives in the little time left between now and my impending departure. In that case, thanks!

Mrs. Renhennie, if you are, by chance, perusing this document, I trust you're enjoying your new nose. I realize apologizing again won't help so I won't repeat myself but please know that I do regret harming you, the archetypal innocent bystander, most of all. To any others who read this, assuming Fallow doesn't just bag the whole project, I have to inform you that I'm not much different from you. I look out through my senses to a world. I have a self full of thoughts and emotions. I'm on the road to oblivion, just like you are, having been expelled from a womb and now facing death, just as we all are, some more imminently than others (ahem).

Samuel Beckett says we're born from a woman who straddles a grave. Our lives are a mere flash of light before we hit the bottom. Can't quote you the exact line because the prison library sucks plus I don't really want to take the time. Guess I can be pretty certain you're reading this, Dr. Fallow, so I'm assured of an audience even if it's someone who thinks Freud explains everything except those problems you can treat with drugs. You probably imagine that a dose of Haldol would clear up all my symptoms. Yeah, but would it make you go away?

Probably it's a good thing I'm being executed. I'm really a danger to society (not). Ordinary citizens would have to sleep with their shotguns under their pillows (if they don't do so already in this firearm-loving nation) were I allowed to roam (with the buffalo, also almost extinct). My death will make sure I never murder Beagle again. If I did somehow escape this fate and actually found him and killed him this time, could they try me for it? Wouldn't it be double jeopardy?

Even if the person I killed wasn't Beagle, I thought it was him so I should have a free pass. Guess I could ask Leonard when he arrives but he probably wouldn't know. How the hell did he graduate from an accredited law school (what was it, by the way? Never did find out). Maybe he specialized in veterinary law given how I'm being treated like a dog by a Beagle. Poor old Leonard is out there somewhere and I'll have him go along for the final procession but I don't want to contemplate his stupid face any more than I absolutely have to. However, I should take this opportunity to say, "Leonard, I forgive you." My fate was always to end up like this. At least I might as well see it that way now.

Time is pumping along yet I have so much I want to construct with these words: entire nations, the geologic histories of continents, the rise and dissipation of empires, the complete biographies of ordinary citizens in obscure countries. Despite my skepticism, what I would like to create, more than anything else, would be some place to go after my neck breaks. Somewhere in my recent scribblings, cribbed shamelessly from a Nabokov novel (The Gift, maybe?), I wrote that we live our lives in a jumbled closet, fascinating in itself but cramped. What if at death the door to the closet opens for the first time and we step out? What could possibly be beyond that door? We can't know. Imagination creates heavens and Utopias according to what we've experienced of the good things in our lives but we can't imagine something completely other, outside of human experience.

What would I want to encounter after that final snap? I think more than anything else, I would like to see the Big Picture, to understand all the whys and wherefores of life, of time, of destiny. I'd like to become the cosmic eye seeing all, knowing all, loving all. Such an outcome would be the only fitting compensation for the pain of our lives: to wake up after death and realize we were everything all along, each of us actually the One taking on the limitations of a body and a personality while forgetting who we really are. This is the basic Hindu myth and I would like it to be true. So let's speculate. The time is now nine thirteen PM, less than three hours left unless they dawdle. Wouldn't it figure that the only thing they'd do on time during my entire prison experience would be my execution? Otherwise the policy is to hurry up and wait.

Let's posit, just for the heck of it, that I was eternal and looking for the greatest amount of experience, of drama, of thrills, so I decided to take on the part of one Isaac Turbot while simultaneously inhabiting trillions of other beings. I'd be born to a woman who lived by waitressing and by random encounters with men. I'd never know who my father was until I saw him at a Seafair parade when I was thirteen. I'd live isolated and in pain, convinced my father was persecuting me, hearing his voice berating me constantly, even in my sleep. I'd kill the man I believed was my father, be arrested for it, imprisoned, and condemned to death. I'd come to believe I hadn't killed him after all, that he lived on while I headed to the gallows for his murder. What an odd story! Who would believe such a yarn yet it's true, it's mine, it's what I am? I believe I've played the part well, to the hilt, you might say.

The third act of the story would be for me to start writing in prison, finding a freedom and a power I'd never known before as I scribbled away until the final split second of my life. What a wild part to play! I'm a great actor, if this is true, because I have absolutely no memory of ever being anyone or anything other than little old me. That's how far I've sunk into my part. Moreover, I'd have to be a brilliant novelist, not to mention the greatest filmmaker of all time, because this story is incredible, literally beyond belief. The experience I'm undergoing is completely absorbing (almost life-like), endlessly detailed. And that's just me. I think of all the other beings alive now, each with an intricate narrative, and I'm staggered.

Of course, the One is playing Beagle's part, Sandy's part, Fallow's part, the hangman's part. We're all in here with each other, or with ourselves, really. By this theory, the common sense view of reality is actually an illusion, a dream of separation. What would be true is our being the offspring of an enormous mystery, amusing ourselves and loving ourselves by creating this drama of life. How vast this is, how marvelous! Just think for a moment of what's happening on the planet right now, all the people being born, making love, hurting each other, helping each other, dying, all the creating and destroying going on in this very moment. How can we stand to live in a work of art so intricate, so frightening, and so beautiful? We stand it by closing down, as I did for most of my life.

I stayed within the circumscribed world of my fears, my negative thoughts, my constant obsession with the persecution I believed was being inflicted upon me. Maybe mercy from some unknown source is dictating my breaking out of it now, as a measure of compensation for being killed. Maybe these words I'm hurrying to write down are a preparation for what's on the other side. In this moment I can think of how vast the picture, the book, the drama of reality is but, after the gallows drop, my dream is to be able to see it all, in both its entirety and in its detail, in its every movement and texture. Maybe if we were to see that now, the sheer magnitude of the truth would explode our senses, cause our heads to burst from all that lovely creativity.

"Do you really believe this?" I can hear the skeptics asking, not as voices, but in my imagination. I don't know, but I do believe what I write down here. I believe in the realities I construct on paper. I know nothing now of whether they have any relation to that massive shambling beast commonly called reality but I believe in this process that's flowing from my hands to this page. I'm way beyond the point of worrying about realism. I just want to live and this scribbling is the only method I have, aside from breathing, for being alive in these final hours.

Now I'm agitated, like my bones are about to break and burst out of my skin. I can't scribble down everything I have to say. I wish I could type a million words a minute to channel the massive flow surging through my brain. I've been lost all my life but now I'm finding something and no, I don't know what it is. Is it myself? Some Other? Just an illusion? Maybe it's Being, Heidegger's old buddy, working through me. I wouldn't call this "faith" in any form. It's so banal to convert on one's deathbed, so easy to believe what you want to believe. This writing is all I have now. I can't go against the words and whether I like it or not, the words are leading me to the source of this (whatever it is), both immanent and transcendent, beyond my own, not-so-cozy world of illusion.

What is this all about? I can't believe I'm asking now, at this late date, at nine thirty-six p.m. when I'm scheduled to die at midnight. Is there anything beyond what we see? I've been alone for so long I can't stand it anymore. I'm losing what I always thought of as myself: the persecuted outcast, the perennial underdog, the paranoid killer (liking those alliterative "p"s) and finding what? The concrete texture of the walls and floors suddenly comes into focus. After being lost in this world of words, I'm suddenly here again, or at least it seems so.

I have a vision (or is it a perception? No matter) that I've not in my cell. Instead, I'm sitting up on a mat in a dimly lit room surrounded by sleeping men. The smells are strong, of layers of sweat and dirt on human bodies giving pungency to the odors beneath. A range of snores, from the light and glancing to the deep and thunderous, punctuate the fetid air. A cockroach scuttles across what appears to be an aisle in front of me. Fleas bounce up from the blanket of the huddled figure to my right. Could this be reality and prison a dream, or the reverse? Am I oscillating between the IMU, where I wait for imminent execution, and a life in some other forsaken (don't know by whom) place where my prospects appear to be almost as dire but not imminent.

Excuse me again, Pontius Pilate, but I still have to ask, what is truth? Must I really consider that I was paranoid the whole time and Beagle wasn't my father? Are the voices I've been hearing mere hallucinations? That would take everything away from me. Isn't ending my life enough? My whole identity was built around the persecution I felt but if it was just me doing it all, perpetuating my own pain, then I have less than nothing. All my fear, rage, and effort would be pointless, ridiculous, absurd. Fallow must be coming in his pants about my defeat (kind of like Beagle, come to think about it). Well, he'd be right to come. That's what I should have been doing instead of fighting wars inside my mind. I should have been pumping sperm into the womb of the world. I should have been creating. Emotions grab me, tears spatter the notebook page as if I were in some sentimental melodrama (and really, isn't that what this is?). I have to stop writing.

For better or worse, I'm no quitter. Mere moments later, I pick up the pen and go on. The bitter truth may be that I killed a man who hadn't harmed me. I won't go so far as to say an innocent man because, if he was of the same species as me, he wasn't innocent. Beagle didn't bring me here. The governor didn't put me in the IMU. I'm the only one responsible and the guilt is fierce. In killing Beagle, I killed myself. I feel like half my head has been sawed off and carried away, leaving brain fluid to leak down upon my shoulder. No voices anymore, except this one, the one writing here. That's the voice I'm hearing, but it isn't Beagle's voice, it's mine. I'm listening to myself and that's all there is. I feel incredibly empty.

How could I have constructed such an elaborate illusion for myself? The world is lovely, dark, and deep, deep, deep (apologies to Bob Frost). Why did I construct something so limited, so hateful, so pathetic? I don't know. Maybe I did it for the clarity of this moment, suddenly taking away the poison of a lifetime in order to have a few hours of truth. I'll bet Dr. Fallow and the sensation seekers who read this will be disappointed.

They want to delve into the perversities of a sick mind at the point of death but all they will find is revelation. I'm still afraid. My body does not want to die and has been listening to my mind about my immediate prospects. The flesh knows what is about to happen. Waves of fear batter at me. In less than two hours, I'll be dead, and all the words I pile up won't change my fate. Unless, a miracle...

Okay, no major miracles this second. A cockroach (the same one from my recent vision?) scuttles behind the toilet and although his (or her? female cockroaches? I guess so) life is miraculous, I don't see its relevance to mine. I'm feeling a bit desperate (how do you like the understatement?). No doubt I deserve to die for killing Beagle but I just don't want to. If I were to be set free, I'd be able to live. I could fill my thoughts with other people, with creation, with love, and not with paranoia. Just as I'm about to die, I'm finally ready to enjoy life. What a farce! I'm not even as old as Jesus was when he began his ministry. I don't suppose I could say his life was wasted by dying so young. But look at what he accomplished! He changed the world while I'm just scratching away, obsessively, in a notebook. Still, this is what I have.

One hour and fifty-five minutes and counting. Will they do it on time? Midnight is the hour of evil deeds. However, my death is no worse than any other. They all just happen. The curtain of this particular drama is falling. Does everyone who dies wake up to realize they were never separate from the One despite how real the divisions seemed? I don't know but what a good joke on us if that's the truth. We spend our entire lives searching frantically for the fulfillment we've had intrinsically all along. Better take a shit and wash up now.

Just the moving of my bowels and the feel of water on my hands and face are magical in making me feel renewed. My legs are shaky. A band of tension stretches across my forehead. I can truthfully say I've been through a lot today. I take in a deep breath and feel a burst of joy spread out from my heart. Suddenly everything feels like it's happening precisely as it should, as if everything has been planned out from the beginning. I don't really have to say anything anymore. I was blurting out these words (scribbling, always scribbling) to keep fear at bay but now I accept it as part of the show. I feel the fear at the center of my skull, stretching out to my brow and down my spine to make me shiver. The fear is real. I am real. The words are real.

Something in another cell hits the floor with a ringing sound (maybe a dumbbell dropped a dumbbell, sorry fellow prisoners, can't help it) and the purity of the tone comes as confirmation of the perfection of everything here. Let me sustain this to the end, for another hour and three quarters. I take another breath. I suppose I could actually count how many are left now. Why doesn't someone show up with a stay of execution? What if the mountain roads are closed by avalanches (in May? Yeah, right) and the messenger can't get through? The reprieve might still arrive by helicopter or carrier pigeon but I suspect it's not going to happen. Fear is just the gristle on the very fine meat, so I acknowledge the fear and try to let it go (not so easy). I wish now I'd chosen lethal injection. When I made the choice, I let my rage act against me. Still, this is perfect, right? Right? Sure, why not? This is all there is, for me anyway, so let's just call it perfect.

Somewhere, they must be busily preparing for this great event but I don't have much to do. I'll just be along for the ride. Wish I could dress up a bit. The old prison uniform isn't very flashy. They really should be televising this. Fallow suggested I talk into a tape recorder but I insisted on writing this all down (like I won't be?). If I'd been on video, I could have acted everything out. Maybe I said this before (but I'll say it again), people should see what an execution looks like if they're going to vote for capital punishment. By the same thinking, a meat eater should see what goes on in a slaughter house. I wonder if the meat here in stir will taste funny a few days from now. No, they said they would cremate me (care for some barbecue?).

The mood shifts and I'm feeling kind of abandoned (big surprise). Everything I thought I realized just now could be total bullshit and maybe nothing at all is real, but I don't actually believe that. Something is happening here. Something lives through us, and in us, and around us. Its identity is a mystery but some try to turn it into a deity. I'm not going to be stoic and pretend I'll go into nothingness unconcerned. What was that old Warner Brothers movie where the tough guy, Bogart himself, I believe, pretended to be afraid as he was taken to the electric chair so the Dead End Kids wouldn't think he was cool (or maybe it was Cagney)? I'm not going to pretend to be cool (obviously I wouldn't want to be in the chair. That seems horrible, with flames bursting from eyes and ears. At least hanging has the potential to be quick, unless they screw it up. And whoever heard of a large bureaucracy making a botch of things? Hah!).

I don't want to be obliterated. Having had a taste of being a Self, I don't want it to stop. I just want to go on there's no way to be sure I will. I just have to take the plunge. And then what? Go towards the light, says the Tibetan Book of the Dead: don't let the monstrous apparitions frighten you off or you might have to come back for another lifetime. Frankly, I don't want any more lives. This one has made me a bit tired of the process. No, I won't take the living room set or the sports car. I want to go for the really big prize, the awareness of all that is. But here I am with only ninety minutes left worrying about what comes next. Some French guy, when asked if he'd prepared himself for the next world, said: "One world at a time."

What should my last words be? These are my last words, as rambling and confused as they are. People can make what they want of them. But I should say something on the gallows. I like what Emily Dickinson is reported to have said:"I must go in. The fog is rising." Hard to compete with that. I could say, "Never split an infinitive," something I may have been guilty of in the last few days. A bit late to hire an editor, who'd have to climb the steps to the gallows with me, red pen slashing away even while I'm writing. What the hell would I have written about if I'd decided to become a writer, if I hadn't been insane? I don't know. Maybe I'd have made something up, told a story about someone completely different from me, although wouldn't the character and I sort of grow together as I told the story? (How many rhetorical questions have I asked in this document? Three hundred and thirty-three? Thanks to me for keeping that last question from being rhetorical).

I don't have anything to leave in a will. This document in itself is my only legacy (aside from the clothes I gave to the Kims). Fallow, if you try to screw Sandy out of her share, I will reach a cold and scaly hand from beyond the grave to crush your testicles. The night guard is looking inside my cell with a sympathetic expression. Events must be moving. Soon I will be lifted up and out of my humdrum boring life (not really) in order to pass into history, although down is the actual direction I'll be taking. My name has been in the newspapers and my face has been on TV. What more can a modern man hope for in terms of fame? On the whole, I'd rather have anonymity.

The thread of words keeps unspooling here but will soon be broken. Is this really happening? Maybe I'm a Galapagos turtle sunning on a beach somewhere and this is a bad dream I'm having because of a stomach full of rotten seaweed. But I know this cup will not pass away from me.

If this document was a story, in book or movie form, I'd wait until the last second for the stay of execution to come through, so there's no use expecting anything this early. I think I'm ready to die. I've lost everything, including both my tenuous grasp of reality and my firmly held illusions. I do have this writing but, like my breathing, I can't take it where I'm going. Besides, I will be selling this for the good of science (another hearty ha!). Despite it all, I'm acquiring an undeniable sense of perfection. It's like I'm in a play and I'm acting brilliantly. This, the critics will say, was a consummate performance by an actor at the peak of his powers. He was born to play the part of Isaac Turbot. Too bad he couldn't have been a bit more swashbuckling (confession: I've never buckled a swash or swashed a buckler in my life although my one sword scene was very effective).

I've known love with Sandy, I've known friendship with B-day, I've had an enemy named Beagle, even if he had no idea of who I was. Maybe that really was a grunt he emitted as he died, and not my name. Must have been quite a surprise to die at the hands of a stranger. But he's in good company with that, as such deaths happen all the time on this globe, on streets and in battle. Wonder what his reaction will be if I show up in the next world? Will he embrace me like a father or give me a clout on the head? I'll soon find out.

One hour left. Not enough time for all I want to say. Of course I don't know what's going to come out until I write it but I feel like I could go on for years. Wonder if, as a last request, they'd wait until I finished a really long novel about prison life? Uh oh, here's the good Reverend Acksel right on time. They let him in the cell, holding a twenty pound Bible, his expression as grim as the Last Judgment (and I guess that's what this is). I ask whether he minds if I keep on writing while he's here. He says he doesn't mind but would like to talk over my fate with me. Hypocritically (yet hopefully?), I tell him I've accepted Jesus as my Lord and Savior. His granite face crumbles and he bursts into tears, insisting I kneel down on the floor with him to thank the Lord. Less than an hour left and here I am cracking my knee caps (still scribbling) on a concrete floor next to a blubbering middle-aged man. Where are the dancing girls? At least

John the Baptist was able to see a hoochie coochie dance before he lost his head.

I sit back on my bed and tell him I'll keep on scribbling. He asks if he can read from the Bible. I tell him sure, just not too loud if he doesn't mind. He's actually a pretty good guy. He certainly seems to care a lot more than I imagined he would. I'm back on the bed while he sits in the chair. He keeps trying to make eye contact when I look up from the pad. Fine, Acksel, you're a very good minister, you've saved another one, just stop getting in my face every second. Maybe I should have gone defiantly and alone to death but I enjoy having another person here even if he's a fool for an ancient Hebrew.

Now I can hear some bustling at the end of the corridor, causing a corresponding stir among my fellow inmates. The warden must be assembling the guard team that will escort me to the execution room. The end is closer now, only forty-five minutes away. What shall I do during this time? Pray? I have my own minister here for that. I'm a man so wealthy I don't even have to pray. I keep people on staff for that sort of thing. Kneel, you lackey!

Guess I'll just keep on writing. If some prayers pop up in the midst of everything else, so be it. Now a guard brings Leonard in. Leonard looks shabby, as usual, and painfully embarrassed, as any lawyer in this situation should be. I think it's been twenty years since a convicted murderer in this vast country of ours has gone so swiftly to death. And yes, I am including Texas in that statistic (although I'm actually just making it up). But I have to stop blaming Leonard. I'm responsible for this, I recall all too well, both on an individual level and in this sliver of awareness I call my self, therefore on a cosmic level as well.

I peer inside the Pandora's box of my mind, hoping for an answer from something, someone, larger than myself. I receive lots of echoes but no definite reply. That's okay. This was not constructed to be a world of certainty. I am in a state of oscillating, vibrating tension, mingling excitement and pure fear. I've given Leonard the same spiel about wanting to write so he and Acksel have begun to exchange small talk, about the weather, for fuck's sake (warm apparently). Neither of them is going to die tonight, so they can waste their time any old way they want. If they were home, they'd probably flip on the set and check out I Dream of Jeannie. I could use a genie now but I don't have a bottle to rub. I can hear the preparatory activity at the end of the corridor getting more intense.

Wonder what the executioner is thinking now? Will I encounter an archetypal grim presence, hooded and unresponsive, or will he be off several rooms away (maybe in a cardigan and chinos, puffing on a meerschaum), pulling on the trap door cord but unable to see the results of his tiny action? Occasionally, Leonard or Acksel glances at me, thinking probably that my scriptomania is another sign of my psychotic tendencies. This thought reminds me to apologize to Leonard about the insanity defense, telling him he was right to want to go for it. I tell him this and he's stunned and begins to cry. Can't I talk to anyone tonight without causing tears? He's begging my forgiveness for his shoddy work. I lie and tell him he did the best he could given the circumstances (probably true but nevertheless not good enough to help). Reverend Acksel claps me on the shoulder. "Stout man," he says although I've actually lost considerable weight due to the execrable prison food. (Sorry, sympathetic kitchen staff).

I almost feel peaceful now. I've enjoyed having people close by me, even these people, as I breathe deep of pomade (the Reverend), deodorant (both of them), and anxious sweat (my legal counsel, naturally, overcoming with his effluence the chemical buffer he's slathered on). I'm about to walk the plank off this planet and sink into the depths of the universal sea (a little purple in the prose, maybe? Why not? I'm allowed).

Just half an hour left and a contingent appears outside my door. Let's see, we have the warden (dark suit, frayed at the cuffs and around the neck but clean) and four elite guards, men I've never seen, spit and polish killers from the looks of them. Two of them carry rifles and the other two have the covers on their holsters unbuttoned to reveal the black pebbling on the handles of their revolvers. This display of weaponry is unusual in Walla Walla because of the fear the inmates will grab their guns and take over. Obviously, the risks have been carefully weighed. I'd like to see that memo.

The warden reminds me I can keep writing if I don't cause trouble but one false move and it's cuffs and shackles for me. My, I love a masterful man. I stand up and stretch. This writing game is tough on the spine. Must keep chiropractors in business (something pops in my neck). Leonard and Acksel line up behind me and I step out of the cell. The two guards with sidearms step to the left. The warden gestures for me to walk in front of them, writing away, writing this very sentence, as a matter of fact! The two riflemen step in behind. The warden follows and, after him, Acksel and Leonard.

As we pass by the other cells, I see that each of my colleagues is pressed to the bars. To a man, they bid me farewell. I look at each of them, smile, and nod. Their faces, bearing the marks of lifetimes of pain, both given and received, are astonishingly beautiful. I never noticed that before. I always assumed they were a bunch of assholes. At least the guards aren't dragging me crying and screaming out of here. Such behavior is considered very bad form as it depresses the others. I feel good to be walking. I haven't had much exercise in the past week so my legs are just a little bit wobbly (or maybe the fear is kicking in?)

The light in the corridor outside my cell is diffuse, softening the edges of everything in my line of sight. I squint as if I've been in darkness the whole time although the amount of light inside my cell is pretty much the same as out here. Hope it's not my eyes. Wouldn't want to go blind for the final minutes of my life (or would I?). At the end of the IMU, an unarmed guard waits at the thick iron door. He lifts his right hand and displays a Marine Corps tattoo on his forearm. He blows a police whistle. The door buzzes open. We step into a chamber with another big grey door on the far wall where a fat face looks through a chicken-wired window. Once we are all inside and the door behind us clicks shut, the door in front of us opens and we pass through a maze of cinder block hallways and thick vault-like doors. What are they trying to do, get me lost? Are they afraid I might run back, retrace my steps, and hide myself in my cell?

No one says a word. The final walk is not a time for idle chit chat, obviously. I'm glad to be in motion. Action is a great cure for the meanderings of thought. If they really wanted to be merciful, they wouldn't even tell someone he was condemned. They'd just do it the way I mentioned before, like the Chinese (I think): no warning, just a bullet in the head. But I don't think mercy is high on their list of concerns. It's okay, really. We're all part of the vast game.

For some reason, reality, fate, Being, whatever you want to call it, wants this to happen so it is happening. Another set of double doors. Another fat guard gives a disapproving look at my notebook where I'm writing furiously. Fuck you, you big baboon (and he's trying to sneak a peek at what I'm writing). Just because you're still printing letters with big pencils on wide-lined paper, no reason to be snotty about my salvation. No, no, wait a second, I wanted to be a center of loving awareness, all-forgiving. Too late for that now, I guess, although I can start again in this new moment, this new sentence. Not many more chances for renewal.

A guard hip checks the push bar on the door and we step outside. I feel dizzy at suddenly being in the open. Even through the glare from the lights on the buildings, I can see up to some of the brighter stars. I haven't been outside for months. In this place, even the exercise room is indoors. The breeze almost knocks me out with its intoxicating coolness. What a combination of smells! I detect stalks of wheat, insecticide, the rusty water sprayed out of irrigation lines, flowers blooming, snow melting on the mountains, honey in hives, the exhaust from airliners, barnyard shit, the ozone around power transmitters, the rich wet smell of high school kids fondling each other on the long bench seats of Ford pickup trucks. An entire world is out here!

Too much going on, really. Even if you're free and wealthy, you can never keep up. You have to decide what you want to explore among a trillion possibilities. How do the un-incarcerated bring themselves to choose? I wish I'd done more exploring in the time I had. A swirl of wind lifts a flock of shredded papers up from the yard to perform a little aerial dance in my honor. A crescent moon with a ludicrous leer skitters behind the windows of a guard tower. From outside the walls comes a sound like static. A few words in journalese drift over to us. I hear someone say, "...as we look at the prison, we can only speculate on what's happening inside. The warden has placed a tight..."

We approach a two-story wooden building that looks like a barracks. I turn to look at Acksel and Leonard and smile. One of the guards shoves me in the back to keep me moving. Oh, yeah, asshole, now would obviously be the time for me to make a break for it, just as every guard in the towers has me in the sights of his machine gun. Maybe I should do it that way, better than hanging.

But we step inside and the moment passes. They would probably just have chased me down and clubbed me anyway. Worst of all, they might have confiscated my notebook. Horrors! Don't take away my literary pacifier. Otherwise how could I stand the fact that you're murdering me, you sons of bitches? Maybe I'm creating an escape for myself in the midst of these words but that doesn't mean I have to be thrilled about being killed (a thrill kill! for some, anyway).

Inside, the smell of newly cut wood fills the air. In one corner of the high-ceilinged room is the gallows, looking much like the ones in the movies I've been remembering, constructed in the streets of Western towns to execute horse thieves and stalwart protagonists (who will soon be saved, just before the large-lettered THE END).

Again, I entertain the fantasy of someone riding in at the last minute and shooting a bullet through the rope just as I'm falling. Really, what are the odds of that? And yet that scene has happened more than once in the movies. Standing beside the gallows (in my particular and personal film) is an interesting group of observers. One of them, the man with the black bag might as well wear a little sign reading "Doctor" on his chest. He has horn-rimmed glasses, a trimmed mustache, and an air of harassment as if he's about to rush off to deliver twins. Fallow, my psychiatrist (?!), stands beside the real doctor, making a little professional dyad together. The AMA would be proud of these boys. First do no harm, says Hippocrates, but here they are in the slaughter house.

Fallow peers eagerly at my notebook and nods vigorously when he sees me scribbling away. Several reporters and state officials stand awkwardly beside him but the real focus of the composition is the man on the gallows with the black hood on his head who's nervously wringing his hands. Shouldn't a hangman be more composed? What if his sweaty fingers slip as he's about to pull the handle? Where is the handle, by the way? Seems appropriate that I can't see it, in the same way we go through most of our lives not knowing where the end is coming from.

The two guards in front of me grab me by the arms. I can just barely put pen to paper. Leonard leaps around them to shake my hand which is a little awkward because of the pen and the goons pulling on my arms. I almost drop the notebook but recover. Reverend Acksel comes up and gives me a long hug, scrunching the notebook to my chest but I manage to keep scribbling. Hey, padre, don't start messing with those choir girls back at church. Ignore the heroin-addicted hookers beckoning from the sidewalks. Don't invite the merry widow back to your office for a little "counseling." He tells me I'll be with the Lord in minutes but I don't share with him the mixed emotions I have about the prospect. Will I find harsh judgment, acceptance, or the void? I guess I'm ready for any of that triad.

The doctor doesn't examine me. Must be more interested in dessert than appetizers. The guards lead me up the steps while the little crowd below looks up as if they expect me to start preaching. Now would be a good time for someone to burst in with the reprieve. No, the protocol as well-established in Westerns is that they always wait until the hangman's hand is just about to move the handle. Even a split-second too soon would ruin the suspense. I do hope the trap door is oiled. I don't want any black comedy scene of the hangman jumping up and down to loosen it, then falling through himself.

The guards move me onto the trap, being careful to stay off it themselves. They take a leather strap and cinch it tightly around my arms and chest just above the elbows as I specified. Yep, I can't raise my arms but I can keep this writing going. You know how it is, some people like to write in cafes, some in mountain cabins; as for myself, give me the gallows any day to spark the creative fires. I feel okay, though. The writing is actually getting me through this. I couldn't have been able to bear it alone. Maybe they should give notebooks to all the men in the IMU, allowing them to express themselves. They committed their murders and mayhem because they never found the creative outlets so important for a well-rounded life.

Okay, so I've admitted I was delusional, quite a shock to my world view. But what if all this current spectacle is delusional as well, a complete hallucination? Maybe after I was in the psychiatric hospital, I stopped attending classes and didn't go to work. Maybe I lost my apartment and lived on the streets, filling my time with thoughts of Beagle and philosophy and landscaping and catering and Sandy, none of which were remotely real. Could it be I imagined the murder and the trial and my prison stay, all of which definitely had an unreal quality to them? Maybe when the trap door opens and I drop, I'll wake up to another vision of life where I'm sitting and scribbling, always scribbling, on a mat in a downtown shelter where my fellow men rise from their slumbers and prepare to embark upon the morning, ready for another absorbing day of panhandling and cadging smokes.

My vision flips back to the gallows. I'm on my way. I sure as hell hope somebody is home when I come calling. Don't want to be knocking around forever in the void. In fact, nothing at all is happening for the moment. People shift from foot to foot impatiently, friends of Beagle perhaps, here to see the administration of justice in its most radical form, a swift descent. I knew it. Nothing comes off on time around here, even my head. I breathe in, breathe out, watch the little patterns the observers make in the room, approaching each other and breaking apart like amoebae. Maybe I should just look at the shapes, colors, and textures without evaluating. I try it, but no way. Neither my mind nor my body will let go of the fact I'm about to die.

The hangman scurries down the steps and then scampers up again. The warden asks me if I have any last words. Yeah, I do, I tell him. My last words for the benefit of the public are: "I'm sorry for what I did. I'll be seeing you all real soon." The guards chuckle at this while the reporters dutifully mark it down in their pads. Fellow writers! Can't they even remember something as simple as that? I'm surprised by the small turnout of the media but then remember the warden said he didn't want to turn this into a circus. No? How about a small traveling carnival? A Punch and Judy show? Street mime? Where, oh where, is the bathysphere now, when I really need it? Gone forever. I'm forced to feel everything happening to me directly, no leavening for this dough.

Reverend Acksel climbs the stairs, Bible in hand, his weight making every step creakily plead with him to lay off the barbecue. He comes up close on the platform and lays a hammy hand on my shoulder (continuing the barbecue theme). The gesture is stiff and awkward but comforting for all that. He launches into the Our Father, a prayer familiar even to someone raised as a pagan like me. But where did I learn it? Surely not from mother. Must have been Gouchie although she would have had to get her ass out of the armchair to put me to bed and I don't remember her ever doing that. What do I remember from all my years in her house? Nothing much now: just a night in bed in Ballard when the moon came through the window and painted everything in my room with ivory light, suggesting some playful presence in reality rarely available to me.

As the Reverend Acksel intones his prayer, the words fall around my head: "Our Father:" he says, inevitably making me think of Beagle, wherever he is, the golden calf I fashioned as a father for lack of a better one. "Hallowed:" bringing to mind Halloween and the mask of delusions I wore for so long. "Thy will be done:" causing me to remember I wanted to make a will, leaving everything to Sandy but I never did, an omission difficult to correct at this late date. Would a statement from the gallows be considered sufficient? I really do want her to have any money from this project and I don't trust Fallow but I have the fewest resources imaginable right now to do anything about it.

"Our daily bread:" making me think of the bread and wine, the body and blood of a single Self, broken up, apparently at least, into all the lonely items in this universe, not realizing they are themselves the whole shebang and what they always wanted in their deepest desires. "Trespasses:" What if an anti-capital punishment guerrilla group is just about to trespass into the prison, firing Uzis with non-lethal bullets containing soporifics to send all the prison personnel and onlookers off to dreamland. And what about the winged pigs flying around the room shitting out snowballs from hell?

"Into temptation:" bringing up a sudden cascade of images of everything that could tempt me, bodies and accomplishments and honors and consumables and entertainment in every media, all dancing around the perimeter of the gaping black hole that is me (writing faster and faster now. Will Fallow be able to read this? Probably not if the friction sets the page on fire). "Deliver us from evil:" That's all I ever wanted. Evil has saturated my life but maybe only my brain. The upside of what's impending is the chance to at least be delivered of all that's plagued me. "The kingdom and the power and the glory:" Oh, yeah, that's what I'm talking about, some massive monarch muscle with the moxie to obliterate everything gone wrong for me, forever and ever, amen.

Enough with the praying. On with the show! Reverend Acksel lifts and drops his catcher's mitt of a hand upon my doughy shoulder one last time and walks down the stairs, making the entire structure shake with each step. The hangman comes up and places the noose around my neck, pulling it snug in what feels like an affectionate gesture, the way my mother wrapped a scarf under my chin so I could go out and play in the snow (huh, finally a positive memory of her). I smell English Leather, the brand chosen by nine out of ten hangmen to keep down the sweat of killing. I look through the eye holes in his hood that are crudely cut out as if he made them with a pair of kid's scissors. I look into his eyes. My God, it's Beagle!

Has my madness reached its full flowering at this final moment? I look again and he returns my stare, directly, with no reticence or filters. He doesn't seem angry or impassioned in any way but why was he so nervous just now? I remember those eyes distinctly from the last time we met: the moment when I stuck the plastic knife deep into his heart. This can't be true. After losing all my illusions today, after dismantling my paranoia, am I hallucinating again? Shit! You can't get anywhere in this life. Yeah, but I'm sorry, that really is Beagle. I whisper to him, "Beagle?" He nods but puts his finger where his lips would be under the hood. Carefully, he places a black hood like his, but without eyeholes, over my head. I keep writing on the pad. Hope it's legible. Did I turn the page to a blank sheet or am I writing over what I've already written? The bag is absolutely dark. All I can see are swirling colors generated by my eyeballs. My heart starts to beat very fast.

What is Beagle doing here? He must have had me kill someone else, just like I said to the reporter. Maybe the whole murder scene was as much of a set-up as my paranoia told me. Beagle walks off the gallows, each step exactly in synch with every fourth beat of my heart, eventually blending in with the murmuring from below. Is Beagle celebrating his utter victory by killing me himself? But his eyes, when I looked into his eyes, they were full of compassion, green and deep like an ocean trench. Maybe he isn't going to kill me. This might be what I prayed for, the last minute salvation. A beefy patrolman will burst into the room any second now, waving the reprieve. A cowboy will shoot the rope in two as his horse rears high in the air. Beagle has infiltrated the prison, using his money and influence to buy his way into the role of hangman. He wants to claim me for his son! He isn't going to kill me at all! In this last minute, he's going to destroy the defenses of the prison. The walls will crumble with a high-tech trumpet blast. He's going to take over everything and help me esca nothing

Tuesday, May 2nd, 1989

To whom it may concern:

I didn't expect the afterlife to be anything like this. Somehow I thought the next world would be radically different. What I'm looking at through my eyes (yes, apparently eyes and a body to hold them came along for the ride through the void) is remarkably like the reality I knew before I went to prison. My death is turning out to be as strange as my life was.

A green backpack is next to me on the bench where I'm sitting. Inside, along with multiple toiletries and miscellaneous objects, oddly familiar, I find a newspaper dated May 1 1989, with an article that says Booth Gardner is the current Governor of the State of Washington. Governor Renhennie (a ridiculous name) apparently does not hold power in this dimension.

I'm in a quiet park beside a large gray building that I somehow know to be the County Courthouse. If pressed, I'd say this is morning. Groups of men, and a few women, sit on other benches, talking and laughing. Some tents are set up along the edges of the grass. One of the old trees in the park extends its branches over me. I'm writing on the backs of documents I found in the backpack. On the opposite sides of these sheets are endless paragraphs about the legal issues involved in a real estate transaction. A thick stack of various papers, held together by twine, turns out to be an exact copy, down to the coffee and food stains, of my writings pre-execution, including a transcript of the television interview (written in longhand, oddly enough). In my pocket, I find an identification card for the main downtown shelter with the name that's followed me through the void: Isaac Turbot.

I have an assortment of memories to shuffle through, many of them from my past life, along with information that appears to apply to my current life: where to get food, where to find a toilet, where to go for shelter in event of rain or cold. However, all these thoughts have a dream-like quality

Is this a moment of lucidity or yet another delusion? The IMU seemed real, and so did my crime and my trial. What about Sandy? I hope she's real because that would mean I'd be able to go and see her. Could I restart my gardening job with Tony? What about my mother and the house in Ballard? More dreams. All I know for sure is that I'm sitting here with the sun on my face and a stack of papers in my lap, as aromatic as if they were scavenged from a dumpster. A cloud passing by bears a remarkable resemblance to a certain nose.

Strange visions arise inside me and fade away again. I was scribbling in a cell in Walla Walla for months (and doing the same while sitting up nights on a mat in the shelter, the scratching of my pen in counterpoint to the snores). I was hung by the neck until dead (and I just woke up early with my fellow homeless men and made my way out to the park). Maybe what I'm experiencing now is a reincarnation allowing me the opportunity to replay and improve what didn't work out in my last lifetime.

No matter. Beagle isn't here, at least not yet. I'll see if he has the ability to follow me into a different incarnation. I wouldn't put it past him as my nemesis, my inspiration. This place I'm in seems to be empty of Beagle's domination. Being shines through every element around me, joining the presence I feel within as I sit on this bench. Under Beagle, I lived in oppression and struggle. Now everything just is: a plume of smoke caught in the wind, a plane cutting through the branches above, a siren echoing off the brick facades of worn down buildings.

For now, I'm enjoying being here. My fingers move the pen across the page, the ink flows from the point, and these words are formed. I don't feel hungry or thirsty or lonely or sad. All those states are potential within my mind and body but they aren't immediate. I apparently have some familiarity with the German philosopher Heidegger and a phrase of his pops into mind: "Language is the house of Being." Maybe that's what I've been doing from the last lifetime to this one, with my incessant scribbling on reams of paper: trying to build a house where I can live. Maybe this is it, as I sit on the bench with the sun caressing my face, the music of what is (composed of bird call and engine sound and human speech) playing for me. No fears or desires rise up to pull me away from myself (for the moment anyway). My hand slides across the page, leaving a trail of ink forming words as I attempt, in my own way, to construct a home.

305

Thanks to Dr. Tawnya Christiansen, psychiatrist extraordinaire, for reading the manuscript and giving valuable comments. Of course, any technical errors (in fact, all errors) are entirely my own. I want to be clear that I in no way endorse Isaac's (or Scientology's) skepticism about the help psychiatry offers.

Thanks to Joe Midgett and Sulo Turner for their helpful critiques, and to Chris Peters for his design expertise. Thanks especially to all those with mood and thought disorders who've shared their experiences during my thirty-five years of crisis work. I appreciate my friends and colleagues for being there and, as always, I appreciate my family, Gail, Joe, and Matt, for being here.

Sam Rogers is a writer and Clinical Social Worker who lives with his family near Puget Sound.